LETTERS FROM A SAILOR

ROGER BAKER

First published in 2023.

ISBN 978-1-3999-4710-7 (paperback)
ISBN 978-1-3999-5109-8 (eBook)

For Felicity

1

The suit seemed out of place. That would have been the thought of any casual onlooker noting that, amid the ranks of yachts and leisure cruisers lining the jetties of the marina, there was a man wearing a business suit and tie. However, as it was as yet early morning, there were few people abroad to make note of this singular event. Had there been, the subject of any such scrutiny would not have cared less. The suit was expensive and well cut of a style favoured by professional men. Its wearer, a healthy-looking young man, was busy about the business of mooring his yacht and had given no thought to any incongruity in his appearance amid St. Helier's Elizabeth Marina, for it had all been part of a well-planned scheme that was about to come to its conclusion. For now, he had but one thought occupying his mind: he had to be in his office by eight.

The plan he had made involved a double crossing of the English Channel. The schedule was tight and success would depend on a number of factors, all of them outside his control. Foremost among these was the weather. He had mentally prepared himself for all of the possible adverse scenarios that he could think of, detailing the steps he would need to take in order to deal with each of them. In the event everything had run smoothly and he had not needed to fall back on any of these.

What might easily have been a wearisome ordeal had proved to be an exhilarating experience. The weather could not have been bettered had he himself arranged it, for the moderate north-easterly at his back had been ideal for the return channel crossing he had just completed. For this return crossing the boat he was using was brand new and he was sailing her for the first time. This had made for a hesitant start, but by the end of the first hour he had begun to feel at ease with his new purchase.

It had proved to be a night of growing pleasure as he had given the boat its head and had begun to discover its capabilities. It was with real regret that he had made out the harbour light of St. Helier and had begun to shorten sail. Then the earlier excitement had given way to a new pleasure as he made his steady controlled approach to harbour against the backdrop splendour of the breaking dawn. It was at this point that he had changed into his office garb in order to save time. Those few extra minutes gained were all that he had needed to moor the craft in his customary berth in the marina. He had twenty-two minutes before the deadline.

He was about to lock the door of the boat's cabin when he remembered the signal hoist he had made before entering the harbour. Momentarily the thought of what his superiors in London might make of it crossed his mind, but was instantly dropped. Now was not the time. Quickly, he freed the line and lowered the signal. He smiled to himself as he untied the furled umbrella and pinstripe trousers that had served as his flag and flung them carelessly into the cabin. Then, after securing the cabin door and picking up his briefcase, he jumped ashore and strode away along the jetty humming cheerfully to himself.

He felt surprisingly fresh after the long vigil of the

Channel crossing. Ten minutes of purposeful walking had taken him away from the harbour area and into the business area, where the elegant town houses of an earlier age had become the home of the many financial services operators taking advantage of Jersey's offshore status. He turned with an easy familiarity through the ornate doorway of a building whose brass plate identified it as the Jersey office of Rayleton Securities. A middle-aged man behind the reception desk in the entrance hall greeted him as he entered.

"Good morning Mr. Rayleton."

"Morning Tom." The reply was uttered without a glance as the speaker strode to the lift at the rear of the hallway and disappeared.

Minutes later he appeared in his outer office. A young woman was preparing a breakfast tray at a side table.

"Morning Charlotte. Mmm! Is that for me?"

"A good secretary has to think of everything, even such non-essentials as eating."

"Quite right. Bring it through. David Kingsbury shown up yet?"

Charlotte nodded towards the inner office with a smile on her face and followed him with the breakfast tray she had prepared.

Rayleton greeted his waiting visitor with a beaming smile.

"Good morning David."

"Ha! The prodigal returns."

Rayleton made a play of consulting his watch.

"I left St. Helier after close of business on Friday in my old yacht, which is now at Hamble offered for sale, and returned in my new yacht which is tied up in the Elizabeth marina. Now, here I am at 7.52am. dressed and ready for business."

Holding up his briefcase, he offered himself for inspection.

"I win our bet, I think."

David nodded in acknowledgement and gestured towards a magnum of champagne on Rayleton's desk.

"I watched you make harbour – I liked your choice of pennant."

Rayleton dropped the briefcase on the desk and examined the champagne.

"Excellent! I like a good loser. Now, I take it you will have no objection to a small breakfast celebration. Look Charlotte. Mr Kingsbury, being a gentleman, has paid up. So, if you can find three glasses, I will offer a toast to my new boat, *Sea Urchin* and her first victory."

"Three Glasses? A look of mixed surprise and alarm crossed Charlotte's face as she replied.

"Of course. As our honest second you must join us."

"Oh no! I couldn't. I get giggly on champagne."

"Good! That should make for a most interesting morning. Banking is far too stuffy a business."

When he went to bed that evening, Richard was finally beginning to feel the effects of his exertions over the weekend. Despite this, sleep did not come immediately. Too much had happened over the past three days. However much his body sought rest, his mind was not yet prepared to fall into line. Every detail of the weekend had to be re-visited and there was much to think over.

Silently his mind trawled through the new additions to its memory bank. Initially there had been the excitement when he had first cleared the harbour and then the slow progress along the eastern coast until he had been able to make full use of the prevailing wind. There had been the difficulty of staying awake as he crossed one of the world's busiest water-ways and the reward of watching the stately passage of a massive oil tanker from sea level at close quarters. Then he had enjoyed that feeling of homecoming as he had made his way up the Solent.

It had been over a year since he had last seen Rob. He was

standing waiting on the landing stage as Richard carefully inched alongside his new boat.

"God, you've taken your time. I've been here for hours," had been his only comment and the old camaraderie seemed instantly resumed.

There was a time when they had been inseparable, but then the patterns of their youth had been broken by the demands of higher education and training as they made the transition from youth to manhood. Their paths had become very different, but, when they were together dealing with boats, nothing seemed to have changed.

But it had changed, he now reflected. Beneath the smiles and laughter, he had sensed something else, but there was nothing concrete that he could identify as the origin of the idea. When people have been in close relationships things do not always have to be spelled out. Small changes are noted as if by some sixth sense. Was this what his senses had picked up, the merest hint that Rob was concealing an underlying discontent.

In the years after the war Ben Maitland had served under Richard's father in the navy. Their two families occupied adjacent married quarters and strong bonds had developed between them. Richard and Ben's son Rob were the same age and had become inseparable friends, spending all their free time together and mad on anything to do with boats. In turn Ben had kept a fatherly eye on Richard after the death of his father and Richard had come to spend as much time in the Maitland house as his own. Only in the years after the boys had completed their schooling had there been any break. True to his great interest Rob had completed advanced courses in marine engineering, while Richard, under heavy pressure from his uncle, had undertaken courses that would prepare him for a role in the family banking business.

When his career in the navy came to an end, Ben had purchased the run-down boatyard on the Hamble and by hard work and a dogged attention to detail had turned it into a successful business offering boat repair, maintenance and berthing facilities. It had been the natural choice of base for Richard's sailing activities. He was a regular visitor there and the spare bedroom at the adjacent house was always available to him.

As a regular visitor, he could not have been unaware of the strained relations between the Maitlands and the neighbouring Baxter Marine Company. He had therefore mooted the possibility of his buying one of Baxter's latest yacht designs with Ben before going ahead with the purchase. In the event Ben had been perfectly open-minded about it.

"I don't like the man and he doesn't hide the fact that he would like to get his hands on our river frontage, but a boat is a boat. Baxter builds boats: we service them. We're not competitors," was how he had summed up the situation.

Thus armed, Richard had bought *Sea Urchin*. Despite Ben's apparent equanimity, he had thought it would be diplomatic to make the purchase through a company of yacht brokers and it was they who had handled all aspects of the deal and the delivery of the boat to the Maitland yard. There had therefore been an element of excitement as Richard had made his way up the Solent and into the Hamble to take possession of her.

In their younger days Rob would have shown the same enthusiasm as the new owner. On this occasion the seeming lack of interest left Richard nonplussed. The expected joshing from Rob about banker's bonuses had not happened. They had worked in silence moving all necessary gear from the old boat on to the new and he had then gone across to the house to speak to Ben and Lou before he set off on the return leg.

While he was in the house, Rob had cast off the bow mooring leaving only a single rope holding the boat to the jetty. It seemed to Richard that he was unhappy about something. On an earlier occasion Lou had mentioned that, after the freedom of college, he was finding it difficult working under his father doing basic jobs that used little of the skills and knowledge that he had acquired. Thinking that this was the cause of Rob's strange silence Richard had decided to tackle things head on.

"What's up with you then? Have you and your Dad been arguing, or is it because I've bought a Baxter yacht?"

Rob had taken a deep breath before turning to face him.

"So, you know about my run-ins with the old man. He's right in his way, but he will not try anything new. It's always his way or nothing."

"Well! What is bugging you? Is it Baxter?'

Rob had paused to consider the best way to phrase what he had to say.

"It's not Baxter so much as his way of operating. Like this boat."

Richard had been momentarily taken aback.

"You don't like the boat. Is that what you are trying to tell me? Well I like her. I think she looks fabulous."

"I agree with you. She does, but that is what we're meant to see. That's how Baxter sells his boats. It's a very slick sales operation."

"Are you saying that I've made a bad buy?"

"No!"

He remembered how Rob had shaken his head, uncharacteristically lost for words.

"Oh, I can't say exactly what I think." He had paused to collect his thoughts. "I think she is a lovely-looking craft, but that is what Baxter wants you to concentrate on, that and the other great selling point – her speed. Right?"

Richard had nodded in agreement.

"So how does he get that speed? I would love to get my hands on a copy of the design plans and specifications."

Over and again Richard's mind ran through this exchange. Repeatedly he examined every word and detail. At the end he remained none the wiser. Nothing seemed to add up. Gratefully he returned to the final stages of the return crossing. Only then as he mentally glided into the Elizabeth Marina amid the lustre of the dawn did he relax enough to allow sleep to finally claim him.

2

Years of service in the Royal Navy had conditioned Ben Maitland to early rising. As was their usual practice, he and Lou had breakfasted early so that he could be in the boatyard by eight. That had been over an hour ago during which Lou had tried to occupy herself by washing the breakfast dishes and other odd jobs. At the end of the dining table the files of the quarterly VAT return documents that she had been working on during the previous evening lay in a neat pile. She had scheduled their completion as her main task for the morning and was anxious to get on with it. However, that was on hold until all of the breakfast chores were complete. At the other end of the dining table an unused place setting provided the reason for the delay. Rob had not yet made an appearance.

The dish washing and tidying that Lou had been doing were all designed as distractions, simple everyday tasks that would draw her mind away from the anxiety that was gnawing away inside her. She dreaded these mornings after one of Rob's nights out. After he had completed his schooling, the plan had been that he would study marine engineering before taking on full-time duties in the family business. He had shown a strong aptitude to his engineering studies and had moved on to the advanced courses that Southampton had to offer, and in particular the applications of computer technology to design and analysis of ships and boats. Returning to the basics of maintenance and repair of small privately-owned yachts and cruisers in a small family business was never going to be easy.

The problem was not made any easier by Ben's naval experience. He was not a martinet, but the navy taught its people that strength and success come from adherence to discipline and above all time keeping. That was how Ben organized his workdays and he expected the other members of the family to fall into line with him. That had always been accepted. The original plan had been that Rob would take a basic course in marine engineering and then join his father in the family business. The earlier ideas were changed when Rob had taken so well to the original course that he had followed this with the most advanced courses in his field and coupled this with applications of advanced computer technology. He was now far better qualified than work on basic maintenance tasks required. Either he would have to find employment that could use his many skills or else the family business would have to find some way of making use of them. She smiled ruefully to herself at the idea of her husband making any such change to his established routines. The result was the uneasy stand-off that had produced repeated clashes.

The weekend must have been hard for Rob, she mused, seeing Richard again with his new yacht, with all the freedom that being in charge of the bank's Jersey operations gave him. It was also easy for him being a member of the Rayleton family. His uncle had never hidden the fact that he would like to see Richard at some point take over from him as company chairman. How strange, she thought, that two young people, who at one time had been inseparable, should now be so far apart.

The noise of a door shutting upstairs suggested that Rob was finally out of bed. Lou took a deep breath. Perhaps now her day could soon begin, but, at some point, there would be the usual clashes between father and son.

Minutes later Rob appeared in the kitchen yawning and bleary-eyed.

Without the need to think, she began a series of long-practised moves. More water was put into the kettle and the switch depressed, the cooker ring beneath the pan she had used earlier was re-ignited and an egg was broken to join the already-cooked bacon.

"I could murder for a mug of tea."

"Well if you will go out drinking all hours." She retorted over her shoulder. "You only have yourself to blame."

As soon as it was ready she brought the requested mug of tea across to the table. Rob eagerly grasped the mug.

"What time did you get in last night?"

"Late... No, make that very late."

Lou shook her head.

"It makes no sense when you know you have to work the next day. Your father has been at work for over an hour."

"I know. I'd better get down to the yard. I can catch up on lost time later."

"Aren't you going to have breakfast now that I have cooked it?"

Rob looked at the contents of the pan.

"Make it into a butty. I'll eat it as I go." Minutes later, clutching his mug of tea and a half-eaten butty, Rob hurried across the yard through the many boats that had spent the winter months out of the water. A stiff morning breeze created the characteristic tinkling sounds in boats' rigging, and he shivered as he made his way to the area adjacent to the yard's slipway where his father stood in the cockpit of a family cruiser applying a coat of marine varnish to the exposed cabin woodwork.

"Morning."

Ben lowered his brush. To address his son.

"I've been waiting for you to help get Bill Martin's boat in the water."

"Right let's do it."

"That's what I like to see, real get-up-and-go. It's just a pity that it has taken an hour-and-a-half to reveal itself."

Rob stuffed the last of the butty into his mouth as Ben climbed down the short ladder set against the side of the boat bearing his varnish can and brush. Once down, Ben replaced the lid on the can. dropped his brush in a can of cleaning solvent and carefully wiped his hands while eyeing Rob.

"And what exactly are you planning to do with that mug in your hand?"

"Sorry. Heavy night."

"Not good enough. This may be a family business, but it is a business all the same, with work to be done. In future, could you confine your debauchery to Saturday nights!"

"I said I'm sorry. Anyway, this isn't the navy and I'm not some poor bloody sailor who has to ask permission to go on shore leave."

Ben ignored the invitation to a verbal scrap and adopted a more neutral response.

"I'm not telling you how to lead your life. I just want a proper day's work out of you."

With that he picked up his painting gear and headed towards the workshop.

"Now let's get that boat in the water."

Lou watched the final stages of their exchange from the kitchen window. She could hear nothing of what was said, but their body language told her everything. Here we go again, she thought, another morning-after to mark up. Once again there was the usual tightening in her stomach.

She breathed in deeply and exhaled slowly several times in an effort to relax. VAT returns, she thought, were difficult enough without these extra distractions.

3

"One-thirty, one-thirty. Who'll gimme one-thirty-five?"

The auctioneer, a stocky figure already balding as he passed into middle-age, glanced around the sparse crowd gathered around the tailboard of his pick-up truck.

"I have one-thirty. Last chance folks."

He paused momentarily, then banged the flat of his hand hard against his clipboard.

"Sold at one hundred and thirty dollars."

It was the last item on his list and chance to wipe the perspiration the hot sun had raised on his forehead. The crowd, released from the discipline of the sale, began to chatter as they dispersed. He looked across the yard and, seeing his client, jumped down from the truck and made his way over to her.

"Well I guess we're all done, Miss Pearson. Didn't get the prices I was hoping for, but that's how it is with sales. Some days folks just don't seem in the mood for buying."

"When will you have the figures ready for me?"

"Later this afternoon I guess." He nodded towards his assistant sitting at the makeshift sales table at the barn doorway. "Ed's taking down names and payments. I'll get it all typed up for you. Will you be in town?"

"No. I'm staying at Martha and Hal's place."

"That's OK. Ed lives out this side of town. I'll get him to drop the list off on his way home."

"Thank you again Mr Lomax." She shook his extended hand.

"My pleasure. I only wish we could have had a better outcome. Now if you'll excuse me, I ought to be giving Ed a hand over there."

With that he moved off towards the barn where a gaggle of buyers were waiting to collect their purchases.

The girl watched him walk away and then turned to look over the yard to the entrance driveway where a slow trickle of cars and trucks were making their exit. It was like the slow closing of the curtains at the end of a play. All morning she had wandered forlornly among the marked lots. She had watched as one by one the miscellaneous items of house and farm were sold off. As the morning progressed the realisation had grown that the sale marked the end of an important phase in her life. Now the buyers were leaving, many of them bearing items that she had known all her life. It felt as if each item was a part of her own being that people were carrying away.

A deep sadness slowly welled up inside her and tears formed in the corners of her eyes. She was spared from openly weeping by an arm placed around her shoulders. Even before she heard her voice she knew instinctively that it was Martha.

"I think we are all done here honey. Let's go home."

Jenny had gone to her room soon after their return and Hal had disappeared among the outbuildings. Left to her own devices Martha had settled on the porch. At this time of the year its shaded warmth made it a favourite spot, particularly at times like today when she had much to mull over. She was still there when Hal re-joined her after his work outside just as Ed Kowalski's pick-up truck nosed into the farm's driveway.

The truck swung to a halt below the porch and Ed climbed out clutching a large envelope.

"Evening Mr Summers, Mrs Summers."

"Evening Ed," Martha replied as Hal stepped down from the porch. "You got the figures for Jenny?"

"Yes ma'am. It's all here."

He paused uncertainly looking around to see his expected recipient.

"She's resting at the moment." Martha replied. "We'll see she gets them."

"Oh! Right". He handed the envelope to Hal. "Thank you, Mr Summers."

He paused for a moment, as if uncertain whether this was the right thing to do. Then, collecting his poise, he made his exit with a muttered, "I'd better be going."

Hal watched his truck as it disappeared down the track to the road and then returned to the porch and handed Martha the envelope.

Moments later Jenny emerged from her room.

"Was that Ed Kowalski's truck I heard?"

Martha handed her the letter Ed had delivered and watched as Jenny opened it and scanned its contents. Then with a sigh she handed the sheets to Martha.

Hal waited, impatient to learn what it said.

"What's it all add up to?" He finally demanded.

"Don't be so impatient." His wife replied. "This is Jenny's business."

"Tell him Martha." Jenny replied, laughing at this matrimonial teasing. "It's no big secret."

Martha took a deep breath.

"The total from this morning's sale net of dealing costs was eight thousand, three hundred and seventy-two dollars.

The real estate sale net of costs came to two hundred and fifteen thousand and sixteen hundred dollars. That makes a combined total of two hundred and twenty-three thousand and six hundred dollars clear of all expenses. Satisfied?"

"Two hundred and twenty-three thousand!" Hal repeated the figures. "It don't seem much for a lifetime's work, but it's something I guess."

Jenny shook her head sadly.

"Not really. The farm was bought on mortgage and grandpa had been borrowing more over the last few years. The bank will get most of the money."

"Goddam banks. What the hell is this country coming to?"

"You will have to excuse him honey," Martha said as her husband stomped off the barns. "He's been fretting all day."

"Is anything wrong?" Jenny asked with concern.

Martha looked at her. "Your grandpa didn't want to worry you, but while you have been away at college things have been going from bad to worse. There's not much of a future for little farms like this."

She paused to wipe a tear that had trickled from the corner of an eye.

"I guess we are in the same financial fix as your grandpa was, except we ain't ready to die yet."

Jenny put a comforting arm round her shoulder and putting on a brave face Martha patted her hand.

"There now. I'm being silly. We shall manage. The question is what are you going to do."

"Me? Oh that's easy. One day soon a handsome prince will ride up on a fine white horse. We'll fall in love, ride off together and live happily ever after."

She laughs. "Well that's the Hollywood version. In the real version I'll have to get a job somewhere and take things from there. First of all, though, I want to deal with this."

Martha looked at the paper Jenny offered to her.

"What's this?"

"It's a letter I found last week going through Grandpa's papers. It had never been opened."

Martha looked over the letter, her face showing first curiosity then surprise.

"Well it seems to have come from some attorney – Lordy it's from London. That's London, England."

She cast a look of complete puzzlement at Jenny.

"Why would a London law firm write to your Grandpa?"

Martha returned to the letter.

"Look it's dated 1942. No wonder it was never opened. That was when your Grandpa was fighting with the marines in Guadalcanal. He didn't come back home until late 1945, and then he wasn't the same man as before."

She shook her head sadly at the reminder of times past.

Jenny directed her thoughts back to the letter.

"It says something about a property that had been rented out if you read on."

"Honey, that was fifty years ago. Things have moved on. Now don't you go chasing rainbows."

"I know, and I know it seems crazy, but I have to look into this. You and Hal have been like family to me since I was a little girl, but now grandpa's gone I don't have any close kin."

She paused as she took the letter back.

"This letter is the only lead I have. So, when everything here is settled, I'm going to try to find out if this law firm is still operating. If it is, I'll use what's left of grandpa's money to pay them a visit. Who knows, I might find out where my folks came from, like Ronald Reagan did."

4

If ever the subject of his chauffeur-driven Bentley came up, Henry Rayleton would brush it aside with the comment that he was a wealthy man and could easily afford the occasional luxury. He might also add that he could not think of a greater luxury than escaping the stress of driving through London traffic. This would produce some form of rueful acknowledgement and a satisfactory end to the topic. It also deflected the conversation away from the real reason for the apparent self-indulgence.

The Rayletons had acquired their Hampshire estate during the course of the eighteenth century and it had remained as the family seat through countless generations. By basing himself there, rather than in some central London apartment, Henry had been able to keep some sort of balance to his family life. While he laboured in the city his wife could indulge her passion for gardening and his daughter had the perfect setting for developing her twin aims of competing at the Badminton Horse Trials and establishing her own riding school.

The key to all this was his chauffeur. By rising at six-thirty, he could spend an hour or so ensconced in the spacious rear seat with his papers and be in his office by eight, fully prepared for the day ahead. This day had been no exception and he was already well settled at his desk when Charles Denning slipped into the room for their customary morning meeting.

The two men could not have been more different. Tall and strongly built with hair greying at the temples, Henry looked every inch the patrician. By contrast, Charles was short and slim. He had kept his boyish looks, but the early loss of much of his hair to balding had left him with a shining dome that was strangely at odds with his youthful features.

Despite their differing appearances the two men made an excellent team. It was not unknown within the many companies headquartered in London for tensions to develop between Chairman and Chief Executive. Rayleton Securities was a family-controlled business. As such ultimate authority lay with Henry. Charles fully accepted this and saw his role, as its title suggested, in putting into effect the policy decisions of his chairman.

Charles had only one matter to report. For some time, he had been locked in negotiations with a Portuguese banking group with the aim of an eventual amalgamation of their respective operations. Banco Cardosa was slightly smaller than Rayleton and its European business was minimal, but it had built a significant arm in Brazil. It was this that had attracted Henry. It was a natural fit. Cardosa would find further growth difficult without access to London and South America was the missing piece in Rayleton's operations.

Negotiations had been ongoing for some time. There had been the usual problems and these were exacerbated by the Portuguese company's fragmented ownership. Not all the parties involved were happy with the prospect of losing their independence. Now after months of tedious negotiations Charles could finally see a positive outcome.

Henry put down the document that he had been reading when Charles had entered and studied his visitor quizzically.

"You're smiling Charles. That usually means that you have something pleasant to tell me."

"I think we are there."

The words were very simple and indefinite but Henry knew immediately what they meant.

"Really. Now that is worth smiling about."

"We had a rough outline of an agreement last week, but as usual, there were the usual small hitches and one slightly larger one."

Henry was smiling.

"The usual 'what's in it for me' queries?"

"Exactly."

"And?"

"I've promised that we will make São Paulo our regional HQ. All the details and figures are in my report. Celia will bring it to you as soon as she has put it all together."

"Good. That's much as I expected. In their position I would have stuck out for the same. I'll give the report a quick run through before lunch and then we can go through it in detail together in a day or so. What sort of timescale are we working to?"

"I thought it best to move quickly on this, so we have pencilled in Friday of next week, if that is convenient for you. We also thought Lisbon for the signing."

"No problem. This is excellent news. I think this will provide the platform for our next stage of growth."

He had risen from his desk as he was speaking and moved towards the drinks cabinet.

"I think a drink is called for. It's a bit early, so we had best make it a sherry."

He solemnly filled two small sherry glasses and handed one to Charles who stood to receive it and then raised it with a toast.

"Here's to luck in Lisbon!"

"I think we can leave Lady Luck out of things. I've had a feeling in my gut about this one all along. Let's just make it The Future!"

Charles, smiling broadly, touched Henry's glass with his own and repeated the toast.

"The Future!"

"Over the years," Henry continued as he returned to his chair, "I've learned to trust my gut instinct. Back in the seventies when I took over, no one gave us a chance of surviving against the big groups that were being formed. My gut instincts told me we could survive if we stuck to what we are good at and did that well. Now look at us. We are stronger now than we have ever been. With Cardosa under our belt, we shall become stronger still, and that, in no small way, is due to you. I feel very much in your debt."

"Not just me Henry. It's been a team effort."

"Well. You and your team then."

He paused for a moment, considering how best to phrase what he was about to say.

"I have been giving a lot of thought recently to what comes next. I have decided that when the dust has settled on the Cardosa tie-up, that will be a good time for me to step down from my current role. When that happens, and this is strictly between the two of us and must go no further, I shall want you to take over full operating control of the company."

Charles seemed a little surprised by the announcement.

"Thank you, Henry. I was not expecting that."

"Well, you deserve it. I'm telling you now to give you time to adjust your thinking."

"Does Caroline know what you are planning?"

"Lord no. She has been suggesting that I should be thinking about retirement for a couple of years or so. I do not want her to get any wind of this until it is all settled."

He toyed momentarily with his sherry glass.

"It's ironic that we are lining up our biggest deal in Portugal. The family were shipping wine out of there long before we became bankers. What followed was pure chance. The government wanted to smuggle gold payments into the peninsular to help finance opposition to Napoleon. With our contacts we were a ready-made conduit. The banking interests developed from that. The shipping business declined with the advent of steam and was sold off last century, but ships are still in the family blood. That has always been the case. Rayleton men have always had to choose between a city desk or the sea."

He paused at this point, his gaze fixed on Charles. The latter quickly picked up on the drift his conversation had taken.

"Which brings us round to Richard."

"Exactly! He is the only Rayleton man of his generation. I can't allow him that choice."

As he had been speaking, Henry had risen to his feet. He now moved behind the seat he had just vacated.

"When you have in turn retired, I want to see him sitting in this chair. So, one of the many jobs you will be taking on is making as sure as possible that he is ready for that role."

Charles chuckled.

"For once I'm ahead of you there. I've already made arrangements to bring him back here when he has completed the end of year figures for the Jersey office."

"Have you now. What do you have lined up for him?"

"I am making him a deputy to John Haslam. In addition to working on existing Corporate Finance operations, he will also have specific responsibility for developing the small companies list. There is a degree of overlap between the two."

"Good! That should stretch him enough to take his mind off boats."

"Yes. He seems to relish anything with a competitive edge to judge by the recent St. Helier episode."

"I could not agree more. That is not the sort of image we should be cultivating."

"Right. I'll break the good news to him after next week's divisional heads meeting. So, if there is nothing else you need to bring up, I'll get back to my office."

"Make the date for the Lisbon signing immediately after the divisional meeting. I shall be overflying Jersey, so Richard can fly back with me. It will be a good opportunity to give him a taste of life at the top while having a friendly chat. So, let me know as soon as there is a fixed date so that Harry can arrange his schedule."

5

From the moment that Jenny had discovered that the source of her grandfather's unopened letter was not only still in existence, but was more than ready to meet her, all Martha's latent maternal instincts had come to the fore. The life she had known had been centred firmly on farm and family. To her the idea of flying across the Atlantic to meet an unknown lawyer in London appeared as risky and far-fetched as attempting to land on the moon. In the weeks that followed she had mustered every argument that her mind could think of against the scheme. Then, once it had become clear that Jenny was determined on her course of action, she had switched her attention to the practicalities of the journey. A joint excursion into town had resulted in the purchase of a large wheeled suitcase and two new outfits together with several hundred dollars-worth of UK pounds. Finally, on the morning of departure, she and Hal had driven Jenny to the airport and accompanied her as far as passport control. Only there, after many hugs and last-minute advice, was Jenny left to herself. Making her way to the departure gate, Jenny was quietly relieved that she was finally on her way.

In the event none of Martha's worries had materialised.

The journey had gone smoothly, and once in England, Jenny had begun to relax and enjoy herself. She had allowed herself a couple of clear days before her scheduled meeting and had spent the time in familiarising herself with the rudiments of London life. Armed with a street map and a map of the London underground, she had set forth on her third morning to keep her appointment.

The street she had sought, tucked away a short distance from the imposing buildings of Britain's government, was the essence of what she had seen in movies. Quiet, discrete and all of a period, it had the appearance of having seen little change over many decades. She was particularly fascinated by the brass name plates that each property bore. Each one was given careful scrutiny. Finally, she found what she was looking for and stood gazing for a moment at the plaque that was engraved with 'Higgs, Camden & Higgs, Solicitors and Commissioners of Oaths'. She hesitated for a moment, then taking a deep breath, she stepped inside.

The reception office of the legal practice was furnished in modern style with clean-cut desks and stylish office machines, but when she was led to an upstairs office Jenny found herself moving back in time to a period that would have been considered dated even when the letter to her grandfather had been written. The office into which she was shown was dominated by a large mahogany partners desk. Behind it an avuncular looking man with thinning silvery hair sat in a large desk chair of similar vintage to the desk. As she entered, he rose to meet her and stepped around his desk. A beaming smile accompanied the hand he extended to her.

"Miss Pearson, it is lovely to meet you. I am James Camden. Please take a seat."

Formalities over, he returned to his own seat.

"Firstly, I must apologise for dragging you three thousand miles across the Atlantic to meet me. Your case is an unusual one and a little complex. I thought it would be best to meet you in person and deal with matters face to face."

As he spoke, Jenny found herself relaxing.

"It's no problem. I would have come to England in any case to try to trace any kinfolk I might have over here."

"Well, I don't know if this will lead you to any family members here in the UK, but I'm sure that you will find the trip worthwhile. It really is all quite extraordinary."

He gave Jenny another of his smiles and then returned to the file.

"Now you said in your letter to us that after the death of your grandfather you had found an unopened letter from this office dated 1942 in his effects. Have you brought that letter with you?"

Jenny took out the 1942 letter from her bag and handed it to him. Camden immediately rose to his feet.

"If you will excuse me for a moment, I'll get Helen to make a photocopy of this. She will hand it back to you when you leave."

Within minutes he was back behind his desk.

"Don't worry, your letter is genuine. It has my father's signature at the bottom. Unfortunately, we do not have a copy. That does not surprise me. Things were very chaotic here during the war – one of our storage buildings was bombed. Luckily, we still have this file, which would appear to be much older."

"Does that mean there will be problems?"

"Not at all. Quite the contrary in fact. Everything seems to be in perfect order. That is what I find so extraordinary. It has all been maintained so carefully for all these years."

Jenny shook her head in confusion.

"I'm sorry, you've lost me. All what years?"

"Forgive me. I have not explained things very well. Now let me see. The first document is dated 1805, which was the time of the Napoleonic War, and then there is a regular sequence until 1941. What is most mystifying is that the original testator, James Edward Pearson, attached a letter to the sole beneficiary, asking that everything should be left untouched. All later testators appear to have simply copied this request."

"Why would they do that?"

"I have no idea. I have never met anything like this before." He gave a shrug of puzzlement before returning to the file. "The last document records the death of William Theodore Pearson."

"That was my great-grandfather. He died on the day the Japanese bombed Pearl Harbour."

"A day to remember indeed, but I begin to see a pattern of events forming. You said in your letter that your grandfather was in military service at the time."

"Yes, he was in the marines. He spent the whole war period in the Pacific."

"I see. And your father?"

"Both of my parents were killed in an automobile accident when I was very young."

"Ah! I'm sorry to hear that."

Jenny put on a brave face. "It was a long time ago and I was still only a baby. So..." She shrugged ruefully at the thought of parents she could not remember.

"Quite so."

Camden was somewhat concerned at the old upsets that had been exposed and quietly steered their conversation back to the matters in hand.

"I'm sorry to have reminded you of unhappy times, but it does explain the break in the pattern."

Jenny looked puzzled. "I don't get it."

Camden returned to the file before him on the desk.

"Well Miss Pearson, we are dealing with the affairs of many generations of your family spread over more than two-hundred years. Yet, in all that time, no one has altered any of the original dispositions; not even the bank account. I find that truly remarkable."

Jenny looked across the desk to him in stunned disbelief.

"You mean there is a bank account that no one has touched since eighteen hundred and whatever it was?"

"Precisely so."

Camden took a document for her to see.

"Here is the original certificate of deposit, dated 1803 for the sum of five hundred pounds with Lablanche Freres of St. Helier.

"St. Helier? Where is that?"

"I'm sorry. I was forgetting that you are new to England," he replied smiling. "St. Helier is the capital of Jersey, one of the Channel Islands. They are English, but operate as self-governing crown dependencies – one of the remaining legacies of the Norman conquest. Actually, they are much closer to the French coast than to England."

Warming to his subject, he returned his attention to the file and extracted further documents.

"There is also a property referred to as 'The Cottage", which is also situated in Jersey. All of the assets were under the trusteeship of Lablanche Freres."

He paused to study Jenny's face.

"You seem a little confused."

Jenny shook her head in disbelief.

"I am, and more than a little. I mean what is this all about and what is it all worth?"

Camden shook his head.

"This is quite the strangest case that I have ever dealt with. I'm afraid I cannot give a straight answer to either question. What I can say is that in 1803 £500 was quite a large sum of money and when the deposit was made, it was stipulated that all money in the account was to be held in gold. So, measured in today's devalued money, we are looking at a figure at least one thousand times greater. In addition, the cottage has been let out for rent over much of that period and all money received from that has also been reinvested in gold over the entire period. The person who made this deposit obviously understood money."

Camden sat back in his chair in order to regard his client.

"I may not be able to give you a precise figure, but what I can say is that you will certainly be very comfortably off."

Jenny had listened to him in growing disbelief, her eyes growing ever wider as the solicitor described the inheritance.

"And you're sure it is mine?"

"Oh yes! Quite sure. The papers that you forwarded from America have been confirmed by your embassy here in London, and I have had a genealogical search carried out. I am quite sure that you are the sole and rightful heir to William Theodore Pearson."

Jenny continued to sit almost motionless, only the slight chewing off her lip showed the mental shock she was under-going as Camden continued his summary of her affairs.

"I have made further enquiries here in London. Lablanche Freres were taken over some years ago by Rayleton Securities, a very reputable private banking group. The account continues to be managed by their Jersey office. The cottage has been occupied until recently, but is currently vacant. So, have a think about how you wish to proceed and let me know. We can of course deal with everything here in London and, if you wish, I can arrange for the sale of the cottage.

"No. Thank you, but no."

Jenny had switched into life at Camden's suggestion.

"I would like to go to St. what-ever-it was and take over my affairs."

She paused for a moment before deciding that Camden needed to better understand her situation.

"Last month I had to sell grandpa's farm to pay off the mortgage. I've been lodging with my grandmother's sister Martha since grandpa died – she and Hal have the next-door farm. That is the address I have been using. At the moment I have no home, no job and no direct family. The big idea in coming over here was to look for any kinsfolk I might have. So, the cottage in Jersey can be home for a while. That will give me time to get my head round all of this and follow up the new leads you have given me."

The remainder of the day after she left Camden's office passed as if in a dream. Returning to her hotel room, she sat for a long time on the edge of the bed lost in thought. Uppermost in her mind was the thought of all the many years the fateful letter had lain unopened. Her mind wandered over all the things that might have been different. Grandpa would not have been so beset by money worries. Perhaps her parents might have been doing something totally different on the day of their accident. She continued in this way for a long time until she realised that darkness was falling and that she had not eaten since breakfast.

Before leaving the Camden office, calls had been made to Rayleton Securities' Jersey office. An appointment had been made for the following week. In the morning she would have to arrange a flight to the Channel Islands and book somewhere to stay. In the morning she thought, a whole new world was opening up.

6

Alan Baxter was not a man of airs and graces. His whole being stated the very opposite. Heavy and square of build, the set of his jaw spoke of a man who would stand neither nonsense nor pretence. In early manhood, after gaining skills as a carpenter, he had decided to work for himself. He had progressed steadily from simple boat repair work at the beginning to now being the owner of a company whose products were featured in many leading yachting publications. At times it had been a struggle, but he had won through by a combination of bulldozing effort and a belief in himself that allowed him to take risks. The face that he presented was, therefore, that of a man whose guiding principle was the belief that you did not get anywhere in life by being nice to people.

This same principle underlay his managerial style. Anyone taking employment with Baxter Marine would very quickly learn that in all matters he was the absolute master. All decisions were made by him and questioning anything, once he had decided on a matter, was something few would contemplate. Even in matters of design, where he knew little of the intricacies and technical details of the more sophisticated craft that his company now produced, he could not bring himself to fully delegate any form of authority and still insisted on having the final say. Thus it was, that today he was afloat on the choppy waters of the Solent in his company's motor launch, watching their latest creation put through its paces.

That the owner of Baxter Marine Ltd should be afloat viewing the performance of his company's latest creation was not in itself strange. For boatyards up and down the country this was standard practice and would be seen as a simple matter of course. At Baxter Marine it was a practice followed as infrequently as possible. From the very first time that he had taken to the water in one of his craft he had learned that, once afloat, his strength and stature were as nothing. Although he would never admit to it and did his best to hide the fact, Baxter suffered from acute hydrophobia. Put simply he was terrified of water, and in particular of the ever-changing and often turbulent variety that covered much of the surface of the globe. He kept his fear well hidden. While such weakness would be seen as a natural enough trait in others, they were deeply at odds with how he saw and projected himself. Rather than seeking ways of overcoming his fears, he had learned at an early age that any weakness or deficiency could be masked by bravado or aggression.

This morning his company's latest creation was having its final test cruise following a number of small modifications. The decision on whether or not to proceed with the craft lay with him. Of necessity he had taken to the water with seeming panache, while all the time fighting to overcome the sense that all his bodily strength had deserted him. Throughout he maintained a tight grip on the edge of the cockpit, while uppermost in his mind was the thought of how quickly he could conclude the operation and return to land.

Alongside him Gary Lucas his head of design was at the wheel. Lucas' designation as head of design covered a mixed role. As the company had no specified production manager, he supervised both the design and construction of the yachts. As such he was one of the few people that Baxter would listen to. Even so, Lucas was enough the diplomat to know how far his authority ran. He could advise, but all decisions were made by Baxter himself.

"She's looking good Gary. How much faster is she do you reckon?"

"In these conditions a good two knots. With lighter winds, perhaps a bit less."

"Is that the maximum we can get from her?"

"Almost, but it would spoil her looks if we crammed any more sail on her."

Baxter thought briefly about the effects such design change would have on his marketing operations.

"No. We don't want that. Tell the lads I'm pleased with that."

Lucas complied by steering the launch to within easy hailing distance and passing the message and instructions to return to base to the yacht's crew.

Beside him, despite his words of praise, Baxter looked grim faced.

"Right. Now take us back in."

Lucas gave a final wave to the yacht and turned in a wide arc back to the shore.

The thought of imminent return to land did nothing to improve Baxter's humour. If anything, his face became grimmer as Lucas eased the launch past a number of expensive-looking boats to the company's single mooring. The boats belonged to clients of the Maitlands. His own business had first been developed on a piece of land with no direct river access. It was only later that he had been able to purchase an old cottage with a garden that gave him the river frontage that he craved, and even that was barely adequate. By contrast the adjacent Maitland boatyard enjoyed a much deeper plot with wide river access providing scope for slip-ways and excellent moorings. Baxter had long coveted his neighbour's property and had made a number of offers to buy it, each of which had been resolutely refused. Now, whenever Baxter had to take to the water, he had the strongest of reminders of this inferior position. The anger that he felt and his inner fears would combine to put him in the blackest of moods for the remainder of the day.

As soon as they touched the jetty Baxter jumped ashore, leaving Lucas to secure the launch. He barked new orders as he strode away.

"Get the two unsold boats modified."

Lucas paused in his mooring to call to him.

"Right. What about new construction?"

Baxter paused briefly before replying.

"Hold fire for the moment. I'm having lunch with a business associate. I'll decide after that."

With that he continued into the modern showroom that stood adjacent to the workshops.

The company's various offices were accessed from a corridor that ran off the showroom. Baxter had already slipped off the storm coat that he had worn on the launch, revealing an expensive suit. As he entered the small outer office where his blonde-haired secretary worked, he threw the storm jacket across her desk without looking.

"Get me a coffee darlin'," was his only comment as he passed into his much larger office and sank into the leather-covered executive chair behind a wide desk that was clear of any accoutrements except for a cigar box and large ashtray. He breathed out for a few moments seeking to find relaxation and then, opening the single desk drawer, took out a cigarette lighter and penknife. Taking a cigar from the box, he cut the tip and flicked a flame from the lighter. Then, sitting back in the chair, he inhaled deeply from the lighted cigar.

It was then that he noticed the figure standing in the doorway. Ron Nugent the company's accountant had been waiting for his return from the sea trial. A slim already slightly balding man in his mid-thirties, Nugent was the complete antithesis to his employer in both looks and demeanour. His voice was uncertain as he addressed the seated figure.

"I need a word Mr Baxter."

"Not now son, I'm busy." Baxter shamelessly batted away the unwanted visitor.

Nugent stood uncertainly for a moment, but necessity gave him the courage to stay and speak up.

"There's a problem."

"There always is. That's why I employ people like you."

Nugent continued to hold his ground and, seeing that he was not to be shooed away, Baxter placed the cigar in the ashtray.

"Right son. Let's have your problem, but make it quick."

Nugent advanced into the room and carefully closed the door.

"We have a cashflow problem."

Baxter was aware that they had been overdrawn for the past eighteen months or more and Nugent had pointed out to him on several occasions that the overdraft was growing, but he had not really given it any attention. When he had been at school his grasp of mathematics had not been strong. As a result, he found accounts deeply boring. As far as he was concerned, growing businesses were always short of money until they reached a certain level of sales. He could not see how there could be a new problem.

"What sort of problem?"

"The bank will not advance any more credit."

"Well borrow from somewhere else."

Nugent shook his head.

I've tried them all. Same story. If our own bankers won't support us, they don't want to know."

Baxter sat back and drew deeply on his cigar as he thought.

"This is a print-out of my cashflow figures for the rest of the year." Nugent offered holding out a paper to him.

Baxter waved away the offered document.

"What do you need money for right now?"

"I have to renew the company's liability insurances."

"Right, stall them."

"I've been stalling them for three months. Cover will lapse tomorrow unless they get our cheque."

"OK. Let it lapse."

"We can't do that. If anything were to go wrong it could cost us thousands."

Baxter eyed his startled accountant.

"How many claims have we had to meet so far this year?"

"None."

"And last year?"

"Jim Dykes made a claim when he lost the top of his finger last year."

"Peanuts. Let it lapse for now and I'll get something sorted. Now run away and play with your numbers."

Nugent slipped gratefully out of the room. Behind him Baxter closed his eyes and drew again deeply on his cigar.

7

Richard closed the file on which he had been working, sat back in his chair, stretched his arms in the air, and yawned. He had long ago decided that end-of-year accounts had to be the most tedious and mind-numbing occupation ever created, no matter how important it might be. As if that were not enough, a steady flow of business continued to pass through his office and the demands of the ending of the bank's financial year had to be fitted in around this. Today had been a typical exemplar of this pattern. A string of meetings in the morning and a sandwich snatched at his desk, had been followed by a two-hour session checking figures that the Accounts Department had prepared. It was a welcome relief, therefore, to lay aside the accounts in readiness for his only appointment of the afternoon.

The daily list which Charlotte prepared for him simply stated, 4.30pm J.Pearson, Higgs, Camden & Higgs. None of the names meant anything to him. Whether J. Pearson would prove to be lawyer, accountant or some financial adviser he could not ascertain, but either way, he assumed, it would be yet another suit. He was, pleasantly surprised, therefore, when Charlotte ushered in his visitor. This new client was refreshingly different. She was not only young and attractive but, in place of the usual dark business attire and briefcase, she wore a simple dress with a short jacket and carried a small handbag. There was also something about the style which suggested that she was neither English nor continental.

Momentarily caught unprepared, Richard failed to take the lead with the usual formal handshake and greeting. Instead it was left to his visitor to take the initiative.

"Hi! I'm Jenny Pearson. I'm here about my Grandpa's estate."

For a moment he was at a loss. His mind was preoccupied with the recognition that her voice was very musical and that her intonation was unmistakably American. He was finally brought to action by the strange glare on Charlotte's face as she held out the file she had carried through from her office.

"Oh, Hi. Lovely to meet you. Please take a seat."

He found himself uttering, while at the same time scuttling for the temporary security of his desk, all the time cursing himself for the unusual loss of professionalism.

Jenny took the proffered seat and Richard turned to the file Charlotte had placed on his desk. He was grateful for the momentary respite it gave in which he could organize his thoughts.

"So, you have come over from America. I assume you came via London?"

"Yes. I was there for almost a week. I flew here yesterday."

"And how are you finding things?"

"Well, I grew up on a farm. After that, London was quite a shock."

"And how are you finding Jersey?"

"I haven't seen much of it yet, but what I have seen I like. It seems so quiet and organized."

Richard smiled.

"Local people might not agree with you on that.

Compared to what it was like years ago it seems much busier. It's now one of the favourite centres for off-shore banking."

"What's that?"

"Tax rates here are low compared to say London or New York, so wealthy people park their spare cash here."

"I'm not sure if I'm classed as one of your wealthy clientele. I have only recently learned that I have inherited a bank account here."

Richard found himself relaxing at the simple openness of her words.

"Quite so, and here it is," he replied indicating the file in front of him. "How much has your solicitor told you?"

"Only that I have an account and an empty property."

"That is not entirely correct. You do have an account and real estate, but the property is not vacant."

He noticed her puzzled look.

"I had better explain. In addition to being a financial centre Jersey is also a very desirable place to live. The result has been strong demand for property at all levels. Properties do not stay unoccupied for long and prices and rents have steadily increased. Some years back, steps were taken to protect local families from runaway property prices. So, there are two markets – one for locals and another restricted market for incomers where the prices are three to four times higher."

"I guess you have to be rich to live here."

"That's about the strength of it."

"And what category does my property fall in?"

"The figures of the rental suggest that it is on the restricted list. The rental is currently £3,300 per month and is currently payable quarterly. Which means every quarter a payment for £9,900 arrives in this office."

"How much is that in dollars?"

Richard reached for his desk calculator and tapped in a quick calculation.

"Give or take a few dollars, around thirteen thousand."

Jenny's mouth had opened in shock.

"Why, that's more than fifty thousand a year. Who would want to pay that much in rent every year?"

"A surprising number it would seem. Actually, your property is occupied on a long-term lease by an Investment Trust Group."

Richard's explanation was greeted with a broad smile.

"Which is what?"

"In this case it is the official address of a of number of investment funds whose shares are bought by the general public."

"And they base themselves here…"

"To take advantage of the Jersey tax rates."

"Well I guess they won't be going anywhere for a while."

"No. I would think not." He paused noticing that his visitor was chewing her lip. "Is that a problem?"

"I only learned about Jersey and my affairs here a few days ago. When I was told that the property was vacant I thought perhaps I could stay there while I tried to track down any kinsfolk I might have."

"I see."

"I guess I'll just have to stay in a hotel. I should be able to afford it with all the rent coming in each month."

"Ah! That brings us to the account. In addition to the property there are the original cash and deposit accounts. They are somewhat unusual in that they have not been drawn on for well over two hundred years, but I'm sure your London solicitor has already explained that to you."

He looked across at Jenny who nodded her acknowledgement.

"The cash account seems to have always been used solely as a conduit to the deposit account. At the moment there is only a token amount in it. The deposit account is where all the wealth that you have inherited is located. The original depositor obviously had a good understanding of money and stipulated that it should be held in gold."

"Is that still the case?"

"Oh yes! Until we receive instructions to the contrary, any new money coming into the cash account is invested in gold via the deposit fund. At the moment that is four times a year as each rental payment is received."

"Is the gold held here?"

Richard pursed his lips as if to discourage such risk.

"No. It has to be held in high security vaults. I believe that currently some is held in London and some in Zurich."

"Gosh! Can I change any of this?"

"Of course. It is your account. Once we have a sample of your signature you can arrange for any amount to be transferred to the current account. I should warn you, however, that bullion banks are like the mills of heaven. They grind exceeding slow. Any dealings with them can take many weeks."

He noticed that Jenny was chewing her lip once more.

"If you need money, then we could arrange for all or part of the rental income to be retained in the cash account."

"I wouldn't want all of it. I've never had much money."

"Should we say £1000 each month."

"That would be more than enough."

"Well it can easily be changed if that proves to be the case."

He drew open a draw of his desk and selected a number of forms.

"Right! Let's get down to business."

It was only after numerous forms had been filled and signed that Richard
returned to the original file.

"There is one final item I must mention. There are two

bundles of papers recorded here. They are not in our modern filing system, so they must relate to the time when Lablanche Freres were in operation. All of their old files are stored in the basement. I was hoping to have your bundles ready for today, but there is a lot of material to sort through. I will let you have them as soon as we locate them."

"Right. What kind of papers? Are there any details?"

"I'm afraid not. The file simply lists them as assorted papers. So! There you have it."

"They are probably nothing important."

Richard put his papers in order as she spoke and then looked at his watch.

"Golly! Time has flown."

He rose from his desk and stepped across to the door to the outer office. Opening the door, he peered inside.

"As I thought. Charlotte has already left."

Jenny reached down to pick up her handbag, which she had set by the leg of the chair, rose to her feet and took up the large envelope which Richard had provided to hold the various documents the meeting had produced. That done she extended her hand to Richard.

"Thank you for explaining everything to me. It's all so strange and I'm such a dummy on financial matters."

Richard took her extended hand in a gentle clasp and looked steadily at her.

"I would not agree with that for one moment. From what I have seen, you have been dealing with a massive upheaval in your life extremely well, and for what it is worth, I think it took real courage to come to Europe, as you have, to sort things out."

She smiled and her head made a brief nod of acceptance.

"Thank you."

He held the clasp a moment longer and then withdrew his hand.

"Right then. We have taken longer than I had anticipated

and we have gone past our normal closing time. The front door will be locked and the other staff have probably gone home, so I will see you out."

As the elevator took them to them to the ground floor, a thought crossed Jenny's mind.

"I hope that long session with my affairs has not upset your timetable."

Richard chuckled.

"Not in the least. The bank's end of year is fast approaching and I had a spell of record checking and summarizing pencilled in. Our meeting has saved me from that fate."

Jenny was smiling as she replied.

"But the work is still there waiting to be done."

The elevator shuddered to a halt and Richard followed into the hallway before laughingly replying.

"Ah, but this time it will be in my favourite armchair with a lovely view of the sea and a beer at my side."

They had reached the front entrance. Richard took a large ornamented key from his pocket and unlocked the door.

"And what about you. Have you any plans?"

Jenny made a gesture of uncertainty.

"Not sure. My funds are limited and I had hoped that I might be able to use the house. I guess I'll have to think again what my best course of action is."

Her face had become serious as she spoke, but she took a deep breath and put on a sunnier look.

"Whatever that will be, now that I'm here I can at least seek out the house that twelve-times-great grandfather Pearson left to emigrate to America."

Richard had opened the door as she made her last statement and followed her as she stepped outside.

"Now we are in the street, I can speak as a private individual. I know your property well. I've had business there at odd times. It is only a couple of miles or so out of town, but it would be so much easier for you if you would let me drive you there and for me it would be a real pleasure."

There was a look of hopeful expectancy on his face that Jenny found comically touching.

"That is so thoughtful of you. Yes. I would like that. What time do you suggest?"

"It's the weekend, so we can choose any time. I could pick you up outside your hotel at midday, then we could have lunch and do the house viewing afterwards."

"That sounds great. I'll see you tomorrow at twelve then."

She walked off down the street and then, thinking of something, turned to call back to him laughing.

"I'm staying at The Radisson Blu."

There was a seeming nonchalance about her walk that hid what she was really feeling. Behind her, Richard stood watching her walk away, his mind turning such somersaults that he almost forgot that he had to pick up the work files to take home and lock up the bank premises for the weekend.

Jenny had remained on the café terrace while Richard was settling their lunch bill. She sat quietly musing over the previous twenty-four hours. So much seemed to have happened in such a short space of time and all of it so different from the life she had known. It all felt unreal. Was it only yesterday that she had learned that she was worth several hundred thousand dollars and, in addition, owned a property here in Jersey, that for the foreseeable future would provide her with a very comfortable income. There was this morning's foray into St. Helier's shops looking for new clothes and then being whisked off to the coast to lunch in a café quite unlike anything she had known in America, where she had been inveigled into sharing a large platter of seafood, another first which she had enjoyed enormously. So many facts and sights and tastes she thought and linking them all was this man, whom she had met only yesterday. She giggled to herself at the thought of what Martha would make of it all.

Her thoughts were broken by the arrival at her side of the man in question.

"Right, all done and dusted. What would you like to do now?"

"There is so much, but first of all there's something I'd like to know before we go down to the harbour."

"And what would that be?"

"I would like to know your name. Yesterday you simply introduced yourself as Richard."

"Ah! Yesterday I was in a bit of a muddle."

She laughed.

"Yesterday I think we both were."

"Yes, disorientating but very enjoyable."

"Whereas today it is simply very enjoyable, and I shall enjoy the experience even more when I know the name of the man responsible."

"My surname is Rayleton."

"Mm. Richard Rayleton. Sounds good ..."

She paused as a thought struck her.

"Rayleton. Isn't that the name of the bank?"

"Yes, but don't jump to any conclusions. It's a family business and I belong to a junior branch of the family. To the bank I'm just an employee."

Jenny said no more on the matter as they made their way down to the centre of the little town and moved through the colourful main street and along the harbour wall. She was engrossed by everything around her, but she was particularly fascinated by the constant movement of the sea against the base of the harbour wall.

"Doesn't it ever rest," she queried as she peered down at the grey-blue water.

"Not really. There is always some form of movement. First time by the sea?"

"Yep. It's pretty well first time for everything over here."

"Come, let's go back and go down on to the beach for your next great seaside revelation."

"What's that?"

"You'll find out."

They descended from the solidity of the harbour wall on to an area of dry sand. Jenny quickly discovered that it was a treacherous surface on which any progress was laboured.

"Is this the revelation that you meant. My shoes are full of sand and I'm in danger of breaking either my heels or my ankles."

Richard was already sitting down and untying his shoelaces. He smiled happily at her complaints as he proceeded to remove his socks and stuff each one into a shoe and tie both sets of laces together. This done, he proceeded to carefully turn up the ends of his trouser legs to mid-calf height. Then rising to his feet, he slung the tied shoes across his shoulder before turning to display himself, arms raised wide.

"Voila! We are ready to walk on the beach. All you have to do is slip your shoes…"

His voice trailed off as he noticed that Jenny was already bent over removing hers. As she straightened up he took the shoes from her hand.

"You have a bag. I'll carry the shoes. That way we each have a hand free in case we want to hold hands."

"And do you want to hold hands?"

"I think so. Do you?"

In reply she slipped her hand into his. It seemed the most natural thing in the world and needed no thought. Hand in hand they began to walk. Their progress was slow with frequent stops to examine items washed up on the beach or to ask questions which required looking at the other's face. Ahead of them the beach stretched into the far distance and measured time had ceased to exist.

. . .

It was many hours later that they exited the sands as dusk began to close in, and much later still after a meal of take-away fish and chips in the lively atmosphere of the harbour that they finally made their way back to the car.

Richard drew in by the entrance to the Radisson Blu and slipped the gearstick into neutral.

"Enjoyed your day?"

Jenny nodded.

"All of it. It's odd to think that this one day is the whole time we have known each other."

"I know, and yet I feel that I've known you all my life."

"Me too."

She alighted from the car and shook her head at the strangeness of it all. Then she began to giggle as a new thought crossed her mind.

"We forgot to look at my property."

Richard chuckled loudly.

"Perhaps it's just as well. It might have been a let-down for you. There are trees screening it from the road these days, so there is not much to see. You get a better feel of the place from the sea."

A thought struck him.

"We can do that tomorrow. I'll meet you here at 10 am. Wear something casual, jeans or something similar. Oh, and bring something warm."

With that he slipped the car into gear and with a cheery wave drove away.

The following morning, as on the previous day, Jenny was standing waiting at the entrance to the hotel as Richard arrived, his face glowing as much from the anticipation of a seeing Jenny again and showing her his new boat as from the ten-minute walk from his flat.

They exchanged greetings and looked at each other momentarily.

"How do I look?"

Richard was pleased to see that she was dressed much as he had suggested.

"Every inch the able seaman."

"How are we travelling. I can't see any ferries."

"We don't need a ferry, and in any case, they keep well offshore. We need to get in closer. So, a boat is the order of the day. Come I'll show you."

Surprise, curiosity and concern assailed her in turn as she followed him across the road to the marina. Her concern abated somewhat as she found herself in the midst of this strange array of boats of all shapes and sizes. Finally, Richard halted at the stern of a sailing boat and, after jumping aboard, offered her a hand. Once she was aboard he unlocked the cabin door.

Right. You can settle down here or have a look around down below while I unmoor her and get ready. He stopped, aware that she had not moved.

"Are you OK with this?"

"I didn't expect this. I mean, is this boat yours and do you know what you are doing?"

Richard gave her a reassuring grin.

"Yes. This is my boat, and yes, I do know what I'm doing."

He took both of her hands in his.

"I know this must all be very strange to you, but trust me. I've been messing around in boats most of my life and that includes ocean sailing. I'm also a qualified yacht master."

Jenny had let her hands rest in his.

"I do trust you. It is just that you're asking me to jump through too many hoops all at once. Just give me a few minutes to get used to everything. Don't forget my family were farmers. We have no connection with the sea."

She sat in the cockpit while Richard made his preparations.

What's the name of the boat, she called to him as he freed the mooring rope.

"*Sea Urchin.*"

"Urchin?" she called back. "How does that square with being a qualified yacht master?"

"That's for the off-duty times."

"And how would you class today?"

"Very much on-duty while we are afloat. Any sailor will tell you that."

"That is reassuring."

"Good. Are you ready to set off?"

As Richard had expected, the direction of the prevailing breeze made for slow progress until they had rounded the long Noirmont headland. As they approached, the yacht rolled from side to side in the swell. He glanced across at Jenny and was pleased to see that her moving with the boat.

"The motion doesn't seem to bother you."

"No. It's a bit like riding a horse. You just go with it."

"Have you done much riding?"

"Horse breeding was one of Grandpa's side lines. I grew up with them."

"You will have to meet my cousin Sally. She's mad about horses."

Once round the headland, with the breeze at their backs, sailing became easier. As they passed into St. Brelade's Bay conversation lapsed while Richard busied himself reducing sail. With the boat scarcely moving he was satisfied that Jenny would have ample time to take in the details of the shoreline.

"This is as close in as we can go," he said as they came abreast of St. Brelade's.

"The stone building directly ahead is St. Brelade's Chapel.

It's the oldest church on the island. The church behind it is much later. Your property lies just a little to the right. It would have been much quieter back in eighteen hundred. A lot of the buildings you can see have been erected since the war."

Jenny had come to stand next to him. Richard put his arm around her shoulder.

"You're very quiet."

"Am I? There's a lot to take in."

She paused to look around the sweep of the bay before continuing.

"It's strange. I'm getting mixed feelings. It's all so very beautiful that I'm asking myself why did twelve-times-great Grandfather Pearson ever want to leave this behind. Yet at the same time, ever since we came around the headland back there, I've had this feeling that something bad happened here."

She looked directly at Richard.

"Maybe the two things are connected."

8

During the period that he had been based in Jersey, Richard had found the monthly divisional meetings at the bank's London headquarters a welcome break from regular routine. The huge difference between the relative peace of Jersey and the constant bustle of the capital he had at different times found interesting, fascinating, even maddening and sometimes all three, but never before had he found it dull. In the past he would have flown to London on the evening before the meeting and spent the night at his Richmond flat, which he currently allowed his friend Alex to use. This allowed for a more relaxed journey that avoided the worst horrors of the London rush hour.

In the weeks since the last meeting so much had happened. Meeting Jenny had turned his life upside down in a way he could never have imagined. They had seen each other every day since their boat trip. Each day had seen their relationship steadily deepen. Both realised it's lasting nature and Jenny had needed little persuasion to relinquish the room at the Radisson Blu and move into his company flat. There was no way the London meeting could be avoided, but his absence from Jersey could be minimised by catching the first flight of the day. He smiled to himself as he pictured how she had looked, fast asleep with her hair strewn across the pillow, as he had tiptoed from the bedroom.

The simple beauty of that memory was in total contrast to the mayhem of London in the grip of the morning rush hour that followed his arrival. It was a relief when he finally entered the bank's Head Office and joined the familiar surroundings and routines of office life. The feeling of relief was not to last. He was able to join the scheduled meeting with few minutes to spare. After the usual survey of results, section by section, they had moved on to a number of issues presented by Harry Iverson the Head of Compliance. Harry was not a man to fail to dot an 'i' or cross a 't' and compliance offered ample opportunity to exercise this particular skill. The meeting had dragged on, the mass of detail creating as much new confusion as the old concerns it settled. By the time the meeting had closed, the lunch break was fast approaching.

Richard made his way to Alex's office. He was sitting at a desk with his back to the door. His eyes were fixed on the screen of his desk computer which was displaying Test Match coverage. Richard entered as silently as he could.

"I read recently that Top Guns in the city earn their employers thousands of pounds every minute. Obviously, a gross exaggeration."

The figure at the desk swung round. A broad grin creased his face.

"Rest a while young man and I will perform some mundane financial miracle for you."

Richard gave a casual glance at the screen.

"Anything happening?"

"Australia have just taken another wicket. Anyway, what brings you to the big bad city?"

"Usual monthly meeting and then some compliance matters."

"Harry on good form?"

Richard raised his eyebrows in in mock supplication.

"Oh yes! A real three-yachter."

"What's a three-yachter?"

A young woman had followed Richard into the office. Alex laughingly explained.

"When Richard is bored in meetings, he draws yachts."

"I managed three this morning."

"Bad as that, huh? Well this should liven up your day. Charles wants you in his office. Pronto."

She reinforced the message with a jerk of her thumb as she turned and walked out.

Richard exchanged a look with Alex and followed in her wake.

"We'll be in Giulio's." Alex called after him.

Charles' office was a grand affair on the upper floor that was dominated by a desk of a size that was in proportion to its surroundings. Behind it, Charles was scanning the file that Celia had procured from the personnel department. He glanced up as Richard entered and waved him into a chair. Being summoned to the Chief Executive's office normally meant that something serious was afoot and Richard was momentarily taken back to school days and a summons to see the Headmaster. That was normally bad news he thought.

As if reading his thoughts Charles straightened up and smiled.

"It seems that you have been in Jersey for a little over three years. How have you found it?"

This is just play-acting Richard thought, and he does not need that file as a prop. He knows exactly what goes on in this company. These were the sort of things one does not say at times like this however, so he smiled and remembered the lines his character was supposed to say.

"It's been good. It is all very different to London and I've learned a lot."

Charles nodded approvingly.

"Excellent. Henry and I are both pleased with what you have achieved there. Revenues are up strongly and you have made a number of very useful contacts. You would also, it would seem, found time to have fun."

He pointedly closed the file.

"But, time moves on, and we have to move with it. I now feel you are ready for a new challenge. I'm putting you at the head of a new team that will focus on attracting smaller companies and grooming them for stock market flotations."

"That sounds fine. I've had some experience with small companies in Jersey."

"Good. You will report to John Haslam. You will also be a member of his takeover team. So, if anything big develops in that field, he can call on you to help man the pumps. I'm expecting quite a lot of action in that area, so you should find it more interesting than this morning's meeting."

There was a hint of a smile on his face as he looked directly at Richard.

"Any questions."

"Only the usual ones. What will my salary be, and when do you want me to start?"

"Salary will be Jersey plus twenty per cent. As regards start date, there will be a slight delay. I had hoped for Rachel Hindlip to replace you once your accounts were complete, but I have just learned that she will be off work for a week or two with injuries from a car accident at the weekend. Once she is fit again and ready to take over, Celia will send you formal notification. In the meantime, I would like you to have your end-of-year accounts ready by the end of the month."

Richard nodded his understanding.

"Thank you, Charles. I'll give it my best shots."

"Good. I would stress that this is an important position

whose success is vital for the bank's future. It will require your full and undivided attention. Fortunately, you have no domestic ties, but your yachting interests will have to be put on the back burner. It goes without saying that success would be a huge boost to your career."

His pep-talk over, Charles relaxed back in his executive chair.

"Not a word to anyone for the moment."

Richard took the signal that the interview was over and rose to his feet.

"Of course, and thank you again Charles."

He had almost reached the office door when Charles stayed his progress.

"Oh! I had almost forgotten. Were you planning to fly back to Jersey this afternoon?"

"Yes. At four."

"Henry is overflying Jersey on his way to Lisbon in the executive jet. He would like to fly you back. Be here at three. As you go out ask Celia to cancel your flight."

Once outside and out of earshot Richard released his feelings in a prolonged 'Aaaagh!'. He had a heartfelt dislike of manipulation, especially when it was done in company time when there was little that he could do about it. All through the meeting with Charles he had felt that somehow his uncle was behind the proposed move. The end piece about getting a ride home in the executive jet was the final confirmation. It was right from the Uncle Henry play book.

As he made his way out of the building on his way to join the group in Giulio's, his mind was busy examining all the ramifications his posting back to London would bring. Eventually *Sea Urchin* would have to be repatriated, he mused and made a mental note to call Ben Maitland about arranging a possible permanent berth. Then there was the Richmond flat. When he had been given the Jersey posting, allowing Alex to have the use of it on a low rent basis had been an ideal solution for both of them. Nothing had been said about what would be done on his eventual return. As things had once stood, Alex would have had the use of the spare room until he had found a place of his own. Now, once he knew about Jenny, he would want to move out immediately. The savings he had been able to make over the past three years should help with any deposit he would need to find. These were everyday matters which time would resolve. For the moment they could be set aside.

What dominated his thoughts was the most important question of all. What would Jenny make of this latest development. Her quest to discover her family origins and any possible relatives on this side of the Atlantic was what had led her to Jersey. As yet she had only scratched the surface of the puzzle that her inheritance had set. She would be reluctant to leave Jersey until she had discovered what more the island had to yield up and, if she chose to stay on, where would she live. For the time being Rachel Hindlip's unfortunate accident gave them additional breathing space. They would have to begin researching in earnest. Sadly, for the moment the only real lead they had to work on was the existence of the two files of documents which had not yet been located. He would conduct the search himself on the morrow. That settled in his mind, he steeled himself for the lively atmosphere of the wine bar.

He had missed the greater part of the lunch break and there was barely enough time for him to grab a burger, which he gulped down amid the noise and confusion. The atmosphere seemed more frenetic than usual and the litter of empty champagne bottles told its own story. Alex filled him in on what he had missed as they walked back to headquarters. An investment banker friend had landed a big fish and wanted everyone to celebrate his success. Into that heady atmosphere the broaching of the subject of a planned inter-bank yacht race had unleashed all the pent-up energies and rivalries of the young people present.

"The idea is that we use the long bank holiday weekend to complete a course that takes us down the Channel, then round the Scilly Islands, back up the Channel on the French side, round the Channel Islands and back home."

"And where is home?"

"Members of Cowes Yacht Club have kindly agreed to act as umpires. They will start us and count us back in. No personal glory. It will be a team race. Everyone will get a finishing position. The positions of the first three from each bank will be added together. So, the bank with the lowest total wins. Simple. I've made a provisional entry for you and *Sea Urchin*."

"Should be fun," Richard agreed. His words tried to sound the right tone, but inwardly his mind was receiving conflicting signals. Here was yet another element of confusion to add to the heap he had already gathered. Where would he be when the bank holiday weekend came about and what would Jenny make of it. Despite this, as they entered the bank's lobby, he found himself smiling at the strange irony of receiving Alex's news within the same hour of being told by Charles that he would have to curtail his sailing activities. Sod's Law is alive and well he reflected.

After the brief celebratory atmosphere of the lunchtime wine bar the journey alongside Henry could not have been more different. The car was luxurious and well soundproofed. It seemed as if they were gliding silently along on air as they made their way to the Farnborough airfield where the executive jet was based.

Henry had stretched out his long frame and appeared to be enjoying the time to relax. As they passed on to the M3 he glanced at his nephew sitting alongside him.

"So! How do you like the executive life-style?"

"The car's great and it is very nice not to have to drive."

"Exactly. I find it money well spent. I use it as an office for about two hours every working day. Having Harry to do the driving leaves me fresh and raring to go."

Richard grinned at him.

"So, it's not just self-indulgence."

Henry laughed. "Not at all. The same goes for the plane and the pilot. They are leased by the day. Much cheaper in the long run than having our own and as you will see it avoids all the delays and stress of Heathrow."

Harry delivered them to the entrance to Farnborough's terminal. Richard could see for himself why his uncle had settled on this mode of transport. Little time was spent completing clearance formalities and they were soon in a car that ferried them to where their small passenger jet was parked. James, their pilot, was standing beside his plane awaiting their arrival and stepped forward to shake hands with them as they emerged from the shuttle car. He and Henry were old friends and they were left to make their own way up the steps into the passenger cabin. James followed them and secured the door.

"It's fairly quiet today. We can take off in ten minutes, so fasten your seatbelts as soon as you're settled."

Henry acknowledged with a nod of agreement and the pilot passed through into the cockpit and closed the bulkhead door behind him.

Richard eyed the soft leather-covered seats and selected one adjacent to his uncle.

"I didn't want to say anything in the car with Harry in earshot, but this is an important trip. Tomorrow, if everything goes to plan, we shall be merging with Banco Cardosa, a Portuguese bank with useful operations in Brazil and other South American states. I used the term merging, in reality as the largest shareholder we shall be calling the shots."

He sniffed deeply as if to emphasize the importance of terminology.

"In deals like this one has to be aware of the 'amour propre' of the other parties involved. Both sides of the deal know this, but the pretence is maintained that it's a merger of equals."

His words were interrupted by the low whine of the engines behind them at the tail of the fuselage as the pilot fired them into life. Henry waited for a few moments for their hearing to become adjusted to the engine noise before continuing.

"In London we shall continue as before, trading under the family name. In reality we shall be the largest segment of a new company to be known as Anglo-Iberian Holdings. The shares we both hold in Rayleton will be replaced by shares in the new company. So, we shall end up with a smaller percentage of the shares in a much larger company. Their value will remain more or less as it is at present, but should grow much more rapidly in the future"

He paused for a few moments to allow time for his news to sink in.

"Needless to say, all this must remain strictly confidential for the time being."

He sat silently for some moments before continuing.

"This will be the last of these trips for me. Once the dust of the merger has settled, I intend to retire from company operations. Charles will take over all of my current work. Of course, as a major shareholder, there will be times when I'll need to be consulted."

It was proving to be a very relaxed and interesting experience. From the outset Richard had not been able to exactly gauge why his uncle was bothering to break his journey by landing him in Jersey. What he had just learned of

Henry's plans, falling on the same day that he had been informed of his pending recall to London headquarters and subsequent promotion, brought matters into a much sharper focus. Now he could only interpret the trip as promotion in a different sense – this is what life at the top is like; one day you will be at the centre of this.

Henry obviously enjoyed the luxury and special treatment that executive life provided, but if highlighting this had been his motive, the ploy had not produced the effect desired. As a first-time experience, Richard had felt some initial interest, but the same sense of boredom that he felt on all flights had soon emerged. Instinctively his thoughts had turned instead to his yacht. Crossing the Channel in a relatively small boat was tiring and often rough and wet, but it was never boring. One felt alive from being in contact with the elements, something that being transported in a sealed cabin could never offer. Above all, the sailor was left in charge of his own destiny.

His thoughts were broken by a slight dip by the plane as it began its descent to Jersey Airport.

As if he had been picking up his thoughts, Henry glanced across at him.

"I gather that you have enjoyed your time in Jersey and have done a sterling job, but time moves on. No doubt you will soon settle back into your old London routine. From what Charles tells me, you will be kept very busy. Are you looking forward to it?"

"It has created a few complications," he began and then paused momentarily as the plane bumped slightly as its landing wheels touched the ground. Then it just came out.

"I've met someone."

"Have you now. Local girl?"

"No. An American."

"Serious I take it, from the fact that you are telling me."

"Yes. We both think so, although it's early days yet."

Henry eyed his nephew.

"That's good. I shall look forward to meeting her. When you are back in London, give your aunt a call and fix up a weekend when you can bring her down to Rayleton."

Richard busied himself unfastening his safety belt and retrieving his briefcase as the plane taxied to a standstill, relieved of the need for further conversation.

By the time that Richard had checked out at the terminal the jet that had carried him back to Jersey was already making its way on to the runway for its departure He did not wait to see it take off, but hurried to the car park where earlier that morning he had left his car. He was not expected back at the office before the day's close and he told himself that there was little to gain by going back for an odd half-hour or so. The real reason was that back at the flat Jenny would probably be counting the minutes until his return. His earlier than expected return would be a pleasant surprise.

Jenny had spent the past hour on the balcony lounger reading a magazine. On hearing the door being opened, she cast it aside before hurrying to meet him.

"You're earlier..." was all she managed to say before Richard's arms were enfolding her in a long passionate embrace.

"This is great," she continued, "there will be time for a walk along the beach before dinner."

As they walked hand in hand along the sand, Jenny told him how she had spent her day.

"I've seen my house," she said proudly. "I took a bus ride. "That was what gave me the idea of this walk."

"How come?"

"It was a tourist rover trip. We started out along the road up there. I'd not realised how close we were to this beach. I saw the house as we were coming into St. Brelade's. You were right. There were quite a few expensive new properties, so I looked for anything that seemed older and had trees screening it."

"Good thinking. What else did you see?"

"We had a short stop by a lighthouse."

"That would be La Corbiere."

"I can't remember the French names."

"Don't worry. It will come. Anyway, what else did you see?"

"After the lighthouse we drove alongside another long beach and ended up at an observation tower where there was another short break. Then we passed the airport on the way home."

"You seem to have covered the western quarter of the island. I told you it's not very big."

"That's what I like about it, well, that and the peace and quiet."

They walked in silence for a short stretch before Richard commented, "You seem to have taken to walks along beaches."

"I think they're great. You never know what you will come across. Last time I found a handsome bum to fall in love with."

It was the signal to stop and exchange another kiss before walking on.

"Seriously, I think a beach walk is great. You have the sea, which is always interesting and the air is so good. I used to feel the same when I was riding in Grandpa's woods."

"Do you miss that?"

"I miss Grandpa more than the riding. I know he was old and worn out and it was time for him to pass on, but I still miss him. I guess it is something I'll have to get used to."

"When my Dad died, I was told that on average it takes fourteen months for grieving to run its course."

"Yes, it's still early days, but there is so much that is new and lovely in my life now, so I'm OK with it."

She gave Richard a knowing look.

"Anyway, you have not said anything about what you have been up to."

He gave her a rueful smile.

"Well, the outward journey was grim and the rest of the morning pretty damn boring. Then I got a summons to Charles' office."

"Who is Charles?"

"Charles Denning. He's the Managing Director."

"I thought your uncle was the boss."

"He is, but he calls himself the Company Chairman. Charles does all the dirty work."

"So, was it anything serious?"

"It was. I am to be promoted and will get a twenty percent pay rise."

"That's great! But I'm sensing there's some sort of catch…"

"Yes. He's moving me back to Head Office to take on a new role. It was all planned to start next week, but my replacement here was injured in a car accident at the weekend and will be off work for a week or two. So, the clock is ticking on our beach walks. Oh, I was also told that I need to spend less time messing around in boats."

"I thought that you were quiet. Are you worried about the new job?"

"No. It should be more interesting than showing rich people how to avoid taxes and enabling international thieves to launder their ill-gotten loot."

"My. You are feeling sour."

"Sorry. I just feel angry at being manipulated in this way. I think that this has all been set up by Uncle Henry. The final proof was being told that he would be flying me back here on his way to Lisbon in a private jet."

"Which is how you managed to get back earlier than expected."

"Got it in one."

"Right! Put it out of your mind for now. Let's enjoy our walk and then, when we get home, I've made a seafood chowder for dinner. After that perhaps we could make it an early night."

"Sounds good. The chowder I mean."

The bedside alarm clock was showing two-fifty when Richard focused on it. He levered himself upright to reach for the glass of water that he always brought to the bedside. He remembered their coming to bed at nine and the love-making which had followed. He smiled lovingly at Jenny lying beside him, moonlight giving her bare shoulders an ethereal hue. Their first love-making had proved hesitant and barely satisfying. Now, as each day passed, they were becoming more and more accustomed to each other. A trust had developed and making love had become what the words suggested, a rich and deeply satisfying experience that ended with both of them drawn into a blessed sleep. Why then, he asked himself, had he awoken in the early hours and why had his first thoughts returned him to yesterday's interview with Charles and the subsequent flight home in the executive jet.

The return of the topic to his mind in turn brought about a return of the annoyance he had originally felt. Lost in his thoughts, he returned the glass to the bedside table with less than the required delicacy. The sound of the glass on bare wood was enough to penetrate Jenny's sleep and still half-asleep she turned to him.

"What's the matter honey? Can't you sleep?"

Richard felt a new annoyance, this time with his own clumsiness.

"I'm sorry my love. That was careless of me. I didn't mean to wake you."

"Something is bothering you. Is it the new job?"

"No. It's not the work. I think I can make a fist of most things if I set my mind to it."

"What is it then? Is it us? Do you think we are rushing things?"

"No, no! Don't think that. You are the loveliest thing that has ever happened to me. In any case we're not rushing anything. We have fallen in love and this is what lovers do. There's a sort of certainty without the need of proof. Isn't that what you feel?"

In answer she pulled him to her and kissed his head.

"Absolutely. Exactly as you put it, 'certainty without proof'. I love you and I want you to be happy, but I can sense that you have something on your mind."

"I was thinking again about yesterday's events."

Jenny was now wide awake.

"What is it that's worrying you."

"It's not strictly worrying. There's a decision that I need to make which I've been putting off. Yesterday brought things into sharper focus. It's nothing really."

"Except that it woke you up in the middle of the night. Tell me what it's all about."

"It's a long story."

"Well you're not going to be able to get back to sleep unless you come clean."

Richard gave a deep sigh.

"I suppose it centres on my decision to join the bank. I had just graduated and was on my own. Dad had died while I was still at school, which meant eventually we had to vacate the navy married quarters which I grew up in. Our next-door neighbours Lou and Ben Maitland had become family friends. Their son Rob and I got on famously: we did every-thing together, especially sailing. I had just started at university when my mother remarried and moved to Australia. There was some arrangement that Ben would keep a fatherly eye on me and there would be a room for me during any weekend or vacation that I needed it."

"So, they were a kind of substitute family."

"Very much so, and still are. After his navy career ended Ben bought a rundown boatyard and has been slowly building it up. Rob has since joined him. Before I was posted here I kept my yacht at the yard."

"I don't get this. Everything you have just mentioned has been about boats and sailing. How come you ended up in banking?"

"I was a grown man and needed to support myself. Uncle Henry offered a job at the bank and I took it."

"As simple as that."

"Mm. I was aware of the bank of course. I knew that it was family controlled and that its operations were different from the high street commercial banks, but that was about the strength of it. What I didn't know, until I was twenty-five, was that I owned the seventeen-and-a-half per-cent of it that had passed to me from my father. Everything, including several year's profit distributions, had been held in an escrow fund until my twenty-fifth birthday."

"Golly! Some birthday present." She paused in thought momentarily. "I can see how you are being pulled in two different directions."

"At the moment Henry is the driving force. I get the feeling that he looks on me as the son he never had. I think that he sees me as the future head of the family's financial operations. The degree course he steered me into after school was strong on finance."

"What about your cousin Sally? Hasn't he considered her?"

Richard shook his head.

"Since the age of four she has had only one thought in her

head – horses. Besides I don't think she was ever considered. The London financial scene is very much male dominated."

He placed an arm around her.

"So that is how things stand. I think the idea of flying me back here to Jersey in the private jet was designed to encourage me, to give me a taste of life at the top. If so, then it didn't work out as planned. If anything, it has had the opposite effect. I spent most of the journey thinking about being on my boat with the wind in my hair and the bows cutting through the waves.

"It seems to me that you have already decided what your answer will be."

Richard smiled ruefully.

"Perhaps deep down I've always known what the answer would be and that I've been asking the wrong questions."

"Which are?"

"How and when can I break from Rayleton Securities without causing a major upset."

9

It was well into the afternoon on the day following the London trip that Richard found time to fulfil his intention to locate the missing bundles of documents. He told Charlotte that he would be in the basement and if anyone rang she was to say that he was with a client.

The basement was how the Rayleton staff referred to what had been the building's cellars in earlier times. At some point they had been upgraded and furnished with rows of wooden shelving each carefully labelled with alphabetical guides. All current client dealings were computerised, but old documents were still retained and were lodged neatly in exact alphabetical order. If the documents were here, they should have been lodged within the Pearson file which he had used at the fateful first meeting with Jenny. Richard re-checked the contents of the Pearson file that was now back in its correct position between files labelled Peachey and Peele. Finding the file as he had left it, he eased a section of the neighbouring folders forward to check for anything that might have slipped behind, but all was as it should be. Nothing appeared to be out of place.

Richard understood enough of the bank's practices to

know that, if documents were listed, then they must still be located in the basement storage. He was left with no alternative to making a systematic check of every shelf. With a deep sigh he began his methodical search, starting with section 'A'.

It proved a tedious undertaking. To his growing frustration everything seemed to be in perfect order. It was well past four o'clock when Charlotte appeared bearing a cup of tea. At that moment Richard was kneeling on the floor checking the lower shelf of section 'N'. He looked up at her with a smile.

"That's a welcome sight. Pop it on the floor."

Charlotte was bending over to do as he had asked, when something caught her eye.

"What's that?"

Hurriedly she placed the tea on the floor and crouched to examine the barely perceptible corner of a dark covered material peeping from the narrow gap below the bottom shelf of the adjoining section. Richard watched keenly as her hand drew out a package which she immediately handed to him.

"It looks like oilskin," he said, turning it over in his hands.

Gently he unrolled the oilskin to reveal an assortment of letters. They were of a variety of sizes and written on ageing papers. All bore the tell-tale creases and wax seal remains of letters posted before the days of envelopes. He looked at them briefly before carefully rolling them back in their oilskin.

"One down, one more to go."

He handed the package to Charlotte.

"Put those on my desk for later. Right now, I need to have a poke under each of these units."

Much later Richard returned to his office bearing only his empty tea cup. Charlotte followed him through from her office and looked at him enquiringly.

"Nothing?"

"Not a sausage."

"Was there any address on the letters?"

"There was no receiver's address. Just a name – 'Elizabeth'."

"Perhaps they were handed to her," Charlotte offered.

"Maybe. Or they could have been sent within another letter. Perhaps we shall find out more when we have read them."

Charlotte gave him a steady old-fashioned look.

"What's this all about. You just used the word 'we'. Is it something that I'm not supposed to know?"

Richard gave her a smile.

"You don't miss much. It's both bank business and a private matter. I think this is part of the Pearson file that has somehow become separated."

She returned his smile.

"Really."

"Yes. Really."

She continued to look at him quizzically.

He sighed resignedly.

"I've been seeing her for the past couple of weeks."

"And is it serious?"

"I think so."

"Good! I'm happy for the two of you. Mind you I'm not surprised. I thought that you had come over all peculiar when I first showed her into your office."

The last comment was made over her shoulder as she passed back into the outer office carefully closing the door behind her.

Only later, when he glanced at his watch after securing the office's front door, did he realise that she had stayed on for almost an hour after their normal close of work. He knew that she would never bother to claim any overtime payment, so he made a mental note to do it for her.

The thought that was uppermost in his mind as he made his way home was how Jenny would react to being presented with a pack of two-hundred-year-old letters wrapped in an equally ancient oilskin. In the event his prepared presentation speech was superseded.

"Have you forgotten that we are meeting your friends this evening?"

The words were spoken by Jenny, already dressed for the occasion and with her hair arranged in a style he had not seen before. It was only then that he remembered that this was the evening they had arranged to have dinner with David Kingsbury and his wife Nicole and were expected at seven-thirty.

"Just look at you. You look as if you have been sweeping the roads or something."

"Dammit woman I've been moving heaven and earth for you this afternoon and this is all the thanks I get."

The words were said with mock severity and were followed by an attempt to embrace her which was firmly repulsed.

"No. You're too scruffy and you will mess my hair up. Go and clean yourself up or we'll be late."

"Well, if I am scruffy, it's because I have been on my hands and knees in the basement looking for these."

He offered her the oilskin package as evidence.

"What is it?"

Jenny took the package hesitantly and unrolled the oilskin.

"Oh! They're letters, and they look very old."

All thoughts of preserving the integrity of her appearance were forgotten as she threw he arms around him.

"I take it all back. You're a darling. Now go change. We can look at these properly when we get back."

In a strange way the discovery of the letters set the tone for a memorable evening. The Kingsbury apartment was situated in a new block only a few hundred yards away, so they had chosen to walk. There was no mention of the letters and, sensing that Jenny was perhaps a little apprehensive about meeting a European lawyer in a social setting. Richard sought to reassure her.

"You seem tense," he began. "Relax. I think you will like David and Nicole. They are two of the most friendly and warm-hearted people that you could ever wish to meet."

"It's easy for you to say that," she rejoined. "Just remember that I have only recently arrived here from a small farm on the edge of Hicksville, USA. Now you're taking me to an evening with a sophisticated lawyer and his wife."

"Trust me. They are not the sort of people who put on airs or judge people by the clothes they wear."

In the event everything proved to be exactly as Richard had said. Their hosts had dressed casually and this set the tone for the evening. Jenny soon began to relax and was happy to respond to the interest they showed in her life in America and the quest which had brought her first to London and now, Jersey. When Nicole rose to clear the dishes at the end of their dinner, Jenny rose to assist her and followed her into the kitchen, where they stayed for a noticeably long time.

"The girls seem to be hitting it off," David offered after a while.

"Good. It's just what Jen needed."

Much later, as Richard and Jenny walked home, she took his arm in hers and squeezed it.

"You were right. They are two lovely people."

"You enjoyed the evening then?"

"Very much, and I liked their apartment."

'Yes. It's very spacious."

They walked in silence for the remaining few yards to their own apartment block. It was as he unlocked their door that Richard recalled what was said as they had bid their hosts goodnight.

"What did Nicole mean by 'don't forget tomorrow' when left just now?"

"Oh, we are meeting up for lunch and she's going to help me find some new clothes afterwards. I can't go on living out of a suitcase."

"That's good," he said with a yawn. "It's been a full-on sort of day and right now I'm ready for bed."

"No chance. We have not looked at my bundle of letters yet."

She took the first letter and examined it carefully before reading it aloud.

> *HMS Tethys*
> *Cape Verde Islands*
> *2ndMarch, 1799*

Dear Miss Pearson,

It was with the greatest pleasure and relief that to-day I received reply to my letter to your father requesting his permission for me to write to you. This he has very graciously allowed.

His letter made a timely arrival. We have toiled all morning shipping casks of drinking water. Within the hour we shall make sail for Freetown and the African coast. Our role is to protect our merchant shipping. I will write at greater length when I have more time. My best compliments to your Father and also of course to you.

Sincerely,

Edward

"Where is Freetown?"

"Not sure. Somewhere in Africa I think."

Jenny lowered the hand holding the letter she had just read to Richard and lay back against the bed head leaning towards Richard's shoulder. For some minutes they sat in silence.

"This is just awesome. This letter is over two hundred

years old. I know it's all so polite and formal, but it's my family. I'm discovering my family."

"Are you going to read them all tonight?"

"No. There are only a few, but I think I'll stop there. If I read and evaluate one each day in the order they were written, I think that way I'll get to know and understand the people behind the names better."

"That makes sense. So, what have you learned from that first letter?"

"Oh, come on! I've only just read it out to you."

"I know, but it's very short. Apart from the obvious, that it is from a young man at sea writing to presumably a member of your family, what other inferences can we draw from it."

Jenny thought for a moment before answering.

"It's well written, so that means that the writer has been educated."

"Carry on."

"It seems that he has already written to seek permission to correspond with her. To me, that makes it sound it like a serious relationship."

"Or the start of one."

"Either way that means he's not too young, but not too old. Then there is the reference to the protection of merchant shipping. That suggests that his ship is some form of warship."

"Exactly. Tethys is the name of his ship. HMS stands for 'His or Her Majesty's Ship'. That is the formal title that is always used when referring to ships in the Royal Navy. To me it all suggests that the writer was a young naval officer."

"It's a pity that he only uses his first name, Edward, but at least that means that he is well known to her."

She raised the letter and re-read it slowly. Then set it down again, her face deep in thought.

"I get the feeling that they have known each other for

some time and that now things have moved up a gear." She finally declared.

"You may well be right. For this letter to have been kept and eventually placed in the Lablanche account files suggests that this is an important family link. If that proves to be the case, then how come your name is Pearson. If Elizabeth Pearson had children she would almost certainly be married and would have taken her husband's surname which would almost certainly not be Pearson."

"Gosh. This is like being in a maze. You no sooner sort one part of the puzzle and then you hit another blank wall."

Richard drew her to him and kissed her.

"We'll get there eventually, but we have to think positively. We've made a cracking good start. Now it is time to get some sleep. Some of us have to work for a living."

As planned the previous evening, Jenny had met with Nicole for lunch and the incipient friendship of the dinner party had deepened further as the afternoon progressed. Jenny happily related the information drawn from the first of the letters. It was then that Nicole had the idea of checking what archive of local newspapers the public library might hold. These could then be culled for news of any Royal Navy vessels visiting the islands. There had been initial disappointment. No one newspaper had offered continuous publication for the entire period that interested them. Moreover, the archive of editions of the paper that appeared in the years either side of the end of the eighteenth century was held by a North of England university. Access was possible online, but Jenny was dismayed to learn that all editions in that period had been in French. Her dismay was immediately brushed aside by Nicole.

"Why are you English speakers so hopeless with other languages?"

"Do you speak French?" Jenny asked.

"Mais oui. Je suis français," Nicole replied laughing at her bewilderment. "My parents are French and I was born in France. We moved here when I was a baby, so I have spent most of my life here. Most people here are bilingual. Bienvenue en Europe."

She slipped an arm around Jenny's shoulder once they were back outside.

"Don't worry, you will soon get used to it. For now, I will be happy to research and translate for you. It will be good for me to have something useful to do, but now I think we need to do some shopping."

The afternoon sped by as Nicole guided her on a tour of her favourite shops. In a ladies' outfitter she surprised Jenny by insisting that she bought a pair of cropped jeans. Jenny was finally persuaded to try on a pair and liked them enough to buy them. As they left the shop she gave Nicole a puzzled look.

"Why was it so important for me to buy crops?" she asked her new friend.

"They are good for the cycling," was the astonishing reply.

"But I have never ridden a bike."

"Then you must learn. Have you not seen? Here everyone rides the bicycle. It is very easy. Tomorrow you shall have your first lesson."

It was not until the evening, after Jenny and Richard had taken their customary beach walk and had their evening meal, that Jenny took up the second letter in her package.

It looked very much the same as the first one she had read, but proved to be one of three posted together from Cape Town. Richard could hear her muttering in puzzlement as she pieced it all together.

HMS Tethys
Cape Town
14ᵗʰ May, 1799

Dear Elizabeth,

It is now three months since I last wrote to you and so much has happened since then that I scarcely know where to begin. We left The Cape Verde Islands on the day I wrote to you. Our next port of call was Freetown which you will find on your globe at the centre of the great westward bulge of the African continent. After the gales encountered rounding Finisterre the weather has remained clement and increasingly warm. The Cape Verdes were hot, but at Freetown the heat was almost unbearable. It is necessary to keep one's head covered at all times although we are yet almost ten degrees north of the equator.

Freeport is a thriving town. The population is almost entirely black with only the occasional white face. Everywhere there is noise and colour quite unlike any European town. Our stay there was short, as the Captain's purpose was simply to obtain fresh fruit and vegetables together with any shipping information. However, it was a welcome break from our normal occupations.

Edward

HMS Tethys
At sea.
18th June, 1799

Dear Elizabeth,

After all the everyday matters I have reported in past weeks, to-day I have real news. After leaving Freetown it was discovered that James Longworth, our Third Officer, was not aboard. He is reported to have been seen ashore in the company of officers of an American trading ship that was in the roadstead at Freetown and sailed two days ahead of us. It is possible that he has met with a mishap, but it is known that he was unhappy with the demands of his position. Thus, the common assumption is that he is now somewhere in mid-Atlantic on his way to America. If so, it is a foolish way to behave. If he is ever found, he will be court-martialled and hanged.

Nevertheless, we are left an officer short. As I am the only Midshipman with enough experience to stand watch, I have been promoted to the rank of Acting Third Officer. I shall remain thus until such time as I can be examined by a board of at least three Captains. If I am fortunate, that could be at Cape Town, a few short days hence. In the meantime, I am spending what little free time I have in studying anything and everything that might be touched on. The ship's Master is also assisting me by questioning me as if he were an examination interrogator.

I look forward to seeing Cape Town. Table Mountain and the varied natural history of the cape are much talked of by everyone who has already sailed there. Even so, my feelings are mixed. There is much that I wish to see, but at the same time I am nervous of the possibility of facing an Examination Board there. It is not the examination itself that concerns me. It is the implications it will have for my future career and all else.

Edward

HMS *Tethys*
Cape Town
26th July, 1799

Dearest Elizabeth,

I feel twice blessed. No sooner had I arrived here than an eastbound Indiaman carrying mail arrived, having sailed direct from home. To my delight there was a letter for me written in your own fair hand. It sounds hopelessly sentimental I confess, but I have read and re-read it many times over. When one is at sea, however busy one may be, thoughts of home creep in. It is so important to receive a letter, however short it might be, to provide that important link.

But I digress. I have news of substance to impart. Our mission here is to join a small squadron that is being assembled to escort a homebound convoy of Indiamen which is expected to arrive here within days. With four Royal Navy Captains on station, one of them a Commodore, it was inevitable that the opportunity to hold my Examination Board would be taken, as indeed it was. As a result, I am delighted to tell you that as from twelve-noon today I will be listed on the navy roll as a full third officer. I know you will wish me joy for we are both aware of the importance of this step. My own celebrations are on hold for the moment, as I am left aboard ship as duty officer while the other officers go ashore. Such is life.

I think much of the walks we took together round the estate in the spring and look forward to the time when we may do so again. I cannot say when that will be. The Indiamen we shall be escorting sail much slower than our frigate and are well laden to boot. Thus, it will be many weeks before we will be able to leave them safe in home waters. Hopefully we might then put into Portsmouth.

What we may not control we must accept with patience. Rest assured that my desire to see you will not diminish, however long the wait.

Edward

As before, Jenny had waited until they had retired to bed before beginning her reading. Lying beside her, Richard heard muttered comments about three letters and then audible intakes of breath and finally the release of that breath with what sounded like satisfaction.

She handed the letters to him and he quickly read through them before passing them back to her.

"So! It was as we thought. They're more than good friends."

"This letter was much less formal." She paused musing. "I would love to know what she said in her letter to him."

"And still no mention of a surname. If the worst comes to the worst we can consult the naval records in Greenwich when we are back in England."

"Mm. It's all becoming clearer. There is a difference in their social positions. I think her family were wealthy and owned the estate he referred to. That is why this promotion is so important to him. He's poor and has to prove himself worthy to her family by earning promotion."

"You make it sound like the script for a Hollywood movie."

"Maybe, but isn't that the way it was in England in the old days?"

"Perhaps. Let's wait and see."

"At least we know that he is the man in her life and it seems to be a love match."

She laid the letters aside and continued with her musings.

"He seems to be a nice, sensible young man. I like him. Equally importantly it would make him my eleven-times-grandfather."

10

As so often happens after exciting events, the following week produced feelings of flatness. No new information concerning Jenny's ancestry emerged. Re-readings of the letters produced no further insights and Nicole's perusal of the online archives of *La Gazette de l'Ile de Jersey* had yet to produce anything of interest. Overlying all else was the notification that Richard's replacement as Head of Rayleton's Jersey office was fit to resume work and would be taking over at the beginning of the following week. As a result, Richard would be required to be in London.

It was a sobering moment when Richard informed Jenny. Although he had been spending working hours each day at his desk in the Rayleton office, the period since they had met had taken on many of the aspects of a honeymoon. For both, his departure for work each morning was a time of seeming loss, his return in the evening a time of joy and happiness. This pattern was now to change and they had to adjust to what would come next. Of two things they were certain. Both the St. Helier flat and the car that Richard had been using were owned by the bank and would be required by the new manager.

John Haslam had telephoned Richard welcoming him to his section immediately after Charles had outlined the planned move. In the intervening weeks he had followed this with a series of emails on all current and new developments. To Richard the unspoken message was quite clear. He would be working at a whole new level and there would be little time to acclimatise. He would be expected to hit the ground running.

With his new duties already taking shape, Richard had used what free time he had to decide on the logistics of his return to London. Alex had wasted little time in lining up a place in a shared house and could vacate the Richmond flat at a moment's notice. There had also been good news from the Maitland yard. Ben had assumed from the outset that Richard's Jersey posting would not be permanent and had used his vacated berth on purely short-term arrangements. It was a relief for Richard to learn that his old mooring was still available. With his mooring fixed, he would be able to return in the yacht with all his gear. Now that he had a firm date, he had also been able to cancel his berth at the Elizabeth Marina.

They were left with the planning of the move itself. Jenny's effects consisted largely of clothes that could be fitted in two suitcases. Despite Richard's larger accumulation, these and Jenny herself could be easily included in *Sea Urchin*. When Richard broached the idea, he could immediately see the uncertainty written across her face

"What's the matter?" He asked. "Are you worried about using the boat?"

"No. Not at all. It's just that I have not finished what I came here to do. Nicole and I are scarcely half-way through the local paper archive. We are so close. I can sense it."

Richard could see her dilemma.

"Sorry. I've been concentrating so much on the move, I hadn't thought of that side of things."

He thought for a few moments before continuing.

"How long do you think it will take to complete the archive search?"

"A week at most."

"Well, it would not make sense to leave it half-finished and have to come back. So, stay on and get a flight back when you're finished. I don't like it any more than you do, but it will only be for a week and, to be honest, I'm not going to be much company for you. The new job is going to be very different to the current one and I have a lot of boning up to do. I'll be bringing loads of work home to begin with. In any case, we can easily afford a week at the Radisson Blu and a plane ticket."

As he finished speaking she put an arm around him.

"It's not the money that concerns me you bonehead."

The week after Richard had sailed proved to be eventful. After Richard had returned to London, when Jenny had told her of her plan to stay on to complete their search, Nicole would not hear of her staying in any hotel and insisted that she stayed with her and David. That way, she said, there would be opportunity to give Jenny her promised cycling experience and complete their archive searches.

She had borrowed her mother's bike for Jenny to use. Each afternoon they took a break from the tedious work of combing the newspaper archives to take to the local road. As she explained to Jenny after her first wobbly effort, motion produces balance. Once one had the courage to press hard on the pedals, however wobbly she might be at first, balance would take care of itself. All other aspects of cycling would soon become second nature. The real problem was getting one's leg muscles accustomed to the new demands made on them and building up sufficient stamina. After several afternoons of practice, she judged that Jenny was ready for a longer excursion.

Nicole said nothing about her plans before they set off. They took the coast road to St. Brelade's that ran alongside the beach that Jenny had walked each evening with Richard. They soon left behind the decorative gardens with their statuesque palms and Jenny found that a longer ride gave her a feeling of confidence. She began to relax and was soon happily chatting. It was when they turned off, at the point where the main road turned inland, that the road signs told their own story. It was with some excitement, therefore, that she and Nicole stopped at a gateway that hosted a board bearing the name 'London & Overseas Investment Group'. Through the gateway the drive, bordered by well-tended lawns, curved to the left behind the trees that shielded the house from the road.

Pushing their cycles, they ventured up the driveway. Ahead of them the drive terminated at a small parking area to the side of the front door. The house was a handsome building of medium size. Constructed in the local stone, it had the look of a family home built by a comfortably secure merchant or professional man of its time. Mid-way along the drive they stopped to take their first proper look at the house. Jenny stood motionless, soaking in its every detail and committing them to memory. Beside her, Nicole refrained from comment, aware of the building's emotional significance to her new friend. Only then did they become aware of the car that was quietly following them up the drive. The car drew alongside them and a window was lowered.

"Can I help you?" the suited driver enquired.

"We just wanted to see the house." Jenny ventured uncertainly.

"I am sorry, but this is private property. I must ask you to return to the road."

Nicole intervened at this point.

"My friend thought that you would make an exception in her case as she has recently discovered that she is the owner of this house. Richard Rayleton will vouch for her if you care to ring him."

"Oh. My apologies. Could you come up to the house while I park."

With that he wound up the window and drove up to park alongside the front door where the ladies joined him.

"I am sorry. It's all my fault." Jenny began. "I'm Jenny Pearson and this is Nicole Kingsbury."

"Nice to meet you. I'm Will Hendry," the stranger began before a thought struck him. "You're David Kingsbury's wife. I think we met once at some function. But you're American," he continued turning to Jenny.

"Yes, my family lived here before they emigrated to America some time in 1805. The house has been rented out since then."

"That explains it."

"Explains what?" Nicole interjected.

"We've been here for some years now, but when we first took out the lease everything was very old fashioned, you know, dated."

"It's an old house." Jenny observed.

"Of course, but I was referring to the furnishings. It must have been let as a furnished house before we took out the lease."

"Do you still have the furnishings?"

"Yes. The owners could not be traced, so we had everything stacked out of the way in the top rooms under the roof. Everything is all there, but I'm afraid the confidential nature of our business means that I'm not allowed to let anyone in. As owner you are allowed to inspect the property once a year, but you will have to make a formal request to arrange that."

While Jenny and Hendry were speaking Nicole had been peering in through a window.

"It is all very quiet. What exactly do you do here?"

"Not a lot actually."

A broad grin creased Hendry's face as he replied.

"The main purpose is here behind me."

He stepped to one side to fully reveal a large plaque fixed to the wall that bore the names of four companies.

"Your property is the registered address of the four trust funds in our group until such time as our lease expires. It works well. We have enough space to allocate a separate room to each fund."

"Impressive. But what exactly does a registered office do?" Jenny enquired.

"At its simplest it's the official address through which a company may be contacted. It also determines what laws and tax rules the company operates under."

"Oh, I see."

"We take things a little further here. London handles all investments and our registrar handles all shareowner matters, but we keep updated lists of all shareholders and all official documents relating to the companies together with the official copy of their audited accounts."

Nicole looked on impressed, but Jenny's face bore a more thoughtful look.

"How much trouble would it create for you if you had to move out?"

Nicole's expression underwent a rapid change at the boldness of the question, but Hendry's smile continued to dominate his features.

"Very little. The work we do here could be done anywhere." He shrugged dismissively as he spoke, but followed with a direct question of his own.

"Are you thinking of evicting us when the lease expires?"

"I don't know. There is a possibility, but I've only recently learned that I own it and I've not made any firm plans yet."

"Well, let us know in good time of any change you decide on. Now I must get back to work. It has been nice meeting you ladies."

With that he opened the door and disappeared inside leaving the two girls standing outside.

They stood for a moment looking at the now closed door and then gathered their cycles and began to walk back down the driveway.

"It is so frustrating," Jenny exclaimed. "He and his staff can go in and any Tom, Dick or Harry on business can go in, but I own it and can't enter my own property."

"That's the way things are."

"Makes good business for lawyers," Jenny replied grinning at her friend.

"Mais oui, very good business. All the same, it is a lovely house."

They had reached the end of the drive. Nicole looked at her questioningly.

"Are you ready to make the ride home?"

"Not yet. I think I would like to see what St. Brelade's has to offer. We ought to be able to find a drink somewhere."

Richard had been standing at Gatwick's arrival gates for some twenty minutes before the first trickle of arriving passengers began to emerge. He finally caught sight of her trailing the wheeled case she had taken for her stay with Nicole. There was something forlorn about her appearance that was in stark contrast to her usual gay liveliness. As she came closer he could see that she had been crying.

She made no hurried rush to embrace him, but simply buried her face against his chest. He could feel her body shaking with silent sobs as she clung to him.

"Whatever is the matter," he murmured, folding his arms protectively around her.

"Let's get home," she said. "I'll tell you there."

Richard said no more, but led her quietly to the new car the bank had financed for his use. Jenny took little notice of the surroundings as they made their way north to the motorway and on to Richmond. Once there she took little interest in the flat which would be her new home for the time being, but sat quietly while Richard made them both a large mug of tea.

She sat as before for a while, nursing the mug in her cupped hands, seemingly drawing comfort from its warmth.

Finally, she looked at Richard with sorrowful eyes.

"I'm sorry. I thought I was done with crying, but seeing you somehow brought it all back. It's all so very sad."

Richard sat beside her and put a comforting arm around her shoulder as she took a first sip from her tea. He had no idea of what the 'it' she spoke of was, but realised that there was no point in hurrying her. It would all come out when she was ready.

"I'd managed to keep a lid on things on the plane, but seeing you again was too much."

She sniffed again and taking a tissue from her pocket, cleared her head before continuing.

"I'd been working all week on the online archive with Nicole. We had found nothing until this morning. I had almost given up and then suddenly there it was."

"You found a story?"

"There were several, and they were all connected. The first was about a shipwreck. A small Royal Navy ship had been in a fight with a bigger French ship. They had broken off when the weather deteriorated and the smaller ship was making for the nearest harbour."

"St. Helier?"

Jenny nodded.

"They didn't make it. They sank a little way off Noirmont. You remember, I shuddered there when you took me out in *Sea Urchin*. The weather was very bad and there were no survivors. The ship's commander was named as Lieutenant Edward Weybourne."

"Edward!" Richard exclaimed. "You think this is..."

Jenny waved a hand for him to stop.

"There's more," she said brokenly. His wife was living in Jersey and at the time of the shipwreck she was well into a second pregnancy. The shock and upset caused her to miscarry. She lost the baby and two days later she also died. Her name was Elizabeth."

"Edward and Elizabeth and a Royal Navy ship. These must be the two young people in your letters."

"I'm sure of it. It all happened in early September, 1805. It must have been sometime after that twelve times grandfather Pearson sailed for America."

She began to weep again.

"It's so sad. They were young and the letters show how much they loved each other. Then in a few short hours their family was ripped apart and that poor boy was left without parents, and I know how that feels."

"So, they already had an older child?"

"Yes, a little boy. The newspaper said that he was left in the care of his grandfather who was also in Jersey."

Richard sat quietly taking in the ramifications of what he had just learned.

"If this Edward and Elizabeth are the people in your letters, then this surviving child is the missing link in your family tree. So, we have to find some proof of identity and then we have to establish something else."

Jenny looked hard at him.

"I'm not with you. What are you thinking?"

'When I read through your account file, I noticed that every holder of the account over two hundred years was named Pearson. If Edward and Elizabeth's surviving son is the link in your family tree, then all of them, yourself included should be named Weybourne."

11

Back at his desk on the following Monday morning Richard had time to reflect on how little London headquarters had changed in the three years he had spent in Jersey. Operations were organized much as they had been earlier and the faces that greeted him each morning were for the most part faces that were familiar to him. The only real change was that he was now positioned in a more central role in the bank's hierarchy. Formerly he had shared an office with Alex on the first floor adjacent to the dealing room with its constant comings and goings. Now, in line with his more senior position, he had moved up a floor where he had an office to himself and where there were fewer distractions.

If anything had changed, he reflected, it was in himself. On the surface he might not show any signs of this, but in subtle ways he was aware that he had. He had enjoyed the relative freedom that being in charge of the Jersey office had given him. As he had adjusted to the demands of that position, he had come to enjoy working in his own space, free from the noise and interruptions he had known in earlier years.

Nor was it simply the freedom that Jersey had offered. His

own maturation over this period had played a part. The line between youth and adulthood is ill-defined and by its very nature will develop at different speeds between different people. He had moved to St. Helier as a relatively young man and responsibility had brought him to full manhood. His growing sailing experience had been an undoubted aid in this process. Above all else, so too had Jenny. Meeting her had provided the final ingredient of emotional maturity. With Jen at my side, he thought, I can now face anything.

What that anything might be was yet to be decided. It was obvious that she had taken a deep liking to Jersey, regardless of the family links that they were still unravelling. The few weeks they had had together there had been blissful. Deep down, Richard knew that at some point he would have to make a break with the bank. Both of them were agreed on that, but while London was not where they wanted to be long term, for the time being they both accepted they would have to put up with it.

His reminiscences about Jenny and Jersey, in that strange undirected way that the mind has, had produced new lines of thinking into his head. Why was Edward Weybourne's ship making for St. Helier at the time that it sank? The newspaper coverage had indicated that the action had taken place in the waters off Guernsey. Why then, he thought, had the ship not headed for Plymouth or Portsmouth, where much better repair facilities would have been available. Was it because he was anxious to avoid being stuck in England when his wife gave birth to their second child, or perhaps were he or members of his crew wounded and in need of immediate attention. The reasons behind his course of action would never be known. The one new fact that had emerged that they could be sure of was that Weybourne's family were living in Jersey at the time of his death. That presumably also included his Father-in-Law. A new thought struck him. In that case, he mused, it was possible that

Weybourne too held a bank account with Lablanche Freres. If that were the case, there was a possibility that the missing letters had been filed under the name of Weybourne.

A glance at his watch warned Richard that the time for his scheduled meeting with John Haslam was fast approaching. Without further delay he rang the familiar number of the Jersey office. Charlotte took the call and immediately put him through to Rachel Hindlip, who was happy for him to press-gang Charlotte for a few minutes. She in turn was only too happy to help her old boss and promised that she would check for any possible Weybourne file and, if any such file existed and contained the missing letters, she would immediately email him.

There was nothing further to be done for the moment. With a deep sigh he extracted the files that he had taken home to study over the weekend from his briefcase and made his way to the larger office at the end of the corridor.

In his earlier years Richard had not had any direct dealings with Haslam, but, now that he had experienced a few days of working with him at close quarters, he had begun to form a very favourable opinion of the mettle of the man who was his departmental boss. Now in his late forties, Haslam had an open face that was rarely without a smile. The smile, however, could be misleading, for it belied the firm resolve that underlay all his actions. His grasp of detail was legendary and he was quick to pinpoint flaws in both detail and thinking. Never known to raise his voice in anger, anyone found to be taking shortcuts or generally slacking would be admonished in a perfectly calm manner that somehow seemed to achieve more effect than any amount of red-faced bellowing might produce. During his first week Richard had taken careful note. Here, he thought, was Rayleton's next General Manager.

Reaching the end of the corridor, Richard tapped briefly

on the door and opened it enough to put his head into the room.

"Come in and take a chair," Haslam called from his desk and proceeded to tidy away the papers he had been working on and select a new file.

"Everything OK? London can be a bit of a shock to the system after a few years away."

Richard nodded his affirmation that all was well.

"Good. I thought it best to give you a few days to settle in and work up to speed. Now we can start to crack on. Have you studied the papers you took home at the weekend?"

"Yes, I've worked through them in detail."

"Good. We can have a look at those in a few minutes, but before that there are a couple of points I need to put across."

He gave Richard a meaningful smile before continuing.

"First of all, I do things by the book and ask that everyone in this department does the same. While you are in this department I shall ignore the fact that your surname is Rayleton and will treat you accordingly. If you do your work in the way I think correct, I will sing your praises to Charles. If you do not, then…"

He left his last sentence unfinished and treated Richard to another long smile.

"All clear?"

Richard nodded his acceptance and smiled back, while inwardly thinking that this exactly what he was expecting him to say.

"Good. Now let's get down to business. There are three basic principles I want you to work to. Summarised they are the client, the business and the bank.

So, let's examine what lies behind each of these.

We'll start with the client. Each client should be chosen carefully. What we are looking for is the right mix of character and know-how to make a success of the business. Once chosen, we do our best to help them prosper and develop, so long as it is within the law."

He paused briefly so that this could sink in.

Richard was tempted to point out that the work he had been doing in Jersey on many occasions meant dealing with money that had little if any legal provenance, but a glance at Haslam's face led him to think that this would not be well received. He settled on a simple, "Right."

"Banking is a business not a beauty contest. You do not have to like your client and there will be times when you may have to sup with the devil. The reverse is also true. Be wary of clients who know how to lay on the charm."

"Finally, we come to ourselves, this bank. As you know, Rayleton's is what used to be called a Merchant Bank. We are not as big an outfit as most of our competitors. In addition, we are not a registered commercial bank that creates new money when it makes a loan. All the money that we lend out is the bank's own capital. Therefore, take great care not to waste it. Examine every angle, put everything in writing and make sure that everything is legal. Above all, make sure the bank's back is covered."

He sat back in his chair to let his words sink in before beginning on a new tack.

"We can now turn our attention to the documents which you took home at the weekend. These are actual cases which we have handled in the last twelve months, but with all names and identifying information edited out. We can start with Case A. How would you have dealt with that?"

Richard took the relevant papers from his folder and glanced over them before replying.

"My initial reaction is not very favourable. The business cashflows over the years shown have been weak. Asset values have dropped over the same period, which suggests that perhaps assets have been sold to stay afloat. In my view that is a probable rejection, but I would need to know more about the applicant and the use the loan would be put to. I would also want to see a detailed business plan."

The answer earned a wide beaming smile from Haslam.

"Good. The applicant was a fifty-two-year-old man running the family farm with his seventy-eight-year-old father. They had come up with the idea of developing a gin making business using part of their potato crop."

"Any qualifications or experience in distilling?"

"None. A search also revealed that the son had been in court on two separate occasions on drink driving charges."

He looked directly at Richard, his eyebrows arched questioningly.

"I would make that a definite rejection."

"Yes. That one was quite clear-cut. We did not need to meet the applicant. Now Case B, let's see what you make of that."

Richard again cast an eye over the relevant file before replying.

"I liked the look of this one. The figures show a small business that is slowly expanding. Profits are small but rising slowly. The asset base is sound, again with gradual small increases which I would think is the result of profit retention. Overall, I get the impression of a well-run business that is looking to expand. My only reservation would be that the asset cover is weak, so I would need to know more about the type of business and what purposes any loan money would be put to."

"And if I told you that the applicant is a youngish woman?"

"My answer would be the same. She obviously knows her business and runs a tight ship. The question is, what is the business?"

It was his turn to look questioningly at Haslam.

"Fashion," was his reply. "She has a small design studio here in London and employs a team of three young designers.

She herself took an initial degree in Design & Technology before starting the business ten years ago. Her aim is to move into the international market. Still keen?"

"Overall yes, but not yet."

"Hedging your bets?"

Absolutely. I like the look of the business, but a break-through in the fashion business would not come overnight. I wouldn't judge that she was ready for a sizeable advance. Perhaps a small loan to be used in strengthening her team and a continuation of the current rate of progress until the business is stronger is what is called for I think. Fashion, from what little I've read of it, can be a tricky business."

"Excellent. That is exactly what we decided. Who knows one day she might be on your list of stock market flotations."

As he spoke he closed the file he had been using and reached into a desk drawer for a new one.

"Right. Last on the list is Case C. This I might add, is an ongoing case which has yet to be finalised."

Richard sat back and waited for him to continue. As he had approached the meeting he had been a little wary, not really knowing what to expect. So far, he thought, I have not made any major gaffes.

Haslam beamed at him as he prepared to resume.

"This case concerns a small to medium manufacturing company. It has been built up over a period of more than twelve years and its products have been well received. I would also add that its owner is a hard driver who does not take prisoners."

Richard glanced at the third file to remind himself of its contents.

"I think that I can see where you are going with this one. It's an interesting record. It was obviously having difficulty getting established in the early years and profits have not been consistent. The most noticeable waiver in profitability coincides with an increase in asset values which suggests a period of expansion which has put a strain on the company's finances. I would need to know more about the market the company operates in. Overall, I would be cautious with this one. I think there is a possibility that this company has been expanding beyond its means."

"Well read. What you have just said sums up the situation exactly. Had it been left to me it would have been rejected, but your Uncle Henry is very keen on it. He thinks that, with the right guidance, we could be looking at a stock market flotation in a year or two, which is why I've included this case. It could well land up on your desk. Apparently, the owner approached Henry in the bar at his golf club. Henry said that he didn't like the man as a person, but thought that he had the drive of a real businessman."

As Richard listened, a strange feeling of foreboding began to infiltrate his mind.

"Who is he and what is the business?

"You're a yachtie aren't you? You may well have heard of him," Haslam replied. "He's a boat builder based near Southampton named Baxter. Makes the Baxter yacht range."

"Yes. I've heard of him." Richard replied, trying to sound as non-committal as possible. "As it happens my new yacht is a Baxter model."

"Well there you are," said Haslam with another smile. "Inside knowledge. The question is," he continued returning the file to the desk drawer.

"How do we cover the bank's back?"

"Exactly! You will learn a lot from this one. Gerry Thomas is handling the case and he will fill you in after we have finished here."

It was towards the end of the morning that Richard joined Haslam's deputy to complete his briefing. He was intrigued at the prospect of meeting someone he had heard much of, but had not as yet had any direct dealings with.

Gerry Thomas was not the sort of person that fitted the popular conception of skilled banker or financier, although as Richard would come to learn, that is what he actually was. His dark hair now etched with greyness, he had been with Rayleton's for almost thirty years and was known as the man to go to if problems arose. Despite the wide recognition of his abilities, he remained in a position of middling seniority. All attempts to move him into more senior roles he had met with polite refusals. Where other people he had worked with had moved on, seeking more senior or better paid positions, he had been content to remain and do whatever was asked of him. As he had once explained to John Haslam, he did not crave promotion. As a bachelor who had inherited a house on the Thames near Kew Bridge he had no need to push for more money. The salary that he earned was more than enough to satisfy his needs. Seniority would simply result in bringing more demands on his time and that would eat into the time available for him to pursue his long-standing passion for art and in particular for painting the human face.

Richard knew little of his life outside of the bank. He was surprised, therefore, to find that he was being carefully studied as he took his seat in Thomas' office. He found it disconcerting and changed his position. Thomas noted the movement.

"Don't mind me. In my spare time I paint — portraits mostly. I like to study faces. They tell you a lot about the person. That is what a good portrait does."

Richard gave him a surprised look.

"Do you think so?"

"Oh yes! I can't remember who said it, 'The face is a window on the soul'."

"And what does my window tell you?"

Thomas grinned.

"I haven't studied you long enough. Besides, we are in company time and we have work to do."

Richard opened the file he had used earlier. Somehow the task seemed easier all of a sudden. This is a man I can work with he thought.

Gerry turned immediately to the matter in hand.

"How much has John told you about Baxter Marine?"

"Not a lot. There appears to be a cashflow problem, probably the result of trying to expand too quickly."

"That would be a fair general summary. All developing businesses have the same problem. In Baxter's case the problem has been intensified by the misallocation of what cash he has had available."

"How do you mean?"

"It's a peculiar set-up. Workshop space and equipment are both below average, but fronting it there's a swish modern showroom. In my book that is the wrong way about. Overriding all of this there is a problem with the site. It is small and its water access is far too restricted for a successful yacht builder. So, even if he gets more finance, he will find expansion difficult. You ought to drive down and take a look at the place."

He looked directly at Richard who sat for several moments in silence. He was feeling the same sense of uneasiness that that first appeared earlier in John Haslam's office. Then he had been able to steer away from it. Now it had reappeared stronger than before. There seemed to be no alternative to revealing his connexions to the Maitland family who would be in the way of any future expansion of the Baxter business. He sensed that Gerry Thomas was someone who could be trusted not to divulge information given to him in confidence.

"There are things I need to tell you. They are confidential and I do not want anyone else to know anything about what I am about to tell you."

Gerry nodded his acquiescence.

"Agreed, but not here. What say we take an early lunch-break. Then you can tell me over a pint. I always think there are too many ears listening-in around this building."

Settled in the corner of a local pub with a beer and a sandwich Richard proceeded to proceeded to tell him of his close relationship with the Maitland family and his unease with his involvement in the Baxter loan application.

"You know Baxter then?"

"No. I've never met him, but I've heard a lot about him."

"But you said that your boat was one of his."

"Yes. I bought it through a brokerage. It seems a cracking good little boat."

"At any rate, you know the sort of man we are dealing with."

"Oh yes. I get the impression from my friends that he's a man who is not afraid to go outside the law when it suits him."

"You think there could be dirty tricks then?"

"Definitely. There have already been regular incidents of him blocking the access road. I can only guess at what he might try if the stakes are raised."

"Well, I've only met him once, but it was a fairly lengthy meeting and I had plenty of time to study his face. I would say that he is not a man to tangle with. His sort only see self. Any opposition they meet is seen as something to be bull-dozed aside."

He drained the last of his beer and looked at Richard.

"Come on. Drink up. We should be getting back."

On the walk back to the office a thought struck Richard.

"Have you completed due diligence on Baxter Marine?"

"Not yet. It's work-in-progress. Something you need to know?"

"Not exactly. I was wondering if you checked out the company's products. I would love to get a copy of my boat's design plans and specification."

"No problem. We are almost ready to have a closer look at his production plans. We can simply ask for design details and specifications as part of our checks. I'll make it all current models and you can take a copy of the ones you want."

They walked in silence for a while. It was as they neared the Rayleton building that Richard broached a subject that intrigued him.

"Given the demands of our work at the bank, how do you find the time to paint?"

"I make the time. If most people looked carefully at what they have done over a given period, they would probably be shocked at all the time spent on trivia. I guard my free time so that I can do what I really enjoy doing. So, most evenings and every weekend I paint. Tonight, there will be an exception. I have just completed a work, so this evening I shall be taking a break."

He glanced at Richard as he spoke.

"Are you interested in art?"

Richard nodded.

"Of course. I've heard about you sketching through Harry's meetings. Been tempted to myself at times. Anyway, come around to my place this evening. It will give us a chance to get to know each other better. Oh, and bring your new partner. Jenny isn't it?"

"How come you know about Jenny?"

"As I said earlier, there are always ears listening-in in this building."

He grinned at Richard as they passed through the bank's main entrance.

"Any time after seven will be fine."

• • •

After a day spent alone adjusting to her new surroundings Jenny had been happy to accompany Richard and meet his new colleague. The address they were seeking proved to be a Victorian cottage that for over a century had escaped the clutches of London's property developers and still stood in its own garden. The sound of a lawnmower suggested that their host was busy outside and gaining no response to the door-bell, they followed a path around the side of the cottage between strategically placed rose-clad trellises to the rear garden, where they found Gerry mowing the final patch of the lawn that stretched down to the river.

He was busily unaware of them and they were happy to wait and follow the distraction of a family cruiser making its way up river. It was only when, mowing completed, he detached the grass box and turned to empty it that he noticed them. His face immediately broke into a broad grin.

"Sorry. We must have the wrong house. We're looking for an artist chap who lives around here."

"Mea culpa. I thought I had time to fit the mowing in before you arrived. Still, I wasn't far out."

He waved an arm to indicate the open French windows.

"Go in and have a look around. I'll join you as soon as I've put the machine away and washed my hands."

They made their way through the open doorway into the cottage's sitting-room, a medium-sized rectangular room with a large stone fireplace facing the French windows. A large settee dominated one of the shorter side walls and a pair of armchairs flanking a glass cabinet faced it. The armchair nearest the fire had extra cushions and this and the small side table with a book and spectacles case alongside suggested that this was the owner's usual seat. The overall impression was of an unpretentious comfort, although somewhat dated, that had passed to Gerry when he inherited the house.

The one feature which stamped the room as different was the pictures which decorated the walls. Flanking the glass cabinet was a pair of portraits of a man and woman dressed in post-war style. The wall behind the settee carried a similar pair of pictures of an older man and woman dressed in between-the-wars style, while on either side of the French windows were smaller pictures in black and white of two people in much older style and obviously based on early photographs. In pride of place above the fireplace and noticeably different from the others in size, style and colour was a picture of a young woman. She was in a sleeveless summer dress standing in front of a rose trellis and was pictured reaching for a rose.

Gerry joined them as they were still taking it all in.

"Did you paint all of these?" Richard asked.

Their host nodded his agreement.

"The early ones were based on old photographs."

Jenny was still looking at the portrait above the fireplace. She spoke to Gerry without turning her head.

"This picture is different from the others. Who is she?"

"She was my wife."

"Was?" Jenny turned to put her question.

"She died in the first year of our marriage."

Oh! I am so sorry. I had no idea…"

Gerry indicated with his hands that there was nothing to apologise for.

"She was diagnosed with an inoperable brain tumour some months after we had become engaged. She very much wanted to be married, so we brought forward our wedding plans. We had a few blissful months before…"

He paused to swallow the lump which had formed in his throat.

"Anyway, it was a long time ago."

"She was very beautiful."

"Yes, she was. I loved her very much and I still do."

Richard had said nothing during this exchange, but had listened with interest. All that he had learned about his new colleague at the bank had now acquired a whole new meaning.

Gerry was ready to move on to different matters.

"Come. You've not yet seen my studio."

He led them through a hallway decked with numerous watercolours and upstairs to what had once been the main bedroom.

"I took over this room after my parents passed away. It has the best light for painting."

The room still had the radiators from its earlier existence, but all else had been removed. In place of the customary bed, wardrobes and drawer units were an easel holding a portrait and a simple deal kitchen table holding cartons of oil paint and an assortment of brushes. Completing the décor were more pictures of various styles and genres, some mounted on the walls, others stacked in twos and threes beneath them.

It was the picture left on the easel that caught Richard's eye as he entered the room.

"Ah!" he exclaimed. "Uncle Henry."

He studied the portrait carefully.

"You've caught him well."

"I've just completed it, which is why I have time to receive visitors."

Jenny moved forward alongside Richard in order to take a closer look at the finished picture.

"So! This is what your uncle looks like. Is it a good likeness?"

"Yes. I would say that it gives a real understanding of him."

"There is a sense of steel in his face. It suggests to me that this is a man who likes to get his own way."

"I think it's the strong jaw line and the structure of the nose," Gerry added. "It is a feature of all the Rayleton portraits hung in the great stairwell at Rayleton House, as you must have noted Richard."

He looked questioningly at Richard as he spoke.

"I wouldn't know. I have only visited the place once. I was about seven years old and more interested in cake and running around outside."

"Well that is where this work is heading. It was commissioned with that in mind. The size had to fit a pre-determined position."

"I'll look out for it when I get the chance. We should be getting an invitation before long."

As he spoke Gerry had already begun to move towards the studio door.

"I thought we might sit out in the garden."

It was a short time later, with a glasses of chilled white wine in hand that Jenny returned to the subject of Gerry's paintings.

"Do you only paint portraits?"

"Not entirely. There are certain buildings and some of London's more interesting townscapes that tempt me from time to time, but portraiture is my first love."

"And what do you charge for one of your portraits?"

"I can't give an exact answer. For a start I don't depend on my painting for a living, so I can afford to charge less than a professional artist might."

He thought for a moment before continuing.

"The basic factor common to every commission is size. The bigger the picture, the longer it takes and the more materials you use. In some cases, travel might be involved. Other than that, it's not easy to define how I measure things. I suppose it boils down to how much I like the subject or the person placing the commission or even how much that person can afford to pay."

He smiled at Jenny as he finished speaking.

"It's just that I was wondering about getting a picture of my Grandpa painted."

She bent over to the handbag she had placed beside her chair and retrieved two photographs, one small black-and-white shot of a happy smiling young man in military uniform, the other a larger photograph in colour of an older man pictured with a horse.

"These are the only pictures I have of him."

Gerry took the two photographs and studied them.

"Yes, I could produce a portrait from these. The larger one would make an excellent informal picture. Who is the subject? A relative?"

"He was my Grandpa. He and my Grandma brought me up after my parents died in a road accident. Then Grandma got sick with cancer, and after she died it was just Grandpa and me."

"He obviously meant a lot to you. Tell me about him."

"There's not much to tell. His father died on the day Pearl Harbour was attacked. Soon after that he enlisted in the Marine Corps. The smaller picture was taken after his passing-out parade. A few weeks later his unit were shipped to Guadalcanal to prevent the Japanese from invading Australia. He was in action in the Pacific all through the war. I guess he was lucky to survive. Even so, Gran's sister said he came home a different man to the one who had enlisted."

"Today it would be described as post-traumatic stress. You can still see traces of a haunted look in his face."

Jenny nodded in agreement.

"After the war he just wanted a quiet life. He bought a small farm and produced most of the food we ate and anything that that would raise cash to pay off the bank loan. His great love was horses."

"Very wise. That would have been therapeutic."

"I guess so, but after he died I had to sell the farm to pay off the bank loan."

"And this picture is your link to him."

"It's my only link."

All through this exchange Richard had been sitting quietly nursing his wine glass. Now Gerry turned to him.

"Well, I would say that warranted a portrait, wouldn't you Richard?"

"Certainly, but on what grounds? War record or child rearing?"

"Both I would think."

He turned back to Jenny, a faint smile playing around the corner of his mouth.

"Leave these with me now and I will get larger prints made of them tomorrow and pass them back to Richard."

Jenny looked totally shocked by this sudden turn of events.

"But we haven't discussed the price...."

She tailed off, aware that Gerry, now openly smiling, was shaking his head.

"No price, I shall enjoy the work. I will simply ask you for the cost of materials when it is all done to your satisfaction. All you have to do is decide on what size you would like."

12

Jenny lay in bed for a long time after Richard had left for his day at the office. She had a whole day to fill and felt in no hurry to get up. It was an ideal time to spend reflecting on the previous evening and their visit to Gerry's riverside home. Uppermost in those reflections was the portrait of his late wife. It was a striking and very lovely portrayal that somehow brought the room to life. There was no doubt in her mind that this effect had been deliberately planned. This was how he had kept his love for her alive and why he would never move from that cottage. What a lovely man she thought.

Inevitably her thoughts turned to his promise of a portrait of her grandfather. That would, in a similar way, keep her memories of him alive. It was what a good painting does so much better than any photograph. When I gain possession of my Jersey house, she thought, grandpa's picture will be hung there. It would provide a link between past and present.

She stopped, aware that in her reverie she had formulated plans that had not previously been thought about in any settled way, but which had obviously been lurking at the back of her mind. It was a topic that she and Richard had never formally discussed. So many other things were happening that they had inevitably concentrated on the here and now. In any case, she reminded herself, she would not be able to regain possession of her property for many months. Yet it was something that they would need to see settled.

It was fortunate they neither of them held fixed views or had a personality that demanded that his or her sole views were all that mattered. At the moment being together was the dominating factor. Nevertheless, the location of their long-term home was a matter which at some point would need to be addressed. She had no doubt that, once he had parted company with the bank, they would be able to come to a decision on this subject that would be acceptable to both. By all accounts Richard had enjoyed his three years in Jersey. He liked the ambience of the island, had made friends there and there was easy access to the sea and good sailing. Perhaps equally importantly they would be spared the cost of buying a property large enough for family living. To her way of thinking Jersey ticked all the boxes. Time would tell whether or not Richard's thinking ran along similar lines. In the meantime, there was this waiting period that needed to be filled.

A similar line of thought had come to Richard as he walked the short distance from the tube station to the Rayleton headquarters. He too had cast back to the events of the previous evening and the subject of portraiture. However, in his case it was the portrait of his uncle, which Gerry was to deliver that weekend, which came to mind. It reminded him that he was pledged to telephone his Aunt Elizabeth to arrange a date for a visit to the family seat. Sighing inwardly, he determined to get the matter sorted at the first convenient opportunity. It was not the act of telephoning itself that had occasioned the delay, so much as the fact that he had only met her on one previous occasion, and that had been at a time when he had been very young.

In the event the call was made and a date was made for

the following weekend. It had been a relief to find that his aunt was a very different type of personality to her husband. From their short conversation she had come across as a warm, home-loving sort of woman with a dislike of ceremony. He had the impression that she was far more interested in his and Jenny's romance than in any manoeuvrings within the Rayleton bank hierarchy.

There was to be no immediate return to the work he had left unfinished the previous evening. As so often seems to happen, other matters simultaneously came to the fore. No sooner had he set his telephone back on its base than Gerry's secretary swept into his office, dropped three folders of documents on his desk, smiled and left as efficiently as she had entered. A note clipped to the topmost folder simply read 'as promised'.

Puzzled, he opened the first file and immediately recognised the Baxter yacht designs and specifications that he had asked for. It would make sense to hand the whole collection over to Rob, he quickly reasoned, and the easiest way to do that would be to make a short detour to the Hamble boatyard when he and Jenny drove down to Rayleton for the promised Sunday lunch. Having been given a brief outline of the irregular pattern of Rob's usual weekend activities, he decided to warn him in advance that they would be calling.

He made the call mid-morning during his usual coffee break. It had been Lou's voice that had answered the call. She would not hear of a flying visit. If they came a day earlier there would be dinner with them in the evening and a bed for the night with an easy drive to Rayleton the following morning. That way, she reasoned, there would be time for everything. Richard could only guess what was meant by 'everything'. Yet the more Richard thought about it afterwards, the more sense it made. They could use the whole weekend and, in addition to meeting both of the families important in his life, it would also allow them to avoid dashing along motorways and for Jenny to see more of rural England.

The remainder of the day passed slowly and with some difficulty. In that first part of the day his other life had come to the fore and he found it hard to concentrate on bank business. His work in Jersey had been relatively straightforward and he had not found it to be unduly taxing. Now he was having to take on board some of the more complex areas of business finance and it was proving to be heavy going. It was not that he lacked the ability to master it. Rather, it was the deepening realisation that this was not how he wished to spend the remainder of his working life.

It was with a sigh that he shut down his computer at the end of the day and prepared to make his way home. When in London, it had formerly been his habit to work into the early evening so as to avoid the peak of the evening rush hour. Now back at the bank's head office this was the practice that he had resumed. He had known that returning to London work patterns after the relaxed life-style of Jersey would not be easy. Even so it was proving more difficult than expected. The one great thing about the return journey was that at the end of it, Jenny would be waiting for him.

He waited until they were eating the dinner she had prepared before he told her of the double visit plans that he had been drawn into for the following weekend. There was an involuntary intake of breath.

"Two visits," she gasped. "Oh Lordy!"

This was followed by the customary lament.

"I have nothing to wear."

Richard smiled to himself. At least, he thought to himself, she will have something to occupy her mind for the next week or so.

In the event other matters were to take pride of place in their minds. It began the following morning with a call from Charlotte in the Jersey office. She apologised for the delay in carrying out the search he had requested, a sudden influx of business had kept her fully occupied for several days. However, she had good news. In the basement she had located an old file bearing the name Edward Weybourne. In addition to account records showing the remaining account balance, it also contained a number of hand-written letters.

Richard began to thank her, but Charlotte cut in. There was a snag. Rachel had ruled that there was no proven hereditary connection to Jenny, therefore the files must remain in Jersey. Having passed on that message, she rang off.

Richard sat back in his desk chair and cursed loudly. The abruptness of the message was so unlike Charlotte he thought. It could only mean that Rachel was in earshot. He was still pondering on these lines when his mobile phone pinged the receipt of an incoming message. It simply read 'taken earlier'. Accompanying the message were photographs of handwritten documents. They could only be one thing.

Making silent thanks for both Charlotte's ingenuity and the usefulness of modern technology, he quickly copied all the attachments to his personal laptop and returned it to his briefcase. He smiled to himself as he put the briefcase back on the floor beside his desk. He would print them out at home. Perhaps these letters would throw light on what had brought Jenny's forebears to Jersey and what had led the surviving members of that family to end up farming in America. He resisted the temptation to read any of the material. This was Jenny's family business he thought; she should have first reading of them. Instead he satisfied himself by texting his thanks to his former secretary.

That evening, after dinner had been consumed and dishes washed, the commencement of a heavy shower put an end to the idea of an evening stroll that Jenny had earlier suggested. She stood looking out of the window at the streaming rain and turned to Richard.

"I'd forgotten about the English weather. So, what would

you like to do? Richard said nothing, but crossed to the settee where he had dropped his brief case on his return home. I came across some material this morning which I need to print out."

Jenny watched as he switched on his printer and printed out a number of documents

"I thought that you might like to have a look at these."

Jenny took the proffered papers with a smile. The smile faded and was replaced by a puzzled expression as she opened it and looked at the first sheet of bank records.

"I don't get it, what is this?"

"It's a two-and-a half page bank account. Read on."

She flicked past the pages of tabulated figures to the first of the handwritten documents. There was a brief pause and then a beaming smile suffused her features

"The letters! Oh, you darling."

"Don't thank me. This was Charlotte's work."

He paused and his face took on a more serious aspect.

"We are not supposed to have these as we cannot as yet claim a proven hereditary connection. So, you must not mention them to anyone."

She nodded acceptance of his warning and read and re-read the first of the letters before handing it across to Richard.

HMS Hirondelle
Portsmouth
29th August, 1799

Dearest Elizabeth

You will have noticed immediately, I am sure, the new address at the head of this sheet. The harbour is of course subject to frequent change, but the ship will be my home for some time. It would seem that Dame Fortune has been smiling on me of late.

In my last letter from Cape Town I wrote of my promotion to Lieutenant. Following this we had a long haul escorting our fleet of Indiamen to the safety of home waters. As we neared the Bay of Biscay our ship was ordered to move independently ahead of the fleet to warn of any possible dangers. It was in the course of this duty that we spotted a small French sloop that appeared to have evaded the Brest Blockade. She made off at once, but shots from our long guns brought down her topmast and we were able to take her without further trouble. As junior officer I was placed in temporary command and dispatched to Portsmouth.

To cut a long story short, it would appear that the navy is short of small fast ships and the officers to man them. It was decided therefore to immediately commission the ship into the Royal Navy retaining her original French name 'Hirondelle'. It was also decided that I should remain as her commander.

There, I have given you all my news in a rush like a young schoolboy when I should more properly have begun with enquiry as to the health and wellbeing both of yourself and your good Father. Forgive me, but I wished you to know of my news at the first opportunity. Prize money and command in one fell swoop is a piece of amazing good fortune which will now allow us to begin to plan for the future.

'Hirondelle' will need to undergo repairs to damage sustained in the engagement. Perforce I shall be held in Portsmouth for some time. It is maddening to be so close and yet not to have complete freedom of movement. However, as soon as opportunity presents itself, I shall endeavour to visit.

Please convey my best wishes to your father.

With love,

Edward

Richard was grinning as he handed the sheet back to her.

"As we suspected, they are more than good friends. This is obviously the real thing."

"Mm. I should be happy tracing the story of my forebears, but unfortunately I know how it all ends."

A tear rolled down her cheek. Richard put a consoling arm around her.

"The end is always the same for everyone. Try not to concentrate on that awful ending. Look at the positives. They loved each other. They had a child to leave behind them and that child was the important link that leads to you. What I hope, is that the remaining letters throw more light on who they were and how you come to end up in America."

"I know," said Jenny sadly. She sniffed deeply and contrived to wipe away a tear before returning to the letters. Her eyes widened in surprise as she read.

> *HMS Hirondelle*
> *Portsmouth*
> *6ᵗʰ November 1799*

Dearest Elizabeth

Dame Fortune, who has been so benevolent to me of late, now sadly appears to have turned against me. I knew, that as a mere newly-appointed Lieutenant Commander, the repairs to my new command would have to fall behind the needs of more senior figures. It is the way of the world and I am left kicking my heels in frustration. It is doubly frustrating that you are a mere day's ride away. Being informed of yet further delay, I decided to hire a horse and make an unexpected visit to my father and at the same time take the opportunity to see you. Alas, I met disappointment in that last respect, as neither you nor your father were at home.

My own father, however, was at home. Brief as my visit would have been, it was to be severely curtailed by unexpected and unwelcome developments. Initially he was in high good humour at the news of my promotion and command. However, his mood changed when I mentioned that I had called at your home. He was at pains to inform me most forcefully of matters of which, hitherto, I had been unaware.

As you perhaps have observed, my family's fortunes have been steadily prospering over many years. In recent years, it would appear, he has been called upon to be of service to Mr Pitt's government. He would not disclose the nature of these services, but it would appear that has been promised due recognition of them in the near future.

The result of all of this is that my father has purchased further acreages of land and is making plans for a much grander house. It would appear that his overriding desire is to move into a higher level of society. With that in mind, he impressed on me, most forcefully, that I would be expected to secure the hand of a young woman of good family. When I attempted to disabuse him of this notion, pointing out that, as a grown man with command of one of His Majesty's warships, I should not be dictated to in this manner, he became totally enraged. In his anger, he went so far as to ban me, on pain of disinheritance, from having anything further to do with you. Rest assured, I chose not to stay any longer under his roof and we parted on the worst of terms.

It pains me to tell you of this, but it is something that I thought you should know. At the same time, you should also know that nothing on my part has changed. The feelings I bear for you cannot be measured in terms of wealth or social standing. I see gold in the love we share and that is wealth enough for me. Should my father carry out his threat of disinheritance, then so be it. With you at my side I will be perfectly content to make my own way in the world.

With best love
Edward

As she came to the end of the letter, she looked across at Richard. Her face registered a mix of surprise and alarm.

"We got it all wrong. It's rich guy: poor girl."

Richard took the sheet from her and quickly scanned its contents. He nodded in agreement.

"Yes. That's about the strength of it."

"And what an awful man his father is," she continued. "I thought from the first that Edward was a straight sort of guy. Now he has gone up even higher in my estimation."

"It's interesting," Richard continued, "but it does not tell us much else. He still signs off with a simple 'Edward'. Other than that he is a naval officer, we know nothing else about him. What have the other pages got to say?"

Jenny was not listening, as she was already concentrating on the next letter.

HMS Hirondelle
St. Peter Port
14th April, 1800

Dearest Elizabeth

I hope that you continue in good health and that the disappointment at being away from home when I last called on you, that you wrote of in your last letter, has now dissipated. It is vexatious I know, but such uncertainties are to be expected, given the nature of my calling. Life for you should go on as usual and I am pleased that you have been able to visit your friends.

In the meantime, I have at last been able to put to sea. More to the point, I shall enjoy an independent role, which will not be constrained by direct attachment to any of our fleets. As Hirondelle has a good turn of speed, she may, from time to time, be called on to carry special dispatches, otherwise I am deputed to spend much of my time in and around the Channel Islands. As they lie much closer to France than to England, the Government is anxious that the navy should make its presence known. A warship of French origin bearing the union flag should send a strong message to Paris, while at the same time reassuring the local population.

My first visit to Guernsey is drawing to a conclusion. To mark the occasion, last night together with two of my officers I was guest of honour at a banquet thrown by the assembled dignitaries of St. Peter Port. Tomorrow we sail to St. Helier where, no doubt, we shall experience more of the same. This is the aspect of my role that I find least to my liking. That said, it is much to be preferred to the boredom and rigours of blockade duty.

I have saved my best news until last. Before sailing to Guernsey, I had first to escort a small convoy of merchant ships eastward to the open waters of the Atlantic. It was on our return towards The Channel Islands that we were able to take a French merchant vessel making for the Seine estuary. She proved to have been carrying a mixed cargo of cotton bales and foodstuffs from France's West Indian possessions. It was not the grandest of prizes measured on any national scale, but is of great significance on a personal level. As Hirondelle was acting independently, I stand to gain the full captain's share of the value of ship and cargo when sold. I have no idea what this will amount to, but, whatever, it will be more than enough for our future needs.

Fellow officers I have spoken to at Portsmouth, who know the Channel Islands, have assured me that they are fine places to live. As the war with France looks to drag on well into the future, I am likely to be maintaining my patrol here for a similarly long period, with only fleeting visits to Portsmouth. When I am better acquainted with what is on offer, I will keep a weatherly eye open for a suitable property here to make our home.

For the moment dearest, this poor script will have to suffice. There only remains for me to say that my feelings towards you grow stronger with each day that I do not see you.

My love as always,
Edward

"That was a lovely letter," Jenny said handing the sheets across to Richard. "He's sticking with her, despite his awful father."

Richard took the offered pages and quickly scanned them.

"Good for him! Now we have two more pieces of information."

"How they came to be in Jersey."

"Uh-uh, and how their Jersey home was financed by prize money."

"Would it have been that much?"

"Oh yes. It would be much like matching the value of a moderately sized cargo ship and its cargo today, with say the average middle-manager's annual salary. They would have been able to buy their house and live off whatever was left over for the rest of their lives."

"But they did not have chance to make much use of it," Jenny said, a rueful look masking her face as she took back the sheets.

"So much love and so much promise..."

Richard reached across to take the last of the sheets, in order to head off any more tears.

"Come my love," he said, offering it back. "You have not read the last one."

Jenny quietly took the letter and was quickly engrossed.

> *HMS Hirondelle*
> *London*
> *29th July, 1801*

Dearest,

Forgive my delay in writing to you. I can only excuse myself on grounds of being called on to sail seemingly to all known points of the compass, often in appalling weather conditions. It was at the completion of the last of these ventures that I received your letter with its dire news. I am left deeply shocked and ashamed on reading of the treatment you and your father have received from my own father.

It is a source of particular pain that I have been the unwitting cause of this. I felt that it was my duty to inform him of our marriage plans and wrote to him, hoping that he had come to accept my views. Alas, it would seem that this was not the case and he has vented his spleen on the parties closest to hand. To dismiss your father from his position and turn you both into the street at a moment's notice is an action that I find utterly outrageous and brings shame on our house. It is a sad irony, that a man who has taken such pains to be looked up to in society, should behave in such a thoroughly churlish and unchristian fashion.

Having made my feelings clear on this dreadful business, I will turn to more practical and I hope more agreeable matters. Since I last wrote I have taken receipt of my prize monies and have been able to purchase a property in Jersey. It is a fine house situated in a village on the coast a little way outside St. Helier and sports fine views looking southward towards the French coast. There should be ample accommodation for a sizeable family. In view of what you have reported, please inform your Father that there will always be a home for him under my roof should he wish it. Apart from all else, he would provide company for you while I am at sea.

The talk here in London is all of ongoing negotiations for peace with France. It is broadly expected that an understanding will soon be announced, with a formal treaty to follow in due course. I believe that both nations would welcome a cease of hostilities at the moment. However, I do not think that the break will be of any great duration as there is much unfinished business. I write of this to make you aware that, before long, opportunity will present itself to arrange our marriage and move our effects to Jersey. Make whatever plans you think fit.

I am due to return to Portsmouth early next month. We shall then have opportunity to discuss matters together rather than through the agency of correspondence. For the moment this letter must suffice. Be brave in the face of adversity, my darling. Eventually we shall together find a new harmony. That is my dearest wish.

My regards to your Father and, as always, my dearest love
to you.
   Edward

"Wow! So that is how the old man ended up in Jersey."

Richard took the final letter and quickly read it.

"It certainly explains a lot, but we still are none the wiser of who the wicked father is or where he lived."

"Maybe we'll never know. Still, we can see how strong the bond was between the two of them."

"It also suggests something else."

Jenny looked at him, puzzled.

"You remember my remarking on the fact that all your forebears were named Pearson although it ought to have been Weybourne."

"Yes. So, what are you thinking?

"Well it might have been a matter of convenience for a newly arrived emigrant to the USA. Yet, I have a sneaking feeling that the change of name might have been deliberate."

"Ah! I can see where you are coming from. You think that it might have been a way of getting back at Edward's father."

"Well, whether deliberate or not, it certainly hid the boy's ancestry."

"But why all the legal fuss and the letters?"

"He was certainly at pains to stay within the letter of the law. He took nothing that was not his and the letters were a way of leaving a guide for future generations to claim their possessions."

"What if..."

Richard placed a finger on her lips.

"Not now. We could be up all night discussing this and we have a busy weekend ahead of us. You remember, people to meet, places to visit."

13

It was late afternoon when they pulled into the Maitland boatyard. The relief at being free from the constraints of the working week had shown itself immediately on leaving the flat. The initial high spirits had continued as the day progressed. Now there was a natural break and for a moment they were happy to sit back quietly, with the engine switched off, and prepare for allowing other people into this private world.

It had been a whirlwind sort of day, Jenny reflected. Petworth, chosen for a mid-morning coffee break, had been well received. What had then followed was an altogether different experience. From what had seemed a very ordinary modern road, Richard had led her to a section of ancient stone wall and had then proceeded to mount it. Only when she had followed him, did its full significance reveal itself.

"Is this the harbour?" she had asked.

He had nodded, and added that this was the entrance to Portsmouth Harbour and the wall was part of the old defence works. They had then parked the car and Richard had shown her what remained of the old town with its inns and harbour jetties and HMS Victory at its centre. For a short period, she was transported back to the end of the eighteenth century. This was Edward's world, she thought. He had walked these old streets and harbour works. This was where he had written some of the letters. At the end, perhaps, this was from where Elizabeth and her father had sailed on their way to Jersey. Or again, that might have been from the very quayside in Southampton where the hotel and its rooftop bar that had provided them with lunch and stunning views over Southampton Water now stood. It had all been a lot to take in. This had been where history had been made, she thought. More importantly, this was also her family history.

She was roused from her reverie by a comment from Richard.

"Time to move, Lou is at the door. She must have been looking out for our arrival."

Lou was already beside the car when they alighted. Jenny caught a glimpse of an elegant dress and a huge smile as she turned from her welcoming embrace of Richard to face her.

"Jenny! I've been so looking forward to meeting you", was all that she managed to say before enveloping her guest in another huge hug. In a different context the words might have been a meaningless formality: the warmth of the hugs showed that the feelings expressed were genuine and Jenny immediately warmed to her.

"Richard has told me a lot about you and the boatyard. Is it always as quiet as this?"

"Oh, goodness no. Summer is our quiet time while people are out using their boats. Winter is when we are hardest pushed. The yard is full then."

Jenny was looking puzzled, so Richard chipped in.

"The yard takes boats out of the water during the winter and carries out any necessary maintenance and repairs. Then they put them back when owners are ready to use them in the spring."

Jenny nodded in understanding as Lou took her by the arm to lead her inside.

"Enough talk about boats. That's all I hear all week. Let's go inside and have a nice cup of tea. I've baked a lovely sponge to go with it."

As they assembled around the kitchen table, they were joined by Ben, scrubbed and shaved after his morning's work.

"Where is Rob?" Richard asked. "Will he be joining us?"

Jenny noticed the quick glance exchanged between Lou and Ben.

"He had to go into town. He should be joining us later."

She gave a reassuring smile as she spoke, but Jenny could sense a certain uneasiness behind it.

Whatever the cause of that might have been, it was soon forgotten as Lou pressed to hear how her visitors had met up. Jenny soon found herself giving an account of her life in America, the discovery of the unopened letter in her grandfather's papers after his death and the trip to London in search of any long-lost relatives.

Lou smiled as she came to the end of her account.

"And you found a pot of gold and yet more old letters," she said.

Ben leaned towards Jenny in a conspiratorial manner.

"This pot of gold you found, you think that is what attracted this fellow?" he said nodding in the direction of Richard. "You know what bankers are like when they smell money."

He was rewarded with a playful thump from Lou.

"Stop it. You are embarrassing Jenny. Why don't you and Richard take a walk round the yard. I'm sure he wants to see his boat."

With that she began to clear the table.

"Jenny can stay here with me. We can have a nice chat while I wash up these things."

Richard and Ben followed their instructions and sauntered

out into the yard leaving Lou and Jenny in possession of the kitchen.

"You must not take Ben seriously. It's his way of showing that he likes you and that you are accepted."

"I guessed that and I was not at all embarrassed. I think that the way you have welcomed me without ceremony is lovely. I can see now why Richard has always felt that this was his second home."

Out in the yard the two men had made their way down to where *Sea Urchin* lay moored.

"We keep a careful eye on her," Ben said. "The fenders are the main concern. The weather is no great problem, but the constant comings and goings of the Baxter crowd are something else. They use a powerful motor launch when they are testing and fitting out their boats and show little concern for the waves it creates."

"You think it's deliberate?"

"Deliberate or not, the speed creates waves."

Richard paused before commenting. He wanted to inform Ben of the boost that Baxter would be getting from Rayleton and this was perhaps the time to air it.

"There is something you should know and I think it's best that you hear it from me. Some weeks ago, Baxter approached Uncle Henry at their golf club with a view to getting a loan. It seems that Henry took a shine to him. Apparently, he sees him as a man with a future."

"What are you saying? He's surely not going to advance Baxter money. He can't properly handle what he has at the moment."

"I agree with you and my departmental head thinks the same, but Henry will not listen. He plans to push the bank into a new area of finance that will involve preparing companies for stock market flotations. This will be the first of what he hopes will be many."

Ben shook his head. "I don't believe it. Lending money to someone like Baxter is akin to pouring petrol on a fire."

A new line of thought occurred to him.

"You're not involved, are you?"

"Not as yet. I have told my immediate boss of my links here and that I want nothing to do with it, so he is handling it. He thinks the same as you, but he is under orders from on high."

Ben placed a hand on Richard's shoulder.

"Thank you for the warning. I appreciate that."

They turned back towards the house.

"I can see that this has put you in a tight spot."

"Yes. I'm still sorting things out in my head. Things have changed. When I first started to work in London it was fun. Then there was Jersey and that was a different sort of fun. Now that I have met Jenny, all of that seems immaterial. We want to make a life together which is shaped by our values and is not dictated by others."

Ben nodded in agreement.

"Lou and I felt the same when we came together. With us it was about the demands that the Navy made. The first chance we had to break away, we took it."

He looked directly at Richard as he spoke.

"Is that the way you're headed?"

"I think so. I know enough about banking now to know that it is not for me. Jen has inherited a house in Jersey which will make a good base eventually, but it's on lease for the next few months. After the lease ends, well…"

He spread his hands in the familiar 'who knows' expression.

"Good for you: she seems a lovely girl."

He paused as they had reached the house.

"Not a word to Lou about Baxter. She has worries enough with Rob at the moment."

"What exactly is she worried about?"

Ben paused at the door seeking the right words.

"Let's just say that at weekends he behaves like he's a naval rating who has been at sea for months and gets a forty-eight-hour shore leave."

"And this is the pattern every weekend?"

Ben nodded.

"We had hoped that your visit would break the pattern but..."

He left the sentence unfinished and they moved inside.

Lou had prepared a traditional roast dinner and had laid the table with five place settings. She delayed serving up the food she had prepared as long as possible, but when Rob failed to appear she removed the fifth place setting and served up dinner with as brave a face as she could muster.

"Looks as if Rob has been delayed in town."

Richard understood the significance of the remark, but could think of nothing to say that would lead the conversation on a different tack. It was left to Ben's wardroom experience to come to the rescue.

"So how are finding England, Jenny?"

"I haven't seen much so far, but I like what I have seen."

"And do you find it in any way similar to the States?" Ben continued.

Jenny smiled.

"The language is the same — well, kind of. Everything else seems different."

She paused for a moment to think further.

"The towns I've seen so far all seem to have a character of their own. Yet, the distances between places are smaller. There's not the same feeling of space."

"Well, if you are going to stay in England, you will have to get used to people being thicker on the ground than you are used to, especially if you are thinking of living in London."

Ben gave her a searching look as he spoke.

"London is interesting, but I wouldn't want to settle there."

Lou had listened with interest to the exchange and now joined in.

"What Ben is trying to ask is if you two have made any plans."

Richard joined in laughing.

"Give us a chance. We've only known each other for five minutes."

After dinner was finished Lou insisted that they retire to the sitting-room where she served coffee. Lou had worn a brave face all evening, but as ten o'clock approached she announced that she needed an early night.

Ben and Richard stayed on downstairs for a final nightcap, but Jenny followed Lou upstairs a little later. As she made her way past the door to the main bedroom, she could make out the unmistakable sounds of Lou weeping.

The morning was well advanced when Jenny and Richard came downstairs to find Lou already hard at work in the kitchen and all evidence of the previous evening's dining gone.

"Sleep well?"

She greeted them cheerfully with no signs of the previous evening's distress.

"What would you like for breakfast. It will just be the three of us. Ben is already out in the yard."

"We shall not want much, we'll be eating at midday," Richard said.

They settled on a simple piece of toast and a pot of coffee and Lou joined them at the table when it was ready.

"Do you always get up so early?" Jenny asked.

"Oh yes. We were both in the Navy, so it's a well-worn practice."

She glanced at the wall clock.

"You will need to keep an eye on the clock if you're lunching at twelve."

Richard pulled a face.

"Twelve's a bit early for me, but it's what some people like."

"What about you Jen?" Lou turned to Jenny who had been sitting quietly dinking her coffee. "Are you an early riser?"

"I used to be when Grandpa was alive. I seem to have been all over the place since I've been in Europe. I guess I don't worry about eating at twelve. It's everything else that concerns me."

Lou smiled comfortingly.

"Now don't you worry yourself. You are going to meet some of Richie's wider family. They are older and live in a big house, but at the end of the day they are just people. So, be yourself. You'll be fine."

"That is what I've been telling her. It's not some grand ceremony. They are not going to be wearing ermine robes and coronets."

After breakfast was over, they returned upstairs to pack their few belongings and prepare for the final stage of their weekend. It was gone eleven when they re-emerged.

"I'll put the bags in the car and let Ben know we are ready to go," Richard said and headed for the workshops.

Jenny and Lou were chatting beside the car when he returned with their host.

"I was just telling Jenny not to stand on ceremony now that we have met. You are welcome at any time."

As she finished speaking she noticed that her husband was looking at the yard's entrance gate where a taxi had pulled up.

"Isn't that just typical," Lou muttered, her face displaying a range of different emotions.

"Better late than never," Ben said putting a consoling arm around her shoulders.

Having paid the taxi driver, Rob lurched unsteadily towards them.

"Sorry I'm late," he mumbled towards his parents.

He then turned unsteadily to Richard standing alongside Jenny.

"Are you going to introduce me?" he demanded, squaring his shoulders in an attempt to make himself presentable that was so utterly comical that Richard could not refrain from laughing.

"You are in no state to be introduced to anyone at the moment," he said taking Rob by the arm.

"What you need is a good long sleep. Come on. I'll see you upstairs."

It was a tricky moment that could have turned quite differently, but to everyone's relief Rob allowed himself to be led indoors. Outside there was momentary silence before Lou turned to Jenny.

"I don't know what you will think of us," she said, wiping a tear from the corner of an eye. "He has only recently begun to be like this."

"It doesn't matter one little bit. I've loved meeting you, and one minor upset is not going to change that. This is the sort of thing that can happen in families."

"Families. Who would have them," Ben muttered grimly.

A few moments later Richard re-appeared.

"He's in bed. He was asleep as soon as his head touched the pillow."

"Thank you for that," Lou said. "I was just saying to Jenny that this is a recent development."

"Leaving university can be very unsettling," Richard said reassuringly.

"One week you are with the big guns, the next you are just

another face in the crowd. In Rob's case he does not even have a new employer in a new town. He's just back at home. At any rate, I'm sure this will pass and I've got something for him that he should find interesting."

He opened the rear door of the car and reached inside for the box of documents that had travelled with them on the rear seat.

"These are the plans and specifications for all of Baxter's current products. We're not supposed to have them, so keep them under lock and key. They should keep him busy between work shifts."

"Do you think it will have any effect?" Lou said to her husband.

"It's worth a try. Either way it won't do any harm. Thank you for that Rich."

"No trouble. Now we really have to be going."

The site for Rayleton House had been well chosen. It was set with its back to a wooded ridge that stretched away on either side providing a natural backdrop that changed with the seasons. For anyone within the house, its many large windows offered wide uninterrupted views over the surrounding parkland.

The house itself was elegantly regular in a style that later generations would term Late Georgian. It was a design that eschewed both the excessive classicism of the eighteenth century and the contrived domesticity of the later parts of the nineteenth. In this way, without any obvious ostentation, it made a statement that its builder was a man of means and local standing. This was the house that the soon to be enno-bled Joseph Weybourne had built on his newly acquired Rayleton Estate in place of the much less imposing original structure, and which now awaited the arrival of its latest visitors.

Two imposing brick pillars capped with Portland stone was how the Rayleton estate announced itself to the outside world. Once within, the visitor was led through several acres of mixed woodland. Traditional wrought iron railings flanked either side of the driveway as it described a long shallow curve that prevented any sighting of the house until the visitor was much closer.

Richard could remember little from his childhood visit. He drove steadily taking in all details until slowing to make a shuddering crossing of a cattle grid. Ahead of them a small stone bridge spanning a stream led them into an area of parkland kept well-grazed by the groups of sheep scattered over it. Behind this the house, rising above skirts of ornamental gardens, awaited them.

Jenny gasped with surprise as all was revealed.

"Oh my!" was all that she managed to say.

A second grid marked by a further pair of gateposts guarded the crossing of a well-concealed ha-ha, the stone walling to its bank nearest the house preventing any egress by the grazing sheep. Beyond this the drive divided into two symmetrical wings that swept in wide arcs around the central section of the gardens. Richard took the left-hand option and followed this until reaching a wide paved area immediately fronting the house. No other vehicles were visible as Richard drew to a stop near the first corner of the house, adjacent to a narrower branch of driveway that led to outbuildings carefully screened by trees.

They made an unhurried walk of the few yards to the ornate front door admiring the view of the route they had just used. They were still enjoying the view when the door behind them was opened.

"It's a lovely view isn't it. We never tire of looking at it."

They turned to find both of their hosts standing in the doorway. To Richard, used to seeing his uncle in immaculately tailored business suits, it was a surprise to see him in a simple linen jacket over an open-necked shirt. Behind him his wife was similarly casually dressed in a sleeveless summer dress with her hair, fashioned in a loose bunch, looped over one shoulder.

The surprise appearance of their hosts had the immediate effect of erasing any stilted formalities and they were soon chatting easily.

"We wanted this to be a nice relaxed family weekend," Elizabeth said to Jenny as she led her indoors. "We get so few free ones where we can be ourselves. I think it is important for Henry to be able to relax. I've warned him there is to be no bank talk."

Behind them Richard was remarking on the garden.

"Oh, there will be plenty of time for that later," Henry replied. "Liz will do the honours then. The garden is her department."

Looking back, it was the appearance of Sally, still clad in her morning riding gear, that was to have significant repercussions. Elizabeth and Henry had been at pains to make everything relaxed and informal, despite this, their visitors were left with the impression of a planned informality in which every move had been carefully choreographed. Jenny's position at the dining table gave her a frontal view of Richard's aunt and, as Sally made her appearance, she could not miss the momentary look of annoyance that crossed Elizabeth's face before being replaced by a beaming smile.

"Ah, there you are dear. Cutting it fine as usual."

"Sorry Mummy. It's difficult to keep track of time when you're riding in rough woodland."

The arrival of a fifth person at the table created an imbalance that, on other occasions, might have created awkwardness. In this instance it had the opposite effect of breaking the ice sufficiently to allow the luncheon to proceed with less formality.

After lunch they were given a tour of the gardens with Elizabeth giving an outline of what had been achieved since they had taken over the property and a brief sketch of what they had in mind for the future. Throughout she spoke of the gardens as if it was a joint effort, yet Richard could not help sensing that the uncle following in their wake was very much a fish out of water in this environment.

Throughout the garden tour Sally had tailed along, although gardening held little interest for her. At one point they stopped, while Richard and his aunt discussed an aspect of design. Standing aside from this, the two girls began to chat about what Sally had been doing before lunch. Once she had discovered that Jenny had grown up with horses, she was determined, at the first opportunity, to draw their guest away and show her what she herself had in the way of animals and facilities. As they reached the end of the garden circuit she seized the moment and casually announced that she was taking Jenny to see her horses.

As she followed Sally around the corner of the house, Jenny was astonished to find, hidden away behind the garaging and other outbuildings, was a completely different world. She was first led into a large stable block between a well-ordered tack room on one side facing equally neat bays stocked with straw and fodder on the other. Beyond them were facing rows of stalls, four of which had horses occupying them.

"This is what I wanted to show you," Sally explained. "There are spare horses. It would be lovely to ride out together. Think about it."

Without waiting for a reply, she drew her guest back outside to show her the former lawn tennis courts, which now served as a dressage practice area and the large paddock with its array of practice fences.

"There. Everything needed to prepare for Badminton."

"What is Badminton?

"Badminton Horse Trials. It's the biggest equestrian event in the UK. So! What do you think?"

"What do I say? It's all wonderful! There is no sign of any of this when you approach the house."

"That's what I like about it. It's my own world, quite separate from the house."

Jenny looked around taking it all in. It was hugely impressive, but a world away from the casual riding she had known before her Grandpa's death. For her part Sally was unaware of these points of difference and was not satisfied until she had extorted a promise to return for a weekend of riding together. Jenny's first instinct had been to decline the repeated invitation, but for reasons she could not understand, she sensed that a bond had developed between them. While the rational part of her brain was formulating polite words of refusal, it seemed as if some other voice was uttering words of delighted acceptance.

When they finally returned to the house the afternoon was already well advanced. The hosts and Richard had returned to the shaded patio and were enjoying tea. After the heat in the garden and driveways they had crossed it was refreshing to sit in the shade.

"Sorry Mummy," Sally muttered, "we got carried away."

"As girls do when they are with horses," her father tartly observed.

"So! What have you been doing in our absence?" Sally asked, ignoring her father's remark. "Anything of interest?"

"Actually, we were showing Richard your father's new portrait. I gather that you have already seen it at Gerry's studio," she added turning to Jenny.

"Mm. I thought it was very good. It will be interesting to see it again now that I have met the sitter," she said smiling at Henry.

"Drink up. I'll show you." Sally was already on her feet.

Jenny followed her back into the house to the entrance hall. She had not taken in any details when they had first arrived. Now she was able to appreciate the scale and impact of the design. On either side of a rectangular alcove, furnished with a small table bearing a large flower arrangement, two separate stairways led upwards to a half-landing from which a further central stairway led to the landing proper with its flanking ornate balustrades. Around this central feature all available wall space bore arrays of family portraits in a variety of sizes and styles. Jenny stopped to examine the lower ones before following her guide to the half-landing. All the male figures, she noted, seemed to have the same prominent jawline that Gerry had remarked on.

Sally waited for her at the head of the final section of stairs. She indicated the portrait alongside of her.

"Here we are. Sir Henry Rayleton (Bart.)"

Jenny recognised the painting that Gerry had displayed to them at his riverside home.

"It's very good. He has caught your father exactly. It also looks very well positioned with him at the top of the stairs surrounded by all his forebears."

"Not quite all. These are all the holders of the Rayleton baronetcy and their families. There is one other painting of the man who actually started the building of the house. It's in an older style from before the baronetcy was awarded. It's further along the landing. Come, I'll show you."

She led the way around a dogleg in the landing and stopped before a portrait of a man dressed in an earlier style, the canvas now somewhat dulled with age. Unlike the portraits surrounding the stairwell, this picture was mounted in a frame that bore the name in gilt lettering of the person represented. Jenny looked at the picture for few moments and then leaned forward to read the inscription. Momentarily her head spun as she read the name Joseph Weybourne Esq.

14

They left Rayleton shortly after tea. As a special surprise for Jenny, knowing of her liking for the works of Jane Austen, Richard detoured from their direct route home to show her the novelist's home in Alton. It was the first inkling that something was troubling Jenny that Richard received, for she looked at the house without showing any interest. Instead she simply stated that she would like to go straight home.

It was the same story when they resumed their journey. The joy and pleasure of their outward journey on the previous day had gone. Whereas then she had been full of excitement, happily pointing out things of interest and bombarding Richard with queries and observations, now she said nothing. Initially he glanced across at her at odd moments, but failed to discern any visible reactions to her surroundings. It was as if she had entirely withdrawn into herself. Receiving no responses to his attempts to draw her into conversation, he concentrated on his driving. The remainder of the journey was completed in silence.

It was with feelings of relief that Richard steered the car into their designated parking space. Jenny immediately went into the property and let herself into the flat, leaving Richard to bring in their luggage from the car. As he entered the hall-way, Jenny emerged from the main bedroom bearing pillows and her dressing gown.

"What on earth are you doing?" Richard asked with a puzzled look.

Jenny looked at him steadily, slowly shaking her head from side to side.

"You don't get it, do you?"

"Get what?" a bewildered Richard replied.

"Us! You and me! What else would I be talking about?"

Richard put down the bags he was carrying.

"You're damn right I don't get it. In fact, I have no idea what you are talking about. What exactly is it that I am missing?"

"The name."

"What name?"

"The name on the portrait — the one of the guy that built the house. 'Joseph Weybourne Esquire'"

"I don't think I saw that one. And anyway, what's that got to do with us?"

"When we were looking at the letters, do you remember saying that my name ought not to be Pearson, as the surviving child would have been named Weybourne. So, I should be named Weybourne. Right?"

Richard nodded.

"Now, let's get closer to home. Your father was named Rayleton because decades earlier the family had changed their name to that of their estate. Right?"

Richard nodded slowly as the situation began to dawn on him.

"But for that change of name, you would also be named Weybourne."

"So, that makes us..."

"...kinfolk."

She finished the sentence for him. "I don't know what the

rules of the game are in England, but, where I come from, kinfolk are not encouraged to marry or have children."

"It's much the same here, but all of this is spread over a period of two hundred years involving a dozen or more generations."

"Doesn't mean a thing. Genes are not bound by dates."

"OK, but we're not certain that the Weybourne who wrote the letters and who went down with his ship in the waters off Jersey is related to the family we have just visited."

"Maybe, but I'm ninety-nine percent sure that he is. So, until one way or another it is proved otherwise, I think we should not continue to sleep together."

"I accept that there is uncertainty, but I don't think the evidence of a name plaque on a two-hundred-year old portrait is strong enough evidence. You could just as easily make the opposite case – until it is proved otherwise, we stay as we are."

Jenny did not respond.

Richard looked at her shaking his head in despair.

"I thought that you loved me."

"I do love you, with all my heart. Do you think this is easy? From the moment I first met you I have treasured the thought that one day we would get married and have children. That is the problem. If we are related, any children that we might have could have any one of a whole bunch of birth defects. Isn't it better to be safe than sorry?"

Richard sighed deeply.

"I suppose you're right. So, what do we do about it?"

"I was thinking about it in the car. I'm sure it must be straightforward to get a DNA test done these days. I seem to think there are labs who can do it all by post. It can probably be wrapped up in a couple of weeks, and we'll know for sure."

She had clearly thought things through and was not about to have her mind changed.

"One thing though," she added, "we'll need a third party from the Rayleton family as a sort of control sample. Do you think that would be possible?"

Richard paused. Two weeks might easily be turn into months of wrangling with the family over something sensitive like this.

"I wonder if cousin Sally might help us out?" he eventually suggested, "— the two of you seemed as thick as thieves this afternoon."

"OK. I've got her number, so I'll give her a call first thing."

Jenny looked at him plaintively.

"Cheer up. It won't be forever."

"No, but it will feel like it."

"I know. I think it will be easier if I'm not around, and anyway I need to go back to the States to sort some things out with Martha and Hal…"

She had begun to move towards the spare bedroom, but checked to turn to face him again.

"If you think about it, either way you win. Heads you have me as before. Tails you get me as a cousin. Can't be bad."

The following morning Richard followed his usual workday morning schedule. The routine was the same, but the experience was very different to that of recent weeks. He had had little sleep as he came to terms with Jenny's decisions. The tube train journey into central London and the short walk to the Rayleton headquarters were the same as on other workdays, but this one was different. Had he been asked afterwards to describe particular details of it, he would have been at a loss to find any picture of the experience. While he carried out all the usual physical motions, his mind was elsewhere. His outward appearance might look much the same, but his mind would give a different account. That story would be one of confusion, doubt, uncertainty and a host of other unpleasant emotions. The world felt disjointed and he dared not seek solace in hope.

Once in his office, he sat flitting through files on his computer, aimlessly searching for something to draw his concentration. The ringing of his telephone broke the confusion and momentarily concentrated his mind. He picked up the receiver and was relieved to hear the friendly voice of Gerry Thomas.

"Hi. Thought that I would get in early before you had settled down to any serious work. I thought that we could have a beer together at lunchtime."

"Sounds good. What time?" Richard tried to sound as casual as possible to hide the mental fog he had been experiencing.

"Good. I'll drop by your office at about 12.50."

"Look forward to it."

Richard replaced the phone on its cradle and sat back in his desk chair. Presumably, he thought, he wants to leave the building. That would mean that he has something to tell me.

Gerry was in his usual good spirits as they chatted on their way towards the bar that they had used before. Richard thought it a good choice, as it was situated off the main thoroughfares and escaped the overcrowding of the more popular hostelries. As before they settled on a table in a quiet corner. Only when they were seated with their drinks did he turn the point of their meeting.

"Things are developing on the Baxter front. John and I have been working together on the loan. I've been down to the Hamble site. I've inspected the facilities and held talks with Baxter and his Accounts Manager."

"And?"

"He certainly needs money. The boats look good and the

showroom is a very slick modern place, but the workshops are cramped and the equipment looks a bit dated. More importantly, I talked off the record with the fellow who keeps the accounts. I'm tempted to say manages the accounts, but he told me that no one at the company has any say in anything that goes on. It's a one-man band — and that one man flies by the seat of his pants with no real idea of what he's doing. The company is currently flat broke and they are surviving by means of their bank overdraft and cutting out anything that needs immediate cash spending. The latest move has been to let their non-statutory insurances lapse."

Richard looked at Gerry in astonishment.

"I had no idea that it was as bad as that."

Gerry nodded.

"Bankruptcy next stop…"

"… without a cash injection."

"Exactly."

"Did Henry know about all of this?"

"Oh yes! Both John and I recommended that we stay well clear of the whole Baxter scene, but he overruled us. God knows why."

"What did Charles think?"

"He's ready to slip into the top seat when Henry chooses to retire, which, from what I hear, will not be too long coming. So, he's not minded to rock the boat at this stage in his career."

Gerry took a sip of his beer and looked Richard directly in the face.

"That's now past history. It's all done and dusted. As from this morning, bonds secured by Baxter's properties are quoted on the London Exchange."

Richard was momentarily lost for words and simply shook his head in dumb amazement.

"How could he be so stupid? A bond issue would have to be in millions."

"You're quite right. Your uncle may be pig headed, but he's not stupid. The arrangement is for an initial million to be issued with more to follow as and when needed."

Richard reacted furiously

"A million! Doesn't he realise the mayhem a man like Baxter can create with that sort of money."

"Relax. Baxter will only get a fraction of that up front. If he uses it wisely, more will be made available. If he doesn't, then we can foreclose on him and take possession of the assets."

Richard sat quietly as Gerry finished his explanation, his mind quickly running through all the implications of what he had just heard.

"It's very clever. I'll give him that, but what about the human factor. What about the Maitland family business next door? That stands to get swallowed up if the Baxter business expands."

"That's what you have been put in this department to learn. If a business does not make the best use of its assets, it gets taken over by someone who will It's the rules of the game. It is not something that anyone can control, but bear in mind, it's not a case of getting pushed out, most are simply bought out. In this instance, if Baxter's business develops it will make the Maitland property all the more valuable at the same time. Could make for a valuable retirement fund."

"I see what you mean. Even so it still seems to me more like the laws of the jungle."

"Agreed. They are one and the same thing. The Rayleton bank is subject to the same rules. If we can't match the pace of the big guns in the financial world, then we risk being swallowed up."

The barmaid brought over their sandwiches, and ate in silence for a short period before Richard turned conversation to non-business matters.

"We were lunching at Rayleton yesterday. We saw Henry's portrait in its designated setting. It looked very grand."

"Yes, to judge by the hanging arrangements, Henry seems to take this baronetcy of his very seriously. It's as if he's lording it over all of the family."

Richard's thoughts immediately swung back to the issue that had followed from Jenny's viewing. He hesitated for a moment before speaking.

"Not quite all of the family. There is another picture, from an earlier period, hanging on its own. It's a portrait of the man who made it all possible. He knew that the baronetcy was to be his reward for services to the crown during the wars against France around the end of the eighteenth century. However, he died before receiving the award, so it passed to another branch of the family."

"Mm, interesting.

Richard paused for a moment before deciding to continue.

"There's more. The picture bore a name, Joseph Weybourne. We think that is also the name of the writer of the letters that Jenny discovered in the inherited account in Jersey."

"Yes, I remember her saying she was hoping to find out more about her family."

He stopped to look at Richard as a new thought entered his head.

"Hold on a minute. That would mean that she is descended from the original branch of the Rayleton family."

"Yes. Had their existence been known, Jenny's forebears would have inherited the Baronetcy and, under the current rules, Jenny would be Lady Rayleton."

"Oh my goodness. I would love to be there when Henry hears of this. That is, I assume he's not yet been told?"

Richard nodded.

"I don't think that he would take the news very kindly, but we are saying nothing until there is cast iron evidence. In any case I don't think Jen gives two hoots about fancy titles. She is far more concerned about the genetic implications."

Gerry hadn't given a thought to biological matters.

"Of course. You'd be sailing into troubled waters there."

"I'm afraid we're already in them. Jen wants us to keep away from each other until we can settle this one way or another."

Gerry stopped eating and glanced at his unhappy colleague.

"I thought you hadn't seemed yourself today. I couldn't put my finger on it. I thought perhaps you were worried about the Baxter situation."

He looked Richard squarely in the face, recognising in him the need for some moral support.

"Would it help by telling me the whole story when we have more time? How about dinner tonight?"

15

There had been little sleep for Jenny. When she had told Richard of the need for them to be apart she had tried to be strong. Continually she reminded herself that it was the correct thing to do. At the same time her heart was taking an opposing view. The result had been hours of anguished tossing and turning before a fitful sleep finally claimed her.

The silence in the flat when she awoke suggested that Richard was probably already left for work. She remembered the look of absolute anguish when she had told him of her decision. His love for her had been written all across his face. Now the very thought of it brought tears to her eyes. What did he think of her now she thought. Would he see her as hard and unloving? Would he realise how hard it had been for her? With that she took a deep breath and then pushed back the sheets.

Making her way to the bathroom, she took a long look at herself in the mirror. She remembered what her Grandpa had said when, as a young teenager, she had asked about his wartime experiences. Weren't you scared, she had asked. She could picture him and remember his voice as he had replied:

"Sure. We all were. In the minutes before you went into

action you could not help wondering whether you would come through it in one piece. Then, once things started, something else took over and you just got on with what needed to be done."

That's it, she thought. Good old Grandpa. You have to just get on with what needs to be done.

Once dressed she made a pot of coffee. Then, while she drank a large mugful, she made a mental list of all the things that she needed to do.

First on the list was to carry out a search for DNA tests. There were a surprising number to choose from, but, after checking out what a number of them had to offer, she was able to settle on one which would provide a personal analysis and also checkout ancestry and search for other persons with similar genetic make-up. That settled, she bookmarked the link to the site ready for use once she had spoken to Sally.

She had no idea of the pattern of Sally's daily activities and assumed that, even though she was ringing the mobile phone number she had been given, she would probably need to leave a message or call repeatedly. In the event she was pleased to get an immediate response from her new friend.

Her plan was to make the call as short and simple as possible. However, what she had hoped would be a simple request for Sally to agree to provide a control sample for the DNA tests, soon became something bigger. Sally had no reservations about taking part in the DNA analysis, but was naturally curious to know why she and Richard needed it. There was no way of avoiding the question and as briefly as possible Jenny outlined what had brought her to England, the unusual bank account, the letters from a bygone age and the naval officer buried in Jersey who bore the name Weybourne and who had links to a country estate.

Sally had said nothing as she listened to Jenny's story, but at this point she responded.

"I don't understand. How are you connected to this?"

"There was a direct line of inheritance linking me to Jersey at the time of the wars with France. I think the naval officer who is buried there was a great grandfather of mine, but it is not certain."

"The old portrait I showed you…"

"Yes. It had the same name."

"So you think the country estate could be Rayleton… I thought that you were behaving strangely when you saw it. Gosh, this is exciting. What does Richard think of it all?"

"He was all for tracing my ancestry at first, but he's not so keen now. I had to explain to him that for the time being we would need to separate because we might be blood relatives."

"I can see now why you need the genetic analysis and what part I will play in it." She paused for a moment. "So where are you now?"

"I'm using the spare room at Richard's flat in Richmond for the present. It's not ideal, but I haven't had the chance to sort anything out yet. I can go back to the States while I wait to take possession of my Jersey property, but for the moment I need to be here for the DNA testing. I'll probably end up in a hotel somewhere."

"I've got a much better idea. Why don't you come and stay with me?"

"I couldn't do that. Your mother would have to be consulted."

"No need. I have my own flat. It's part of the stable block, I think it was once servants' quarters, but it has been modernised and has plenty of room for guests. You could lend a hand with the horses. That would help you relax."

"Are you sure?"

"Perfectly. Besides, who knows, you may end up part of the family."

"All right then. Thank you. It will be lovely."

"Tomorrow then."

"Wait. Where is your nearest railway station?"

"Of course, I was forgetting. You don't have a car. Give me your address and I will pick you up. Will eleven o'clock suit you?"

Momentarily Jenny was taken aback by the offer.

"There's no need for you to go to that trouble."

"It's no trouble. The distance would be much the same if I had to pick you up off the train at Portsmouth or Southampton. This way we can have lunch somewhere on the way back. So, eleven tomorrow."

After the call Jenny sat quietly digesting the latest turn of events. Sally's offer had come as a complete shock, but that feeling was slowly subsumed by a sense of relief. Nothing was yet settled, but some sort of order had been established. She would now have a second member of the Rayleton family to match DNA with, but at one and the same time she would have good company and a roof over her head until she was ready to leave for the USA. It would be hard to walk away from Richard, but, with matters so uncertain, it would in a way be easier than the strain of being in close proximity.

It was a little after eleven next morning when a ring on the doorbell announced Sally's arrival. Jenny moved mechanically. Everything this morning seemed unreal. She was leaving, but did not want to leave. Yet her bags were grouped in the hallway ready for an immediate departure. She had not seen Richard. She had heard his return late on the previous evening and he had already left for work when she had aroused. It was strange to be feeling relief at not having to see him, but it was relief that carried a strong tinge of guilt. Again, she reminded herself of her Grandpa's words and sat to write him a letter that explained where she was going and what she would be doing about the DNA tests. There was a moment's hesitation about how she would sign off when she came to the end. In the end she simply signed her name.

They had stopped for a leisurely lunch at a roadside inn and it was mid-afternoon when they arrived at Rayleton.

When reaching the spot where she and Richard had parked only two days earlier the same feeling of unreality returned. Sally had slowed as they approached the house and swung away to their left and followed the drive extension to a point behind the garage building where she parked.

"Here we are. Home sweet home. This is where I live."

Jenny looked around.

"I can't see anything but the garage."

"That used to be the carriage house. If you look behind it, you will see another building. My flat uses the whole of the upper floor. Daddy had it converted. It's now quite swish and thankfully away from the grandeur of the main house. There is also plenty of space and it is so handy for the horses. Come, I'll show you."

Later, after a leisurely cup of tea, Sally was anxious to check that all was well in the stables. Jenny followed in her wake taking in all around her. It helped of course that this was in the setting of the estate and backed by a wealthy father, but even allowing for that, she had to admire how organised it all was. She was only half-listening as Sally detailed the daily routines for she had begun to realise that she too could do something similar at her property in Jersey once she had taken possession of it.

"You will meet her on Thursday."

She was brought back to the present by the last comment.

"Sorry. I was somewhere else for the moment."

"I was telling you about my friend Jo. The fourth horse belongs to her. We ride together every Thursday. That is her half-day off."

"Really. What does she do?"

"She and her husband run a company that provides a range of services to estates like this one."

"By services do you mean estate management?"

"Mm. The whole shooting match. Accounts, legal issues, employment."

"And do they handle the Rayleton estate affairs?"

"Oh yes. The business grew out of the former Rayleton estate office. They occupy the Old Mill House at the far end of the estate. What was once the mill is now their offices and they live in the adjoining house. I think that was where my family originally lived before Rayleton House was built."

They had moved to greet the horses.

"I thought that you wouldn't mind taking my place on Thursday. There's a big equestrian event at the end of the month and I need to do a lot more work with Bonnie before then."

"Sure, I'll look forward to meeting her."

Jenny tried to sound casually interested, but her mind was working overtime on what she had just learned. There was a strong possibility that the continuation of estate services had left archives intact. If so they could well provide evidence that linked the eighteenth century to the present.

With one of those random changes in the weather that had fascinated Jenny since she had first arrived in Britain, Thursday had dawned overcast with light cloud. It was ideal for a lengthy tour of the estate's many woodland trails. It had been many months since she had last ridden, as her Grandpa had sold his remaining horses when he had become unable to care for them. Now she was eager to be in the saddle again.

Sally had asked her to ride Rusty the third horse. He was a young horse that Sally planned to develop in time to replace the ageing Clyde, but was still inexperienced and in need of strenuous exercise. Jenny was saddling him up when an open sports car came to a halt in front of the garage. It's driver, a slim dark-haired lady got out. She was dressed simply in blouse and riding breeches which disappeared into a pair of black riding boots. Simultaneously Sally emerged from the stables and introduced them.

She was bearing a riding hat which she handed to Jenny.

"House rules. Riding hats to be worn when riding. It sets an example when we have the riding classes in at the weekend."

Jenny tried on the hat.

"At least I look the part a bit more," she said, conscious of the well-worn jeans and trainers which made up her outfit.

"Don't worry about that. This is not Horse of the Year Show."

The three chatted together while Jo led Bess out of the stable and saddled her. She had a relaxed no-nonsense way that Jenny soon warmed to. By the time she and Jenny had left the immediate surroundings of the yard they were chatting like old friends.

Jenny was wondering how she might be able to introduce the topic that had been uppermost in her mind since hearing of Jo's occupation of the Old Mill House. In the event it was Jo who brought up the subject as they rode in close proximity along a broad track that was obviously used by vehicles.

"You must tell me about the letters you have been investigating. They sound fascinating," she remarked. "Sally tells me you think there is a link to the family."

Jenny laughed.

"I've been wondering how I was going to bring the subject up, but now you have done it for me. Yes, I'm fairly sure there is, but there are a few details we need to track down before we can say definitely. I was hoping to ask you if you had any records from the past that might help."

It was Jo's turn to laugh.

"All of them," she said. "There has been no break. Current matters are kept in the office cabinets, but all the old files are stored in the corn store above the grinding room. It is ventilated and dry, so everything is in reasonable condition. So, what is it you are hoping to find?"

Jenny briefly explained that she was trying to establish

whether one of her forebears had been estate manager at the Rayleton estate at around the Jane Austen era.

Sally thought for a moment.

"I don't think there's a formal record of estate managers, but there may well be letters and other documents with signatures. You're welcome to look through any of the files from that period. If Sally can spare you, come tomorrow afternoon. It's always quiet on Friday afternoons."

The following afternoon when she took up Jo's invitation, Jenny was in good spirits. The weather was still fine and she was looking forward to the walk. The track that she had been directed to use followed the ridge against which Rayleton stood. After fifteen minutes or so she was able to make out a small smudge of structures in the distance. Gradually as she walked the smudge assumed the shape of two buildings situated on the further side of the stream. A large square block fronted the stream and a second less bulky one, whose several windows suggested that it provided living accommodation, stood immediately behind it.

As she neared the buildings Jenny could see clearly that this was the Old Mill House. The water wheel that had powered operations in its heyday was still there, but the leat, which had led water from stream to move it, had been permanently blocked and the watercourse was dry and weed-filled. Beyond the small complex a surfaced lane spanned the stream by means of a small stone bridge. Jenny paused for a moment to study the waters of the stream before continuing towards the house.

Seen from the lane, it looked at first sight very much a standard old country house, as the bulk of the old mill was largely hidden from sight. A short drive flanked by well-tended lawns led to a parking area fronting a double garage. A small saloon car was parked outside. She knew from what Jo had told her that the family lived here, but there was only a single door and alongside it a brass plate inscribed with the name Lyttleton & Co. Ltd. It left her wondering whether she was visiting a home or an office.

Once she had opened the door, all was revealed. On either side of a small entrance hall matching doors faced each other. She chose the left-hand door and found herself in a surprisingly up-to-date modern office. A young woman was working at the reception desk. She smiled as Jenny approached.

"Are you Miss Pearson?" she asked. "Jo told me to expect you."

Jenny smilingly acknowledged.

"I'll take you to Mr Lyttleton. He has no clients this afternoon."

She led Jenny to the first of two offices set off a short passageway, knocked and opened the door for her.

"Jo's friend Miss Pearson to see you, Paul."

Jenny mused on the strange mix of the formal and informal while noting that Jo's husband was youngish looking and had fair curly hair that flopped over his forehead as he worked at his desk. He looked up as she entered and rose to greet her while simultaneously brushing back his unruly hair.

"Nice to meet you. Jo had mentioned that you would be calling, but she has gone to pick up the children from school and I'm deputed to do the honours until she gets back. So, how can I help you?"

"Golly, I wasn't expecting a formal meeting. I was hoping to find something that links my great-grandfather eleven times removed with this estate office. Oh, and please call me Jenny."

"Right. Jenny it shall be. Now, eleven times removed, how far back does that take us?"

"Roughly eighteen-hundred."

"Mm. Napoleonic war period. Well I'll show you what we have, but there will be precious little from as long ago as that.

Even then it's likely to be important documents like deeds and contracts."

As he spoke he led her out to the passageway past the second office to a heavy door at the end.

"This leads into the old mill building. The far side has been incorporated into domestic accommodation, but this side is largely untouched."

He guided her past a huge stone grinding trough complete with an equally large grinding stone.

"This was powered by the millwheel on the outside. State-of-the-art in eighteen hundred. The floor above stored the sacks of flour after the grinding. It is very dry, so that is where we keep our documents."

Jenny followed him up a modern wooden staircase into a room that encompassed the entire upper floor. Modern filing cabinets and a shelving unit bearing multiple large volumes lined two walls to their right. In the angle that they made a modern table with two chairs provided a place to work. On the left in the corner three older style filing cabinets stood apart. It was towards these that Paul led her.

"Everything on the other side of the room relates to the present operations of the business and are private. These older cabinets hold all of the out-of-date material. As there were three of them, we allocated one to each century. You may look at anything in those. The first one holds the eighteenth-century material. So, there you are. Help yourself and do use the table if you need to. I'll get Jo to rescue you when she gets back. Happy hunting."

After he had gone, Jenny walked over to the cabinets, rested her hand on the first and breathed in deeply. Since early morning she had had this strange feeling that this day would prove to be significant. As she had walked across the estate it was as if the Old Mill House had been drawing her to it. The feeling had seemed to strengthen with each step that she took. Now it seemed that her heart was in her mouth.

Tentatively she drew open the first of the drawers and, taking out the first folder, began to check its contents.

Everything had been stored as a series of suspension files. As Paul had warned the documents were of a formal nature. All were hand-written and seemed to be related to companies and other organisations that the estate had had dealings with. None of the documents bore any signature. It was the same with each of the other drawers. Each was opened in turn and its contents inspected. Each in turn was closed as being of no further use. As she returned the last of the files and closed its drawer, she felt puzzlement and dejection strike her in equal measure.

Refusing to accept that the feelings she had experienced could have been so wrong, she made one final examination of each drawer in turn. In each case she compressed the files that it contained to the front of drawer so that she could ascertain whether anything had become misplaced. The first three revealed nothing. It was as she pulled the contents of the last drawer forward that she saw it, a modern brown A4 envelope. Too thin to stand upright, it lay on the floor of the drawer where it was hidden by the suspended files passing over it. The feeling she had earlier experienced returned. This has to be it she thought.

She drew the envelope from the cabinet drawer and carried it to the table and sat on one of the chairs. Then very carefully she slid out the contents of the envelope on to the table top. The nature of the material that emerged surprised her. This was not the records of dry and uninteresting business transactions but a miscellaneous jumble of papers. She scanned quickly through them. She smiled at the poster advertising a fete to be held in the estate grounds to mark the completion of the house. The next item, a folded newspaper cutting reporting on the death of the son of a local landowner, drew only a cursory glance. Then came two pages that caused her to draw in her breath. The first was headed Employment

Roll and dated April 6th 1798. Below this was the subheading Weybourne & Co. She quick skimmed through the list of ship's masters, warehouse men and hauliers arranged on the left-hand side of the sheet, with the name of the corresponding employee alongside it on the right. Her heart beating, she hurriedly flipped it aside to scan the second sheet. It bore the sub-heading Rayleton House Estate. There followed a list of first the household staff and then the grounds staff. Finally in a section all to itself she read:

Estate Supervisor: James Edward Pearson

How the document had come to end up in the cabinet archive and in what circumstances it had been compiled she could only guess. What mattered was that it had survived. The link she so needed was here. More to the point this was in all likelihood the house where her forebear had lived and where his daughter Elizabeth had received the letters that had started this whole enquiry. Sitting here in the Old Mill House she felt that humility that follows whenever people are confronted with the basic aspects of their own human existence.

She was still sitting at the table in quiet contemplation when Jo came to look for her. Jenny gave her a wan smile as she approached. The tear stained face that confronted her told Jo all that she needed to know.

"You look as if you could do with a cup of tea. You can also meet the children. You will be seeing them tomorrow when they have their riding lesson."

16

The weeks that followed Jenny's departure were a strange period in Richard's life. In his earlier period of working in London he had enjoyed the buzz that London had to offer. It was exhilarating to be working in the centre of one of the world's great financial centres. It was also equally exhilarating to be working with many people of his own age and with a salary large enough to enjoy what the capital had to offer. Now everything seemed different. London had lost the lustre and appeal that it had once held for him. What was left to him now was a sense of loneliness and feelings of indifference.

Among his colleagues, it was noted that he no longer joined the boisterous wine bar lunch groups, choosing instead to slip out alone for a takeaway sandwich. In similar fashion, he excused himself from any proposed evening activities, preferring to spend his evenings at home in the Richmond flat. When there was pressing work to be done, he would take that home, otherwise his evenings were spent reading or listening to music. All else seemed dull and tasteless to him.

The initial gloom he had felt immediately following Jenny's departure had deepened after he had received a short note from her briefing him on the arrangements she had made for their DNA testing and outlining what he would have to do when he received his package. When the package duly arrived, he had immediately sealed the required saliva sample and returned it. If anything, it deepened the gloom that had engulfed him since their visit to Rayleton. A second note telling him of the evidence she had found of great-grandfather William Pearson's position at the Rayleton estate provided further confirmation of what he dreaded. Much as he tried to remind himself that the DNA analysis might well prove that Jenny was not related, deep down he could not believe it. It would be several weeks before they would receive the results. In the meantime, he felt like a condemned man marking off the passage of each day to the date of execution.

It was some days after the return of the saliva sample that he received an evening telephone call from Rob Maitland. He had been studying the files that Richard had obtained for him and was ringing to confirm that Richard would have no objection to him crawling all over *Sea Urchin* to check on all required measurements. The call had ended with the suggestion that Richard might like to join him in this work at the weekend. Richard's immediate thought was to decline, but second thoughts persuaded him to accept.

It was inevitable that the drive down to Hamble would awaken memories of the same journey completed a few weeks earlier in happier circumstances. There were moments when it all came pressing back to him, but he had deliberately chosen a different route and with the aid of the car's radio the trip was completed with only limited angst. The thought uppermost in his mind as he turned into the Maitland boatyard was that there was no way that he could avoid telling them of his problems.

It must have been written all across his face he thought later, when he reviewed the day's events. As usual when visitors were expected Lou had kept an eye open from the kitchen window. She was already advancing to meet him as he climbed out of the car.

"Whatever is the matter?" were her first words. "Where is Jenny?" quickly followed when she realised that he was alone.

"I'll tell you inside," he said after giving her the customary hug.

She led the way into the kitchen and filled a kettle to make a drink. Then she turned to him. Nothing was said, but the set of her face told him that an explanation was required.

"We've separated," he said quietly.

"You've what?" was her immediate response. "I thought how good you two were together."

"Yes, we were." Richard said quietly taking a seat at the table. "That's the problem."

He outlined the reasons for their separation while Lou busied herself making mugs of tea. She brought the drinks to the table and took a seat alongside him.

She gave him a sad look.

"Oh dear! This is rotten for you. But, under the circumstances, although it is hard, I think it is the right course of action."

She patted his hand reassuringly.

"I think Jenny is being very brave and sensible. Now you must do the same. Remember that we are all here for you. Come down as often as you like."

A further thought came into her mind.

"Do let me know when you have definite news."

Richard gave a helpless shrug of the shoulders.

"It's all virtually cut and dried. We are just waiting for the DNA confirmation."

He was anxious to change the subject.

"How has Rob been?"

"It's early days yet, but those files you got for him have

been a big help. There have been no drinking bouts since you were down last. He's been immersed in the files when he's not been needed in the yard. He's out on your boat at the moment."

"That's great," Richard said reassuringly. "It sounds like it was just what he needed."

He finished his tea.

"I'd better go out to him to see what he's up to."

He stood up and began to move towards the door, but then paused and turned to face Lou.

"Don't say anything about what I've just told you to Rob and Ben while I am here."

He found Rob in the cabin, busy taking measurements and making a careful note of each one in a notepad.

"How's it going," Richard greeted him.

Rob turned from his work with a grin.

"Hi. I thought that I would make a start on the straightforward bits before you got here. It's interesting."

"In what way?"

Rob paused in his work.

"There are slight variations with some of the measurements from what is listed in the file."

He waved the file of typed sheets that he had been using.

"These figures are what were listed when the design was registered. Every new boat built to that design should have the same exact dimensions."

"So, is it serious?"

"It could be if it relates to the seaworthiness of the boat. I've only measured inside the cabin, so it's too early yet to say if it's significant, but at least it's a pointer to how Baxter operates."

"Worth looking into."

"Mm. You might need to ask for your money back."

"Don't forget, I have crossed the channel both ways without any hitch."

"True, but don't you forget that we are dealing with Baxter here. I wouldn't trust him any further than I could throw him. So, I have already spoken to my old supervisor at uni. He wants to bring a small team of his current post-grad students down to check it out. He thinks it would be a good start of term exercise for them, and, if they do find anything serious, you will have a reputable third party to back you up."

He shuffled the loose papers into an acceptable order and closed the file.

"There doesn't seem any point in doing anything further on our own. I wouldn't like you to think that I had dragged you down here on false pretences."

A broad grin crossed his face.

"So, why don't we take the good ship *Sea Urchin* for a run down the Solent? It would also give me the chance to get the feel of how she handles."

"Like old times."

"Yeah. Like old times."

It was many hours later that, happy and now ravenously hungry, they returned to the yard and made fast to her customary mooring. Lou and Ben were completing their dinner when they came in, their faces glowing and happy from their sailing. Looking at them both, Lou felt a surge of relief.

Both of them had been under stress, but today perhaps they had turned a corner by returning to their old comrade-ship. She felt like crying with gratitude, but masked this by playing Mum.

"We waited for you as long as we could. So, wash your hands and sit down. Your dinner is keeping warm in the oven."

As soon as they returned from the cloakroom Lou drew dishes of a variety of vegetables and what remained of a huge steak and kidney pie from the oven. Within minutes they were happily chatting. It's like old times Lou thought to herself as she watched them tucking in to their food.

Ben had remained silent until they had finished eating. There was obviously something on his mind.

"Anything further on that loan business?" was his opening comment, which all guessed related to the Baxter Marine business next door.

"The loan's gone through," Richard replied. "The first tranche was paid into his account at the beginning of the week."

"I guessed as much. It's already burning a hole in his pocket. He turned up this afternoon driving a top-of-the range Mercedes. That should go down well at the golf club."

He rose to leave the table, throwing his napkin down.

"Bloody fool. All he thinks of is show. Still, it's better if he wastes his money on expensive toys rather than making trouble for us."

With that he stomped off.

"He's right," Richard commented after Ben had left the room. "The money he has borrowed is secured on his company assets. If he messes things up the bank will simply foreclose on him."

There was silence for a few moments before Lou rose and began to gather the used plates and dishes for washing.

"That's enough talk about that man. Think of something nicer to talk about."

"Like what? Rob asked.

Lou paused in her work.

"Well. Like what are you two going to do tomorrow."

Rob glanced across at Richard.

"More of the same?"

"Yes. More of the same. Why not?"

. . .

It was early evening the following day when Richard drove away from the boatyard. The tenseness he had felt driving down on the previous day had disappeared and he completed the journey home in a much better frame of mind. As he drove, he reflected on the information Rob had given when he had found him taking measurements in *Sea Urchin's* cabin. The variations from the registered specifications that he had noted were an important matter. From what he had already learned about Baxter he could well believe him capable of underhand practices, but surely, he reasoned, he would not be so stupid as to make alterations that might affect the safety or handling of his company's products.

It was later, when he let himself into the empty flat that he was reminded of the problems in his own life. The time he had spent at Hamble had been a much needed and relaxing break, but it would take much more than a weekend for him to accept the reality of his current situation. Coming to terms with the major adversities that life could throw in one's path would take much, much longer. That was what life was like. It was of no use to rail against the unfairness or unjustness of fate. One simply had to get on with living.

The emptiness he felt without Jenny was still there, but he was learning what countless others had learned before him. No matter how bad things might be, the sky does not fall in. Things can and do get better. He was reminded of Gerry Thomas. He had been dealt the cruellest of blows, but had managed to come to terms with it. Thinking of the evening Jenny and he had spent at Gerry's cottage and the portrait of Gerry's late wife they had seen there, the thought struck him that, important as the finished picture was as a reminder of her, the actual creation of it must have been of equal importance in the early months of bereavement. The very act of painting must have served in diverting his mind from unhappy memories until they gradually became less painful. He smiled to himself at the thought of how he whiled away time during boring meetings at work by sketching boats. He went to sleep that night still thinking of what he could do to ease the pain he felt.

When the alarm awoke him for work the following morning, the thoughts were still there, only now they had crystallised. They followed him as he prepared for work and filled his thoughts on the tube. He would not make rough sketches of imaginary boats or even paint them on canvas. He would design them down to the smallest detail. Better still, he could work in concert with Rob. They had always been at their happiest when they did things together, as this last weekend had shown. They had complementary skills. Together they could design and build boats. He got so carried away with his thoughts that he almost missed his tube stop. Hurriedly he scrambled his way to the carriage door and alighted. As he made his way along the busy corridors to the station exit, his mind was saying to him, one day, no matter how or when, we will build boats together.

He said nothing to anyone about his idea. He did not yet possess the capital or experience to put any scheme into practice. There was still the stumbling block of his uncle and the demands of his current employment to deal with. For the moment his scheme would remain just that, an idea that could be nurtured and developed until the time was ready to put it into practice.

In the meantime, he could begin to develop his drawing skills. The freehand sketches that had filled periods of boredom would need to be enlarged and refined. He would need more than an old pencil and a page torn from a notepad if he was to produce any work of professional standard.

With this plan in mind, Saturday morning saw him begin a series of online searches. His subjects were eclectic. Drawing materials, traditional quality drawing boards, professional drawing office equipment, showrooms and stockists in central London and the outer south western suburbs, sizes and prices, all in turn fell under his scrutiny. Lists were detailed on separate sheets under their respective headings. By late afternoon on Sunday, his head spinning from the mass of data he had accumulated, he decided to call a halt and pay a visit to his favourite Indian restaurant for his first real meal of the weekend. Even then the subject of his earlier activities did not entirely desert him. As he sat awaiting his order, his thoughts had turned to computer-aided design. Traditional methods would be fine for developing original concepts, but CAD would be required for final designs and production plans. That, he was thinking, was how their company would have to operate in the future.

17

It was a strange feeling to be coming home again. For a moment it was a as if she was returning from college at the end of semester, but then she remembered that had been last year and the world had turned upside down since then. Even so, it was good to be returning.

Hal had driven into town to pick her up for the last couple of miles back to the farm and had been briefing her on all that had happened while she had been away. It was mainly farming matters and she had smiled and made suitable responses, but she was tired after a long flight and train journey and was looking forward to relaxing somewhere shady with a cool drink. It was a relief when the rounded storage silos of the farm came into view and within minutes they were turning into the farm track.

Martha had obviously been keeping watch from the shade of the porch, for as the car came to rest she was already on the move. As Jenny emerged she was immediately enveloped in her embrace.

"Thank goodness you are back safe and sound. We were so worried about you."

Jenny extricated herself laughing.

"I seem to remember telling you that everything would be fine."

"I know, but England is so far away. What matters is that you are back safely. Now let's get inside out of this heat and you can tell us all about it."

"Did you get my letters?"

"I'll say she did," Hal said as he followed them up into the porch. "She's read 'em so many times they are almost worn out."

"Don't listen to him Jenny. He's read them as much as me."

"The main thing is I'm here, but if you don't mind, I'll just have quick drink and then have a rest. I have been travelling for over 15 hours and I'm tuckered out."

"Fifteen hours?"

"You're forgetting that here we are six hours or more behind European time. My body clock is telling me that it is bedtime."

"I'll get that drink," Martha said as she headed off to the kitchen. "and don't just stand there Hal Stevens. Put Jenny's bags in her room and then let the girl have some rest."

Jenny smiled to herself as she listened to their customary bickering, which she knew was just a front they put on in company to hide the deep affection that they had for each other.

She was not sure of the time when she awoke from the deep sleep which had claimed her from the moment her head had touched the pillow, but the angle of the shadows outside told that it must be late afternoon or perhaps early evening. When she rose and opened the bedroom door, the smell of cooking told her that it was the latter option and that the evening meal was almost ready.

"Hi, honey. Sleep well?" was Martha's greeting as she

made her way into the kitchen to get a drink. "Dinner is nearly ready, so just you go and relax somewhere."

Jenny did as she had been bidden and took a seat in the porch. Nothing appeared to have changed in the months that she had been away. It was strange, she thought, that while her life had been altered so dramatically, life here went on as if by some form of clockwork. Things happened in the same unhurried way at the same times without any apparent planning. In a moment, she told herself, Hal will emerge unbidden from the barn or chicken house where he had been working and wash his hands ready to eat. Martha would serve up their evening meal knowing that he would be there to eat it with her. Yes, she told herself, it was good to be back.

Then she reminded herself that this was not her life. She had known something similar once, but so much had happened to break the rhythms of that old life. She had been away to college and then first her grandma and then her grandpa had passed on. She now had to establish the patterns of her own life. I thought I had made a start she thought bitterly.

For a moment she remembered that first seafood meal at Gorey and the dreamtime walk along a seemingly endless beach holding hands that followed.

Angry with herself, she shook her head to try to dispel the pain that any further exploration of that memory stream would evoke. For the moment, until the DNA results arrived, that part of her memory bank must be kept under lock and key. Afterwards, if the genetic analysis had confirmed the worst, it could be consigned to her mind's deepfreeze.

Thankfully at that moment, Hal wandered in from the yard and went to wash his hands. Almost simultaneously, there was Martha calling her to the table for dinner. For the time being things were under control, but there was no way that she could avoid reawakening forbidden thoughts when she recounted all that had happened since she had flown to England.

Slowly, as they ate, she filled in the details of her time away. Hal was interested in hearing about the famous sites that London was known by, but Martha was more interested in the smaller and more intimate details and more human aspects of London life. She particularly enjoyed the description of the Higgs, Camden & Higgs office with its brass nameplate, antique office furniture and old-fashioned courtesy.

"It's just like you see in the movies", Martha breathed. "It's exactly how I imagined it."

Her thoughts were immediately drawn into an entirely different direction as Jenny gave them the details of her inheritance.

"Oh, my lord," was all that she could manage to say, while Hal sat totally speechless.

"What's it all worth? Martha finally asked.

"Over a million, if you put the house and bank accounts together."

"A million dollars!" said the incredulous Hal .

"No, that's in pounds sterling. It would be nearer a million-and-a-half in dollars."

Hal seemed totally bewildered by the turn of events, but Martha reached across to clasp Jenny's hand. There were tears in her eyes as she spoke.

"Honey, I am so pleased for you. We were worried what would become of you after we are gone. Now, it seems, we won't have to worry."

"What about kin?" said Hal. "Did you find any more family?"

"In a strange sort of way. There's something I'd like you to see."

She rose from the table and went to her bedroom. After a few minutes she returned bearing the file containing the old letters that had been stored by the Jersey bank.

"It will make more sense if you read these. I can fill you in with how this all fits together as you read each one."

"I'll clear the table first if you are going to spread papers out. It would be a pity to mess them up."

Once everything had been cleared away to Martha's satisfaction Jenny opened the file.

"This is the first letter. It is from a young naval officer at sea writing to a girl back home. We think they must have known each other well because after using her surname in the first letter, in the later letters it is only first names."

"Lovely handwriting," observed Martha.

The second and third letter were duly shown and discussed, Martha noting that they became less formal and more romantic. Jenny put all three carefully back in the file and then withdrew the photo copies of the remaining three.

"Up until this point I had thought that it was a case of rich girl and poor young lover, but as you can see from these, it was the other way around."

"And the boy's father wanted his son to find a wife with the right sort of family."

Jenny nodded.

"Yeah. Something like that."

Hal had been following the story without comment. Now he spoke out.

"How did you find out who they were?"

"The letters show that the writer was in command of the only English ship on duty around the islands at the beginning of the Napoleonic war. The obvious place to research was any local newspaper. Sure enough, there was a report of the loss of a warship with all hands about two years later and, two days after that, there was a report that his pregnant wife had miscarried and died as a result."

"Oh, how sad," Martha commented, her face showing that she was in her mind reliving those awful days.

Hal had been thinking on other lines.

"Presumably the girl's father was living with them and took charge of the surviving son."

Jenny nodded in agreement.

"And after that the old man came here to the States with his grandson."

Jenny nodded again.

Hal thought for a while.

"So, you are sure the old man referred to in the letters was the Pearson who emigrated to the US?"

"It was the last thing I was able to check out. I followed the name of the naval officer and traced the estate from that. Then I was able to get access to the estate records that showed that in 1799 a Joseph Pearson was the Estate Supervisor. I also found a portrait of the officer's father, in the big mansion showing the same surname, Weybourne."

Looking at Hal's face she was suddenly aware of how crazy this sounded.

The day was well advanced when Jenny opened her eyes the following morning. For a moment she was confused until she recollected that she was back in the USA staying with Martha and Hal. A hot shower followed by a brisk rub down had not completely thrown off the after-effects of her long night's sleep, when she went in search of Martha. She found her in the kitchen dealing with the breakfast dishes.

"Good morning honey," Martha greeted her. "Had a good sleep?"

"Mm," Jenny nodded. I needed it. Last night I was dead beat."

"We could see that. That's why we let you sleep on this morning. Hal's been at work for three hours or so."

"Is it as late as that?"

"Don't give it a thought. It's not important. Why don't

you go and sit in the porch while I make us some fresh coffee?"

When she joined Jenny with the coffee some minutes later, she deliberately took a seat from which she could study Jenny's face. Jenny took her coffee and took a long drink from it.

"I needed this."

Martha said nothing for a while but continued to look at her. Then finally she spoke.

"That was quite a tale you told us last night. I lay awake for a long time after we went to bed. Things didn't seem to add up. All those places and organizations and you a stranger in a strange country where you didn't know a soul. How did you get to find out so much?"

Jenny made no reply as Martha continued to look directly at her.

"When you were showing us those old letters last night, at one point you said 'we think'. Who was helping you? Somehow, I get the impression that there's something you're not telling us."

Jenny sniffed deeply and slowly shook her head.

"Oh! It's all such a mess. You're right. I haven't told you the full story. It's not because it involves anything illegal or anything that I'm ashamed of. It's just that it is too painful and, in a few weeks, it won't matter any more. Then I'll be able to try to forget it all."

The words came out in a rush and ended with a series of wracking sobs that engulfed her whole body.

Martha quickly moved to her and slipped an arm around her shoulder to draw her close.

"Whatever is the matter for you to get so upset. Just you stay calm and dry those tears. Then, when you're good and ready, you can tell me what's upsetting you."

Hal appeared in the doorway expecting to have his mid-morning break, but Martha shooed him away with her free hand. Slowly Jenny's sobbing subsided.

"It was after the visit to the lawyer's office. He had told me about the inheritance, but the accounts and papers were all held by the bank where they were deposited back in the eighteenth century in the island of Jersey."

"Wherever is that," Martha asked. "I've never heard of it."

"It's the biggest of the Channel Islands. They're British but are very near the French coast. I'd been told that the property I had inherited was empty so I thought that I could use it while I tried to trace all the background."

"So, you went to this island."

"Yes. There are several flights a day from London and other places, so that wasn't a problem. I checked into a hotel in the centre of St. Helier the island capital and went to see the bank the next day. That is when it happened."

"When what happened?"

"I met Richard."

Martha sighed.

"I might have known there was a man involved."

"He was the manager of the bank. I went along there expecting to see some stuffy middle-aged man with specs. Instead there was this very handsome man in his mid-to-late twenties…"

She paused momentarily as she recalled that first meeting.

"It must have been comical to see. My head felt dizzy and happy at the same time and, to begin with, he seemed totally disorganised. But, we got through the business eventually. I found out that my property was let out so I could not go inside, but he offered to drive me out to see it on the outside the next day. He picked me up and drove to the cutest little place on the coast and we shared a huge plate of sea food and then we went down on to the beach, took off our shoes and walked along the sand hand in hand."

She sat silent for a few moments, re-living that afternoon. Martha sat patiently waiting for her to continue.

"And?"

"And that was it. It was like a dream. It was a long beach and we just walked and talked until we noticed that it was getting dark. Then we had some takeaway food and he drove me back to the hotel."

"And you didn't get to see your property?"

"No. We hadn't given it a thought!" She smiled ruefully as she spoke. But the next day he took me in his yacht along the coast so that I could see it from the sea."

"You went in his yacht?"

"Mm. He's very keen on sailing, and yes he knows what he's doing."

"You were very trusting."

"I was. I would trust him anywhere."

Martha nodded approvingly.

"So, what went wrong?"

"It came out of the blue. I had moved into his flat with him in Jersey. I had also become friends with the wife of a friend of Richards. She is French and helped me with the local newspapers from the eighteenth century which in those days were published in French and not English. We discovered from these about the wreck of the letter writer's ship and what happened to his wife. His name was Weybourne, which is quite a distinctive name."

"How do you spell that?"

Jenny spelled it out for her.

"Mm. I like that."

Jenny paused for a moment before continuing.

"In the meantime, Richard had been moved to a job in the bank's head office in London, so we had to move there. He already had an apartment there, which a friend had been using for the time he had been in Jersey. The bank is owned by his family and his uncle, who's in charge, is keen to groom him to take over one day."

"Is that good or bad?"

"Most people would jump at it, but Richard isn't keen. He prefers boats."

"The more I hear about this Richard the more I like the sound of him."

"I think you'd like him if you met him, but that is unlikely unless there is some sort of miracle."

"Well miracles do happen so you have to keep hoping, but it would help if you could tell me what sort of miracle I have to hope for."

Jenny acknowledged that she had ventured off subject with a rueful smile and continued with her story.

"I'll try to keep it short. The name of the bank is Rayleton Securities. Rayleton is also the family name, but it wasn't always that. The family changed their name to the name of their estate when they gained their baronetcy."

"Isn't that some sort of title?"

"It is. It's one above a knighthood apparently."

'A few weeks ago, we were invited down to have lunch with Richard's uncle and aunt at this Rayleton estate in this seriously big country mansion. After lunch they were keen for us to see the new portrait of Richard's uncle that they had recently commissioned to hang in the family gallery around the grand staircase. All the paintings were of the family members who have held the baronetcy. There was also this other portrait there. It was of the ancestor who had built the house and earned the baronetcy, but who had died before it was actually granted. His name was on the frame in gold lettering. It was Joseph Weybourne."

She stopped at that. Martha immediately grasped the significance of the name.

"He was the one threatening to disinherit his son if he did not marry someone of good family."

"I've found since that she was the daughter of his estate manager," Jenny added, but Martha was not listening. Her brain was busy adding two and two together.

"That means that the little boy orphaned in Jersey should have been the holder of the title and the owner of the big estate."

It was then that the further significance struck her.

"O my Lordy. You and Richard …"

Jenny sniffed deeply.

"Yes. I had to tell him that we would have to separate until we had a DNA test to see if we are related."

"So? Are you?"

"We're still waiting for the results, but I think it's pretty near certain that they'll show that I'm a Rayleton."

Martha sighed deeply. Then, wrapping her arms around Jenny, she kissed her forehead.

"I can only guess at what you are going through right now, but you will feel better for telling me. It doesn't do a body any good to bottle things up. What you must do now is keep yourself busy to take your mind off things. Hal and I will try to help you in that, and if you are looking for work to take your mind off things, I can't think of a better place find it than on a farm."

18

There was a discernible change in the atmosphere at the Rayleton Head Office. Richard had noted the same effect when he had worked there in earlier years. It developed at the beginning of any week that preceded a Bank Holiday. Individual holiday weeks might have the same effect, but then it was limited to one particular individual. Bank Holidays, although often just a single day, affected everyone. That single extra day extended the weekend and allowed short breaks away from home, visits to friends and families, important projects in home or garden or simply an extra day when a lie-in could be enjoyed with the alarm clock switched off.

Richard was perhaps the one person unaffected by the mood change. The life that he had started to construct since meeting Jenny had collapsed. Every day was now a challenge to be overcome. Even so, he could sense the change in the atmosphere as he walked in through the main entrance. He noted a greater tendency among colleagues to smile and there seemed to be a slight quickening of pace.

The change was most noticeable among the young men who would be engaged in the inter-bank yacht race that was to take place over the holiday weekend. Amongst these no one was more obviously affected than Alex. He had taken part in a number of smaller sailing events, but this would be his first serious long-distance race. His customary cheerfulness had moved up several gears as each week was marked off the calendar. Now in the final week he was almost singing and dancing.

The excitement that was building in him was evident when he called on Richard's office at the usual coffee break time. He rushed into the room and with flourish that replicated the drawing of a sword from its scabbard, drew a sheet of paper from a sheaf he held in his other hand.

"Taraa!"

Richard looked up from his work and took the sheet.

"What's this?"

"Final instructions for Saturday."

"We already have instructions."

"Minor changes to do with starting times, otherwise it's all go. I can't wait."

"That is perfectly obvious," Richard growled. "However, some of us have work to do, and a lot of it."

Alex looked at him surprised. Usually there was fun and playful banter whenever they met. This was the first time that he had seen Richard so out of sorts and for a moment he hovered, uncertain of how he should deal with the situation. Eventually he dropped the paper on Richard's desk.

"I'll leave you to it," he muttered as he made for the door.

Richard looked up as he went out. It was not in his nature to be disagreeable, especially with Alex, but at present he did not feel fully in control of himself in social situations. If it had been possible for him to see it, the true problem was that he did not feel anything at all. He too was looking forward to the weekend, but the race in itself was of little interest. For him. three days alone on his boat, dealing with the elements and any navigational hazards that he might encounter, would be the balm his mind most needed.

As Friday drew to a close, he could hear junior staff begin to make their exits and he would have liked to join them. The effects of the continuous hard work he had been carrying out all week were now all too obvious, but he chose to ignore them and, after collecting a cup of coffee from the nearest machine, continued to work on in order to wrap up the case he was dealing with. It was almost seven o'clock when his desk telephone rang. It was John Haslam requesting him to report to his office.

Gerry Thomas was already there when he entered Haslam's office and they exchanged nods. Two of his superiors together was not a good sign, he thought to himself as Haslam greeted him with a beaming smile and indicated that he should take a seat.

"I was hoping that you were still in the building," he began. "So, let's cut to the chase. Any plans for the weekend?"

"Well, yes."

"Scrap them."

The abruptness of the order took him completely by surprise.

"Scrap them?" was all he could say.

"Yes. We need you here."

"This is a bit sudden. I'm supposed to be taking part in the inter-bank channel race. It's a three-day event."

"Ah, yes I'd heard something about that," Haslam continued. "However, it can't be helped. Something has turned up and I shall need you here over the whole weekend, and on Monday I would like you to travel down to Hampshire. I'll give you a full briefing tomorrow. In the meantime, get a good night's sleep. From tomorrow onwards we shall be very busy."

With that he began to collect papers from his desk and pack them into his briefcase. It was an obvious signal that the meeting was at an end. Gerry gave a nod of his head to indicate as much, and followed Richard out of the room.

"This may turn into your first takeover battle. You should find it interesting."

"I'm sure I shall, but I would rather that it didn't mean missing out on three days of sailing."

Gerry gave him a sympathetic smile.

"If it is any consolation, I was planning three days of painting and John now has to go home and tell his wife Val that the break in Amsterdam they had planned will have to be put on the back burner. Welcome to the wicked world of high finance."

As the tube carried him home, Richard was still coming to terms with the sudden turn of events. His original plan had been to drive down to Hamble after work in order to be in position to take *Sea Urchin* out early on Saturday morning. Rob would have everything prepared, and this evening Lou would be expecting him and would be keeping food ready. As soon as he arrived back at the flat, he would have to let them know that he would not after all be coming down to the coast this weekend. Overall, he reflected, it had not been the best of days.

When he made the call, both Rob and his mother who soon took over were disappointed in their different ways. Rob was philosophical about the turn of events. The preparations would have been mainly getting the sails out ready for hoisting and loading drinking water and basic provisions. The bottled water would keep, the food would be eaten and as for the sails he had left that as his final job for the day and had not yet done anything. Lou on the other hand had assumed that he would be bringing Jenny down with him and was saddened that they were to be left with just their usual weekend. When she asked about Jenny, Richard made non-committal comments before ringing off with a promise to see them as soon as he was able. With a bit of luck, he thought, they would think his reluctance to say more was the result of his annoyance with the scrapping of his weekend plans.

That done he made a second call for a takeaway food to be delivered and sat down thinking on how he could spend the rest of the evening. He was not left long to his thoughts. The telephone rang and he answered it to hear the distraught voice of Alex.

"I don't believe it. It's not fair. Why is this happening to me? I've been looking forward to this weekend for weeks and then this happens."

Richard tried to make sense of what he was hearing.

"Alex, calm down. Now, tell me slowly what the trouble is."

"It's my boat," he wailed. "You know I'd moved it round to the Solent last weekend ready for tomorrow's start. Well I've just driven down and there's my boat looking sort of strange. Then I realised that some clumsy bastard had run into it and left me with just a broken stump for a bowsprit."

"And no calling card."

"Not even a scrape of paint."

There were a few moments of silence before Alex spoke again. Richard could hear the desperation in his voice.

"I was wondering if I could crew with you on *Sea Urchin* I know the extra weight would slow you down a bit, but…"

The sentence was left unfinished.

"I shall not be sailing tomorrow. We have a possible takeover situation and I shall be on duty over the long weekend. I've only just found out."

"That's rotten luck," Alex responded, his own disappointment forgotten in response to Richard's.

Richard thought for a moment. Nagging away in his head was the memory of his churlishness towards Alex earlier in the day. There was a way offering itself to make amends.

"You can take *Sea Urchin* out by yourself."

"Do you mean that?"

"Yes, of course I mean it. You're not a beginner. Just bring her back in one piece."

"Trust me. I'll guard her with my life."

"Let's not take things to extremes."

"Thank you, Rich. You're a real friend. I'll try to get a good place for us."

"She's lively, so take it easy until you are used to how she handles. Now, you know the setup at Hamble. I'll give Rob a ring and tell him that you will be taking the boat out in my place. I would go straight there tonight. You can sleep on the boat."

"Thanks again Rich. I'll not forget this."

"Good luck. I shall be thinking of you while I'm wading through company accounts."

They ended the call and Richard immediately rang Rob to cancel his earlier message and to ask him to get things ready as before. That done he settled to await the arrival of his take-away. Somehow the flatness he had felt all day had disappeared. It is strange, he thought, how doing something for someone else makes us feel better about ourselves.

It proved to be a strange weekend with just the three of them working in a building which on weekdays hummed with the activities of many dozens of staff. They met as planned in John Haslam's office for his initial briefing. His first statement caused surprise and a degree of annoyance on Richard's part.

"I am concerned about one of our longstanding clients, Venta Media. I've always believed in the old saying that to be forewarned is to be forearmed. That is why I have called you in this weekend. As yet there has been no formal takeover offer for Venta, but there has been suspicious buying of Venta's stock, which makes me strongly believe that the company is about to be put in play."

"In what way suspicious?" Gerry asked.

"Venta is a small company and stock turnover is normally low. However, in recent weeks there has been persistent heavy buying."

"Someone building up a stake?"

"That is the likely reason. So, we have to be ready prepared for it. Gerry, you and I will concentrate on likely buyers. Richard, I want you to immerse yourself in Venta, what it does, staff, finances, everything. Then on Monday I want you to pay them a visit, get to know key staff and look at the current year's trading."

"Will they be operating on Monday? It's a Bank Holiday."

"They operate round the clock, so there will be some staff there. They will be expecting you at eleven."

That had been the prelude to two long days of hard slog which left all of them very tired. It was a relief for Richard on the following morning to not have to snatch a quick breakfast and do battle with tube trains. For the first time in eight days, he was able to enjoy a short lie in and eat a leisurely breakfast before driving down to Hampshire to meet the Venta management.

It was only when he was shaving that he thought of Jenny. Ruefully, he had to admit that days of heavy work had diverted his mind from recollections that brought only bitter-sweet pain.

He found the Venta operations without much difficulty. It was housed in a Victorian period country mansion with later extensions, standing in its own grounds. He parked in the screened car park to the side of the building. He had arrived with fifteen minutes to spare and was happy to sit relaxing until it was time to make his way to the main entrance. A young woman was sitting working at a desk positioned alongside the lower steps of a fine stone staircase. She looked up as he entered the reception hall and gave a smile of welcome.

"Mr Rayleton? she enquired.

"Yes. That's right."

"Mr Ramsden told me to look out for you. If you would like to come with me, I will take you to him."

Richard followed her as she rose and made her way up a stone staircase.

"All the offices are in the old house," she explained. "The technical departments are based in the modern extensions at the back."

Richard was still wondering what was meant by technical departments when he was confronted by the figure of a tall, fair haired man who appeared to have boundless energy.

"Good man. On the dot. I like a good timekeeper. Helps things run smoothly. I'm Geoffrey Ramsden."

A large hand was thrust towards him for a vigorous handshake.

"Richard Rayleton."

"Henry Rayleton's nephew, so I'm told. That's good. I like family businesses. You know what you are dealing with."

Richard turned to thank his guide, but she was already on her way back down the stairs.

"Come, we can talk better in my office."

He led Richard into what he imagined had once been the master bedroom, but was now very much the modern office. At its centre a large desk imposed itself on the room. Ramsden moved behind the desk and seated himself in the large leather desk chair that stood behind it.

"Take a seat," he said waving his hand at the two chairs facing him.

"We both know why you are here, so there is no need for us to go into that. I think it would help if I fill in the background for you. Then I'll take you on a tour of the company before I introduce you to our accounts team."

"That sounds ideal," Richard said, beginning to relax.

"The company was founded by my grandfather. He was a

keen photographer and that was what the company was immersed in. Photography was still the main business when my father took over, but the steady development of electronics and computers was beginning to change everything. Fortunately, we were able to change our business in good time to what you see today."

"There was a problem. Prior to this, the business was privately owned, but the changes meant operating on a much bigger scale. All of the buildings behind the original house were built and equipped at that time. It was very costly and the only way to finance it was to float the company on the stock exchange, as you now see. Before this my father had made a will and did not change it after the company became public. Under the terms of the will my father's shares passed in equal proportions to myself and my two sisters, neither of whom have ever been involved in the running of the company. My elder sister sold me a portion of her shares in order to buy a property in the south of France. She's a writer and augments what she earns from this with the dividends she receives. She is happy for me to vote her shares as I see fit. Special provision was made for my younger sister who was, sadly, brain-damaged at birth. Her shares are voted by whoever is the company chairman at the time."

"And that would be you presumably?"

"Yes. In addition, I have bought a few more shares over the years when they have been cheap."

"So, what would be the percentage of the stock you can muster against any hostile approach."

"It would be approximately forty-two per cent."

Richard made a quick note of what he had been told. Then looked directly at Ramsden. He judged that he would not be offended by a direct question.

"If this develops into a shooting war, where do you stand?"

"Venta is our family business. It has been the centre of my

life and I have put body and soul into it, and that is how I want things to go on."

"Even if a takeover bid develops and a silly price is offered?"

"Look, this is not about money. I have all the money I need at the moment."

"Good. That's all I need to know on that front."

There was a pause as the young woman from the reception knocked and entered carrying a tray of refreshments.

"A bit late, but I thought you would like a drink before you get tied-up with Eric Hancock in the accounts department," Ramsden explained with a smile.

Tied-up proved to be an apt description of the next three hours that Richard spent poring over the general accounts, and the separate accounts showing sales, costs, cashflows and the historic records showing the growth of the company. At the end of it he felt he had a good enough understanding of the company to be able to discuss matters effectively with Haslam and Gerry back in London.

With the heavyweight accounting aspects covered, Hancock took him to see the operating departments in the newer buildings. He was surprised to be taken into a long rectangular room that had all the appearance of a film studio. When he commented on this to his guide, Hancock laughed.

"That's because it is a film studio of sorts. The main business of the company is producing TV adverts. In the early days they were filmed here. Now the filming is done at our London studio. What you see here are mock-ups that are used in the initial design process. You would be surprised to see how much work goes into a one-minute advert.

His work completed Hancock introduced him to the Design Department and headed back to his office. Max Edelson the head of the design team explained to him the various stages that an advert passed through from initial idea to the dress rehearsals, set designs and all the modern electronic wizardry that made up the modern-day advertisement.

At the end of his spiel Richard faced Edelson with the question that he had wanted to ask. Since he had first arrived.

"Who would want to take this over?"

Edelson shrugged.

"Who knows. We are one of several operators in this field. We are good at what we do, but so are the others. It's a cutthroat business."

Richard followed him to the final section of the operations wing. To his astonishment he found himself in a fully operational news studio.

He was introduced to Kate Foxton the head of the news service.

"You look surprised," she remarked after they had shaken hands.

"I am. I was not expecting this."

"We supply news services in various forms to minor TV and radio channels and some of the bigger local newspapers. The big story today is the aftermath of the storm. Come I'll show you."

"What storm?" Richard asked as he followed her.

"Had you not heard? It's been a big one. It developed in the Atlantic, north of the Azores and at first looked to be heading westwards towards the US coast. Then as these storms sometimes do, it made a sudden change of direction. It reached us sometime on Saturday night. By all accounts there has been a lot of damage along the coast. Cornwall has been particularly badly hit."

Richard had vague memories of a strong wind as he had made his way home from the tube station in the early evening on Saturday, but had thought little of it at the time.

Sally had stopped beside a young man sat in front of a large monitor.

"What is happening at the moment?"

"This is film taken from the helicopter we hired to film the aftermath of the storm. It's the last thing they want at this stage of the holiday season. There, that's the Lizard."

He jabbed a finger at the screen and they watched as the film moved on along the coast to Penzance and finally to The Scillies.

"Look. There's the wreckage of a boat that has been washed ashore."

They all stared at the picture of the white moulded stern quarter of a yacht lying amid a variety of smaller objects washed ashore. The camera closed in on the wreckage. The name of the stricken boat jerked into focus. With a terrible wrenching in his gut Richard spelled out the name *Sea Urchin*.

19

It all felt unreal when Richard entered the Rayleton building the following morning. Nothing was said, but he felt as if all eyes were on him. The few that he looked at directly seemed to have questioning looks on their faces, as if suggesting that they thought that he ought not to be there. It gradually dawned on him that a number of his colleagues, knowing the name of his boat and seeing the news coverage, had put two and two together. In the close interlocking operations of the bank, bad news had travelled fast.

Before he had entered his own office, therefore, he went to see the departmental secretary. He quickly appraised her of the facts and asked her to send out a memo with this information to all staff. With that done, he dropped his case on his desk and sought a meeting with John Haslam.

Haslam was working at his desk when Richard entered his office for the customary debriefing.

"Ah Richard!" he said looking up. "Sit yourself down and tell me how you got on yesterday. To be honest, I do not know too much about this company. They came to us years ago when I was still a junior."

Richard gave him a full account of his visit to Venta. He

was keen to know more about the man running the company and nodded appreciatively when Richard described Geoffrey Ramsden and his management style. It was when Richard moved on to the family shareholdings that he really sat up.

"Good. Well done. That is excellent news. The company broker has only given us details of Ramsden's personal holdings. This shows things in a new light. If a takeover ever emerges, it will make any defence so much easier."

"There is one other item of interest," Richard said. "The Studio Manager told me that they have a studio here in London in addition to the one I saw. I've been thinking that perhaps there is a real estate factor we need to consider."

"Good thinking," said Haslam, making a note of what he had just heard. "I'll get Gerry to look into that."

He sat back in his chair and looked at Richard, and then for once, allowed his human feelings to show.

"As you are no doubt aware by now, there has been a lot of talk about you this morning."

"Yes. First thing, everyone was looking at me strangely. It took a while for the penny to drop."

"The question is, what was your boat doing in the sea near the Scilly Islands while you were here over the weekend?"

Richard explained to him about the last-minute arrangement with Alex.

"So! It was Alex sailing her. Is anything more known?"

"No. I'm probably still thought to be the person who was manning *Sea Urchin*, and listed as missing, presumed dead."

"As I remember, you were not best pleased to be called in over the weekend..."

"...yet it may well have saved my life," Richard finished his thinking for him.

"Quite so. Life can be a funny old business at times."

Richard decided this was the opportunity to request what had occupied his mind since seeing the fatal newsreel at the Venta studio.

"I would like to go down to Penzance to find out exactly what has happened and help straighten things out."

Haslam nodded appreciatively.

"Things are still quiet on the takeover front and, in a way, we owe you three days. So, we can spare you until next Monday."

Richard rose to his feet and was already moving towards the door when Haslam called to him.

"By the way, what was Alex's surname."

"Lodz. Alex Lodz. His father is Polish."

Once back in his own office Richard telephoned the police station in Penzance, as the nearest mainland station to the area of the accident, to inform them of the identity of the missing yachtsman. He was informed that as yet no trace had been found of Alex and that he would now be listed as missing presumed dead. The Sergeant that he had spoken to also said that it would help if he could inspect the wreckage that had washed ashore and if possible to confirm that it was from his yacht. The wreckage was to be transferred to Penzance harbour later that day. An arrangement was made that he would report to the Penzance station on the following afternoon.

Later that afternoon Richard drove down to the Maitland's boatyard planning to shorten his drive down to Penzance the following day. As soon as he arrived Lou threw her arms around him sobbing.

"Thank goodness you are safe and sound. It could have been you caught in that awful storm, instead it was that friend of yours. Such a lovely lad. He ate here, had the food I had ready for you. He was so excited about the race. I didn't see him again. He must have been up early and taken the boat out before Ben and I were about."

Richard made no effort to disengage from her embrace,

realising she needed to give vent to all of her pent-up emotion. Finally, she calmed and drew away from him wiping her nose on a small handkerchief as she did so.

"I'll put the kettle on. You could do with a cuppa I'm sure."

Richard followed her into the kitchen.

"Anything more on the storm?"

"No. I'm as much in the dark as you are. I'm on my way down to Penzance to check things out. It was weird going in to work this morning. Everyone thought that I was dead."

"Don't remind me. I'm just so glad to see you sitting there."

She finished making the tea and brought two mugs to the kitchen table.

"Have you had anything back from those DNA checks?"

Richard shook his head.

"No. Still no news."

It was Lou's turn to shake her head in commiseration.

"I don't know. One way or another, you are not having much of a summer."

They were interrupted by the entrance of Ben and Rob from the yard.

"Recognised your car," Ben said as he sat down with them.

"Smelled the teapot more likely," Lou commented, as she rose to make more tea.

"Bad business that storm," Ben began. "Any further news?"

"Not as yet. I'll be travelling down to Penzance tomorrow. I'll let you know if I learn anything new."

Ben was obviously pondering on something.

"As an old navy man, I know full well how powerful the sea and the wind can be, but the sight of that wreckage on the news set me thinking. The Scillies are low lying, but they would have given a modicum of shelter. It would have been when they turned south to clear the Bishops Rock and they had the full power of wind and sea on their beam that the trouble would begin. Apparently, a couple of boats were dismasted and another one was blown on its side but still afloat. Most of the leading yachts reported damage of one sort or another. Quite a few quit the race and made for the nearest harbour."

"Another one ran aground," Rob added."

"That's right," his father agreed. "What I'm getting at is that, while there was a lot of damage done, only one boat sank. That was *Sea Urchin*. Even then, there was only her stern section washed up on a beach. The rest is on the sea bed."

"What are you suggesting?" Richard asked. "Do you think there was something wrong with my boat?"

"Maybe. You had only sailed her in normal conditions. It takes foul weather to find out what a boat is made of."

"Perhaps you are right," Richard accepted, "but we shall never know for certain. They would have all been strung out. Perhaps Alex caught a particularly bad blow."

Rob had remained largely silent up until this point.

"There is one way will help us make a judgement," he added. "I told you I had contacted my old Head of Department at Uni. Well he and a junior colleague came down at the beginning of last week. They spent most of the day on *Sea Urchin*. They bought a camera and other kit with them and logged everything that could be measured, and that included taking out the decking to check out the framework. When all of that data is fed into their machines in the labs, they will be able to measure what levels of stress she could take. Come the start of the new term, they will begin their programme."

Later, when Richard had turned in for the night, sleep did not come easily. His mind was busy reviewing all that had been said earlier that evening. What also came to mind was what had not been said, but which had obviously been on Rob's mind. If there were any difficulties in the future regarding insurance claims, compensation or even police charges, it would be good to be able to call on the respected and impartial evidence of the university's findings.

It had been a long time since Richard had last travelled the road that led from Southampton across Dorset to Exeter and the resorts of Devon and Cornwall. Then it had been the start of happy family holidays when his father had been home on leave. This time there would be no pleasures and no happy memories to carry home, he thought grimly. He snorted to himself at the thought. Now there was no home, only a flat that had at times seen both Alex and Jenny live there. Now they were both gone. Alex was presumably dead, lying in the ocean, goodness knows where, and Jenny too was gone.

The last thought broke the stream of bad thoughts. Where was she? What was she doing? When would this period of bad news come to an end? Would it ever come to an end? With that final thought he determined to concentrate on his driving. As the miles were covered he found his mind becoming easier, and after a short break in Okehampton for refreshment, he drove into the car park at the Penzance police station half-an-hour before the arranged time.

He decided to go into the building immediately and reported in at the front desk. After a few minutes wait, he was approached by the officer he had arranged to meet. He proved to be a cheerful CID Sergeant named Wilson, who seemed pleased that he had arrived early. Introductions over, Wilson glanced through the notes that he had been given at the desk.

"If I have understood things correctly, you are saying that you are the owner of the yacht section washed ashore in the Scillies at the weekend?"

"Yes, I believe so."

"Right then. The wreckage was brought over to the mainland this morning. It will make sense to check that it is your boat before we go any further. Any other matters and the paperwork we can sort out afterwards."

"Paperwork?" Richard queried.

"Oh yes. Every last thing we cover has to be recorded. This one is straightforward, but some …" He raised his eyes in mock supplication.

It was only a short drive to the harbour where Wilson was able to park free of the normal restrictions. They found the wreckage lying against a low wall, marked-off with police tape. They made an initial examination and then moved the wreckage so that the stern was visible.

Richard bent over to make a close observation of the name it bore. Then, taking his mobile phone from his pocket, he proceeded to take a number of photographs from different angles. When he had finished and straightened up, he found Wilson looking steadily at him.

"Is it your boat?"

Tears had formed in the corner of Richard's eye and the lump in his throat left him unable to speak. He could only nod in answer to Wilson's question. Wilson returned the wreckage to its original position and, taking Richard back to the car, drove him back to the police station, where he asked for a cup of tea for Richard to be brought to his office.

Once they were seated Wilson produced the inevitable notepad and began to take note of Richard's personal details. The tea arrived as they were completing this and Wilson took the opportunity to sort out some of the background details that were puzzling him.

"How come you were not with your boat when it was wrecked?"

"I was at work in London over the weekend and on bank business in Hampshire on Holiday Monday."

Richard explained to him about the plans for the inter-bank yacht race and the last-minute changes that had left him at work in the London Headquarters and Alex taking part in a borrowed yacht.

"Was your friend an experienced sailor?"

"Definitely. I would not have given him the use of *Sea Urchin* otherwise."

"And was your boat in good condition?"

"She was almost new. I bought her in the spring, while I was working in the bank's Jersey office. In the few months that I had her, I made two Channel crossings and a number of pleasure trips around Jersey and in the Solent."

"Any problems?"

"No. She handled well."

"Well that is about all for now. Oh no, I've not taken your friend's full name and address."

"He was known to everyone as Alex, but his name was Alexandr Lodz."

"Foreign?"

"No, he was English, but his father is Polish."

Wilson put his pen down and closed the file he was creating.

"Right. I think that will be all for now. Thank you for coming down here. You have been a big help. We'll be in touch if we need anything else."

"There is one thing." Richard said. "I've been thinking about the wreckage we looked at in the harbour."

Wilson looked at him with interest.

"What about it?"

"Well, two things struck me. The first was the obvious one. This was not a case of the stern breaking off. The port side section of the hull was much longer than the starboard side, which was very short."

"Yes, I had noticed that, but it did not signify anything to me. It does to you though, it would seem."

Richard nodded.

"I was looking at it as a sailor. The route planned for the

race passed between Land's End and the Scillies, then turned south to clear the Bishop's Rock. Once past the rock, the route turned east for the second leg back up the Channel. I think Alex was in the process of making that second turn. The wind would have been coming over his starboard quarter, in layman's terms that's means over his right shoulder."

Wilson was nodding his agreement with what he had just heard.

"So, you think that was the reason for the sinking?"

"In part, but I think that there was another factor at work. The second thing that struck me when we looked at the wreckage was how jagged the edges were. This was not a simple case of sections coming apart under stress. To me it seemed as if it had been attacked by a giant tin-opener."

Wilson looked at him in surprise.

"What could have caused that?"

"The mast. Other yachts had their masts broken off, but their hulls remained intact.

I think *Sea Urchin's* mast must have acted like a giant lever as she made that turn."

Wilson now looked uncertain.

"I think that is a lot to read into what you have to go on. There would have to be more evidence to support that."

Richard told him of the suspicions that Rob had of the way that Baxter Marine operated and of the study that was being made by his old university connections. Wilson made notes of all that had been discussed together with names of all concerned.

"If there is anything in your suspicions, it would seem that this might not be a simple tragic accident."

That done, he closed his notebook with a sardonic smile.

"And there was I thinking, when you turned up early, that I could get home in good time for once."

 · · ·

After leaving the police station Richard made his way on foot to the harbour and began to make enquires regarding boat hire. Eventually he was directed to neighbouring Newlyn where he found what he was looking for, a man who would take out paying customers for fishing trips. After a bit of haggling the boat was booked for the following day to take him out to the waters to the south-west of the Scillies beyond the Bishop's Rock lighthouse.

The boatman was surprised when his customer turned up the following morning without the usual fishing paraphernalia, but bearing instead two large bunches of flowers. He had immediately grasped what the situation was and left Richard alone to his thoughts until they were well out to sea.

"Friend of yours was he the, the yachtsman that was lost?" he eventually ventured.

"Yes, he was. A good friend and he was sailing my yacht."

"A double loss then," the boatman added.

"Sort of, except that boats can be replaced, friends can't."

"That's true enough," the boatman added and then remained silent for a short while before continuing.

"Mind you, you wouldn't catch me in in one of them flimsy craft. I'd rather do my sailing in something a bit stronger like this old girl. She may be small, but she's solid. All being well, she'll see me out."

He patted the woodwork as he spoke and lapsed into silence until they neared the lighthouse.

"I'll take us a way beyond the Rock. That way your flowers will float back this way some."

Richard nodded his agreement and prepared for what would follow by removing all the unwanted wrappings.

As so often is the case in the days following a storm, the sea was calm with just the merest suggestion of a swell marking its surface. As the boat began to describe a wide arc to seaward, he began to strew the flowers one at a time, so as to cover the widest possible area. As the boat completed its turn and headed back to harbour, he stood silently looking back over the stern, watching the gentle movement of the floating flowers until they finally slipped out of sight.

Back in harbour he thanked and paid his boatman, before making his way back to the commercial hotel where had spent the night and collected his car.

He remained in sombre mood as he retraced his outward route back to the Hamble boatyard. He drove mechanically, maintaining a steady pace, while his thoughts were elsewhere. It was only after leaving the Exeter by-pass behind that his thoughts moved away from recollections of Alex and the letter to the Lodz family that he would have to write and took a different tack. The words of his boatman earlier that morning had lodged in his mind. The pleasure of sailing did not necessarily rely on speed. More than anything, it was being as one with the water and the elements. That had been the boatman's point. The elements would not always be benign. Therefore, the sensible approach would be to sacrifice some degree of speed in order to increase the sturdiness of the boat. Already in his mind he could picture the boat he would begin to plan over the coming weeks. It would be one which would be capable of undertaking serious travel. That would require a mixture of both yacht and fishing boat and that would combine sails with engine, while generating its own electricity for lighting and cooking. He was still creating mental pictures of this new boat as he reached the commencement of the motorway and recognised the need to concentrate on the heavier and faster moving flows of traffic.

20

As is often the case after periods of eventful activity, the weeks that followed the holiday break were decidedly humdrum. The upsets of the inter-bank yacht race were already receding into the past. The Rayleton office settled into its normal work patterns. Day after day slipped by, each following the same well-worn routines. It would be many weeks before Christmas would mark a cheerful break from this pattern.

Thankfully Richard was kept busy during his days at the London office, but either side of that, without any of the distractions of family life, time passed slowly. The hole in his life that Jenny's departure had left had still to be filled and there was no knowing how many more weeks would pass before the expected DNA analysis results would be released. If that were not enough, he still had to make plans on how he might extricate himself from his employment at the bank. All of these factors seemed to be interlinked in a vicious circle where any idea of action on any one of the factors seemed stymied by the pressure of the others. It seemed to him as if the whole world was holding its breath waiting for something to happen. When eventually that something did happen, it came from an unexpected quarter.

At the time that he purchased *Sea Urchin*, Richard had used the same broker to arrange insurance cover. On his return from Cornwall, Richard had notified the broker of the loss of the boat and had asked them to file a claim for the full insured value of the vessel. That done, he had pushed the matter to the back of his mind. Returning to his flat one evening after a day at work, he found a letter bearing the broker's monogram in his mailbox. The letter was brief and to the point. It simply stated that *Sea Urchin's* insurers had placed a temporary stop on the policy in view of the police enquiry into the boat's loss. Were the police to find anything unusual in the condition of the boat at the time of its loss, then the policy would be declared null and void. Detective Sergeant Wilson had obviously been in contact with Rob.

As soon as he had eaten his supper, Richard phoned Rob to verify that he had been contacted by Wilson. What Rob had to say gave him food for much thought for the remainder of the evening. The police had not only contacted him, but had followed up with a call to the university staff concerned and had asked if they could prioritise their structural assessment, as it might well prove the key to a number of potential criminal charges.

As soon as he reached the Rayleton headquarters on the following morning, Richard made a beeline for Gerry's office to let him know what he had learned. Gerry did not seem at all surprised.

"That would explain things."

"Explain what?"

"Yesterday we fielded a couple of enquiries about Baxter Marine and this morning we have noted that there has been some selling of the bonds secured by the various Baxter Marine properties."

"But I only learned of the police matter yesterday evening."

Gerry sat back in his chair and smiled at Richard.

"You know what London is like. Nothing stays secret for long, and if there are no facts, then the rumour mill supplies them."

"Isn't there anything we can do?"

"Not at the moment. If hard evidence emerges, then things will really start to happen, if not then it will die away. In the meantime, we shall be keeping an eye on things."

He began to sort through various files on his desk.

"Right now, I have an important meeting with John Haslam, but there are private matters I need to discuss with you. If it's convenient, come around to my place this evening. Come early and we can order something to eat in the garden."

With that he collected the files and strode out of the office leaving Richard standing nonplussed by his desk.

Later, in the early evening, after pausing briefly at the Richmond flat to change into something more casual, Richard drove across to Gerry's riverside home. As he made his way around the side of the house to the riverside back garden, he was reminded of the visit he had made with Jenny weeks earlier. It was a mere flash of remembrance, but the pain that it produced caused him to grind his teeth with the determination to blot it out.

Gerry was already sitting where they had sat on that earlier visit, but with the addition of a folding table to cover any possible need. Richard deliberately put on a smile as he made his way across the grass, hoping that it would not appear as false as he felt it. He need not have worried: Gerry was back to being his usual relaxed self as he waved him into the other seat that he had set out.

"I'm sorry if I seemed a bit short this morning, but you caught me on the hop. I really was in a bit of a rush and what I wanted to talk to you about is best said here and not at HQ."

Richard took the seat across the table from him.

"So, what is it you wanted to tell me?"

Gerry put up a hand palm outward in a gesture to head off that particular topic.

"All in good time. First, we have to think about food. I take it you have not eaten yet?"

Richard shook his head.

"Food doesn't interest me at the moment."

Gerry nodded in sympathy.

"I remember that feeling. It will gradually ease with time. In the meantime, we have to carry on putting one foot in front of the other, and eating occasionally. So, what's it to be; eat out or order something to be delivered?"

"Here's fine."

"Good. Give me a moment while I make the order. I'll make it Indian if that is OK with you."

Richard nodded in agreement and Gerry disappeared indoors. Some minutes later he re-appeared with two glasses and a bottle of wine.

"All done. Should be delivered in twenty to thirty minutes."

He took his seat and poured a glass of wine for each of them and handed one to Richard.

"No news yet on the DNA tests, I take it?"

Richard shook his head.

"Not as yet. It could be any day now. Jen said I was expecting a miracle. The evidence that she is a Rayleton is strong, but..."

He left the thought unspoken.

"It is the waiting and the awful uncertainty that I find so hard."

Gerry nodded in agreement.

"Well, here is something else for you to think about. Things are happening."

"What sort of things?"

"Yacht builder type things." He adopted a conspiratorial tone. "No names and keep your voice down."

"What we spoke of this morning is more serious than I was letting on. There has been a definite buzz about our yacht builder. People are getting jittery about him and there is a nasty smell developing."

"How nasty?"

"Back in my office earlier, I said that we had fielded enquiries about the bonds we arranged on his business."

Richard nodded.

"Well they weren't enquiries. People are very annoyed. One was highly abusive."

"I presume this is about the bond issues."

"Exactly. The business concerned is a very small operation that wealthy investors and executives in large insurance companies had probably never heard of. They bought bonds on the strength of our recommendation. Now, only a matter of weeks later, their investments are underwater. The company concerned is being investigated by the police for malpractice and possible manslaughter charges. It's no wonder our clients are annoyed, and it's all down to one man."

He drank the last of his wine and shook his head sadly.

"You mentioned there had been some selling of the bonds."

Gerry nodded.

"Be careful. In markets there is always buying and selling."

"So, what are you saying."

"At the moment no one is buying. There is only selling. Nothing major as yet, but there is a persistent downward pattern in the market price. It is this that I wanted to talk to you about, so that you can be ready to act when the time comes."

Richard looked puzzled.

"I'm not with you."

"This is the reason you were placed in Corporate Finance, there is a lot to learn and understand. It's not just about money and arithmetic calculations. Honesty and trust are equally important."

He paused momentarily while he sought the best way of explaining it.

"Markets are like pieces of knitwear. The individual strands of wool or cotton are not of any great strength on their own, but when they are knitted together the strength of the fabric is much stronger than that of the single strand. But, if there is any damage to any particular strand, the whole piece can unravel. That is how the world of finance operates. It is trust which knits it all together."

Richard nodded in understanding.

"And you think that Baxter is a damaged strand?"

"It is beginning to look that way. We shall only know for certain if the police bring charges against him: that will take time. In the meantime, trust has already started to unravel."

"You think Baxter will go under?"

"You do not need me to answer that. The real issue is how to put a halt to further unravelling."

"What? Do you think Rayleton Securities is in any danger?"

"We shall certainly be damaged by this whole wretched business. What can't be judged yet, is by how much."

"What puzzles me most is why Henry would want to arrange a ten million bond issue for the benefit of someone like Baxter."

Gerry shook his head.

"Oh dear! The bush telegraph seems to have got things mixed up. The plan was for there to be a package of deals involving smaller companies that had development potential. We are still a relatively small fish. The idea was to lever us into a higher league and at the same time make us bigger than our Portuguese partners. The Baxter loan was simply to be the first of several."

"But why Baxter?"

"I'm afraid that your Uncle Henry's keenness to move into new areas of business blinded him to the need to carry out proper due diligence. He had only seen Baxter at his golf club and seems to have taken him at face value. I'm very much afraid that is something he will come to regret. It has undermined our reputation. Instead of growth it has resulted in the loss of established clients."

"I take it then that we are looking at the possibility of a major unravelling."

Gerry nodded in acknowledgement.

"So, am I to imagine no more employment at Rayleton Securities."

Gerry smiled grimly.

"Perhaps no more Rayleton Securities."

"As bad as that?"

"It's possible. At the moment London is the weakest part of the business. If things were to get messy, I would not be surprised to see our new Portuguese partners cut adrift."

Richard paused to think through what Gerry had just said. Momentarily, he pictured the great staircase at Rayleton House.

"So much for the portrait gallery."

"Yes. Indeed."

"I'm in a fortunate position. I was left this house by my parents. With no heavy mortgage payments to make, I've been able to invest the major part of my earnings over the years. Even my painting interests have paid their way."

He took a drink from his wine glass.

"Don't tell anyone, but it has been my plan for some time

to retire at the end of the year and concentrate on my painting. That is me settled, the question is how are you placed?"

"In the scenario you are indicating, I would have no salary and my shares in the family business might have gone."

"So, what if anything would you have left?"

"I own the freehold of my Richmond flat."

"That's interesting. How did you manage that?"

"My father's life assurance pay-out provided the deposit. The rest was covered by a mortgage."

"And is that still the case?"

"No. I don't know if you have ever been told, but I own seventeen and a half percent of Rayleton Securities. It was my father's share of the family business. I only learned of this on my twenty-fifth birthday. For a little over ten years the shares and annual profits disbursements had been held in trust."

"And you took control on coming of age, as it were."

"Yes. A tidy cash sum had built up in the trust fund. So, I used some of that to pay off the mortgage. I have also had two years of profit distributions since then."

"Good. Anything else? Did Alex pay for his use of the flat?"

"No. He was acting as a sort of caretaker while I was in Jersey. He just paid the local authority rate bills."

"Well, that was an extra saving."

"Exactly. What with the use of the company flat and car, I was able to save a lot of what I earned while I was in Jersey. All told, I now have a few thousand in dividends each year."

"Anything else?"

"Yes. There is my claim on the loss of *Sea Urchin*. She was insured, but the insurer may make the policy null and void if the police bring charges against Baxter. I don't know where that leaves me."

"So, *Sea Urchin* was a Baxter yacht? That is interesting. Where it leaves you is as a creditor of Baxter Marine."

"Join the queue. No much joy there then."

"Not necessarily. Let me tell you a story."

He drained what wine was left in his glass and drew the back of his hand across his mouth.

"Some years back in the States, there was a man nicknamed 'the Grave Dancer'."

Richard gave him a puzzled sideways look.

"He was a billionaire. Made his money buying into companies that were on their last legs. Not just any old companies mind you. What he looked for, were companies that were asset rich but cash poor. They also had to have issued bonds secured on the assets of the business. As bankruptcy loomed the bonds could be bought at giveaway prices. He wasn't interested in saving the businesses. In a bankruptcy, bondholders are senior creditors with first call on whatever is left in the business. The Grave Dancer made his money bargaining with the administrators after a company had gone bust. What he usually ended up with was assets worth many times more than the cost of the bonds."

"Mm. Neat, and a very apt nickname."

It strikes me that Baxter Marine is just the sort of business that would have interested him."

"What are you suggesting?"

"I'm thinking that, should we witness a significant unravelling, then an investment in the Baxter Marine bonds might prove advantageous."

He chuckled as he noted the surprised look on Richard's face.

"Don't worry. I'm not thinking of turning you into a big-time gambler. Think of it as putting yourself in a position where heads you win or tails you don't lose."

He paused, his head cocked to one side, as he picked up a sound from the street.

"Hang on a moment Rich. I think I hear the sound of a motorbike in the street."

He made his way out to the front of the house. Richard sat

quietly thinking over what Gerry had been telling him. Sounds of indistinct conversation drifted back from the front of the house and then Gerry re-appeared bearing two carrier bags from which emanated the unmistakeable aromas of Indian cooking.

Gerry placed the carrier bags on the table.

"Sort this lot out while I get things from the kitchen."

He returned bearing a tray with plates cutlery and a second bottle of wine. Within minutes they were enjoying the contents of the carrier bags. As they sat savouring the rich flavours of the various packages that Gerry had ordered, Richard retuned to the topic they had been earlier discussing.

"You spoke earlier of being ready to act when the time comes. What sort of action are you suggesting and why are you so concerned with my affairs?"

Gerry smiled at him.

"As you have probably already guessed, I would recommend that you marshal all your spare cash and buy into the Baxter bonds when they are at rock bottom. Then, assuming Baxter goes belly up, with the bonds and your claim on your boat, you will be in a position to negotiate with the administrator for the Baxter assets."

That said, he helped himself to more of the contents of another of the tinfoil dishes before treating Richard to a broad smile.

"As for the second part of your question, perhaps it's because I shall never have children of my own that I take a fatherly interest in your affairs. Perhaps it's because I think you are being used to bolster your uncle's ego and the family name. Or maybe it's simply because I like your company. Take your pick."

There was no further discussion of work-related business and they settled down to enjoy the remainder of the evening as the light slowly faded and lights began to appear along the river.

21

It had been a hard week, but the weekend was fast approaching. For most people it was this approach of the end of the working week that gave Fridays a lighter, more comfortable feel to them than the earlier days of the working week. For Richard, this particular Friday had lost that feeling as he laboured to complete an assignment that had filled his entire working day and needed to be completed before he left the office that evening. As a consequence, he had opted to eschew all but a single short break at lunchtime in order to concentrate on meeting this deadline. Now, commencing the final stages with the clock showing four pm, leaving him a little time in hand, he felt that he could begin to relax.

Within minutes of his making that assessment, he was annoyed by the ringing of his internal office telephone. He reached for the receiver cursing inwardly as he recognised the voice of Charles Dennings' secretary. Her message was brief. He was requested to report to Charles' office at 4.30. He could not think of anything that Charles would need to see him about. He shrugged to himself and returned determinedly to his work until he reached a suitable point to break off in order to meet his appointment. Glancing at his watch, he saw that he had four minutes. It was only a short walk upstairs to the top floor and at precisely 4.30 he entered Charles' outer office.

Celia, Charles' secretary was working at her desk. She looked up as he entered. The smile that she gave him seemed somewhat wan.

"You are to go straight in."

He tapped at the door of the inner office and stepped inside.

"Ah! Richard."

Charles grunted, sitting back in his desk chair.

"Take a seat. This will only take a few minutes."

Richard sat in one of the visitor seats at the facing side of the desk and looked across at his General Manager. Charles was known for his affability, but today there seemed something in his face and general demeanour that suggested that he was feeling ill at ease.

"There is no easy way to say what I have to say, so I will come straight to the point. Sir Henry has asked me to have this meeting with you. Yesterday evening he was visited by his daughter Sally. I gather that she has her own apartment separate from the main house. She thought that he would need to read a letter she had received that morning."

Richard studied Charles' face as the latter sought the best way to continue.

"It would seem that you and a young American woman named Jenny Pearson together with Sir Henry's daughter Sally had undertaken joint DNA analyses that would show if the American lady was in fact part of a long-lost branch of the Rayleton family. The analyses did in fact show that the two females, Jenny and Sally, were closely related. What it also showed was that the male subject, that is you Richard, had a DNA profile, totally different to the two females, that showed little if any of the Rayleton DNA characteristics. In short, it would seem that you are not a Rayleton."

He paused to allow his words to sink in. If he was

expecting a reaction, then he was disappointed. Richard said nothing. To him the news that he was not a Rayleton meant something totally different to whatever Charles was presumably anticipating. Words could not adequately express what he felt. There was joy, perhaps even exultation. He was free. His miracle had happened. He sat quietly trying to make some sort of order of the incoherent jumble of thoughts and feelings that had filled it.

Charles was a little nonplussed by the lack of any visible reaction on Richard's part.

"No doubt, you were already aware of this…"

"No. I knew nothing of this. We were each supposed to receive a copy of the results. I have not yet received any letter," he stammered.

"Then I am sorry to be the conveyor of bad news, but you can see why Sir Henry is concerned. Above all else, despite the tie-up with Cardosa, Rayleton Securities remains a family business. There has always been a member of the Rayleton family at the head of it. As the only male Rayleton of your generation, Sir Henry looked on you to follow him. It was for this reason that he guided your further education and found employment for you here."

He stopped there, aware of the logical conclusion to what he had said, but reluctant to say it.

You must realise what a delicate position this news leaves him in. We have discussed this and it has been decided that it would be better for everyone if you were no longer employed here. I am therefore terminating your employment as from the close of business tonight. You will, however, be paid your salary until the end of this calendar year. That is a rather more than the your notice period. I hope that is acceptable to you."

"Perfectly."

"The question of your shareholding in the company will obviously take a little longer to sort out. So, please notify us of the name and address of anyone you may use to advise you on this."

"Thank you, Charles, I still have approximately twenty minutes work to complete the assignment that I have been working on all day. Once I have submitted that to John, I'll clear my desk and move on."

"Thank you, Richard. That would be very professional. Oh, and could you leave your office keys and ID pass with Celia on your way out."

With that Charles rose to his feet and walked around his desk with hand outstretched.

"Good luck."

They shook hands and Richard made his way out. He stopped briefly at Celia's desk to drop off his keys and pass. She did not make any comment, but he guessed that she knew in outline what was happening.

Strangely, as he made his way back downstairs to his office his thoughts were not with himself, but were on the man with whom he had just been dealing. What an awful job, he thought, to have to carry out other people's dirty work, and how typical of 'Uncle' Henry to have ordered it.

As he had calculated, the remaining work on his desk was soon completed. He knew that John Haslam had taken the day off to add to the weekend, so as to give his wife the break in Amsterdam he had promised her. However, he was fortunate to find John's secretary still at her desk finishing off a last-minute report he had left with her. He handed the file to her with a simple cheerio and walked away.

As he passed out through the bank's main entrance he experienced a strange feeling of relief. The log jam had been broken. He had no idea what the future would hold, but the future was now his to make of it what he wished.

The feeling persisted as he made the tube journey back home. People crowded into the early evening trains, people were disgorged at station stops and new travellers took their place. The London rush hour was at its evening peak. All around him was noise and confusion, but he seemed unaware of it. He travelled in his own serene bubble as if experiencing a dream. The feeling persisted into the evening when the pangs of hunger began to make the first intrusions into this dream-like state. Even then, there were no thoughts of venturing out or of calling for a takeaway meal. That would have meant meeting and interacting with other people. This night he simply wanted to be alone. A search through the contents of his kitchen cupboards produced three slices of bread and a can of baked beans. These would suffice and were quick and easy to prepare.

It was as he sat eating this simple meal that, thinking back over his interview with Charles, a new thought crossed his mind. All of the discussion in Charles office had centred on the fact that he had no Rayleton genes in his make-up. This is what had mattered most to Henry Rayleton. The suddenness of his dismissal and the enforced change on the pattern of his life this made had been occupying his mind since he had left Charles' office. The other side of the subject had not been considered. Now it began to appear and begged the obvious question. If William Rayleton had not been his biological father – then who was.

The thought unlocked a state of turmoil in his head that stayed at the back of his mind for the rest of the evening. One of the fixed reference points, that underpin our knowledge and understanding of self, had been removed in that one short sentence uttered in Charles' office. It had left him with a gaping hole in his very being. He decided to turn in early, but thoughts of his parentage remained in his head for some hours until sleep finally claimed him.

He awoke late the following morning, feeling refreshed and clearer headed. What he was going to do with his life was a factor that would need to be addressed at some point, but for the moment, the answer to the simple question, who am I, would take priority. His mother was the obvious person to ask, but she now lived on the other side of the world. Her move there and re-marriage had occurred while he was at university and he had not seen her face-to-face since then. Over the intervening years they had relied on the occasional letter or long-distance phone call to keep in touch. Neither of these seemed to him to be a suitable medium for discussion of such a topic. At some point he would have to travel to Australia to talk through this matter with her. It would also allow him to finally meet Matt Keogh, whose name she now bore.

In the meantime, he thought, Lou Maitland and his mother had been close friends. Perhaps Lou might have some inkling about it all. A trip down to Hamble might provide the answer. As he brewed coffee he planned his day. First of all, however, he needed to get in touch with Gerry. It would be better, he thought, if he were given a first-hand account of what had occurred on Friday afternoon before he turned up at the bank on Monday morning. It would be better still, he thought as he sampled his breakfast coffee, if the account was given face-to-face. In any case, there was something else he now wanted to discuss. He decided that he would make a short detour to Gerry's cottage before heading south.

When he arrived at Gerry's home he made for the front door for the first time and rang the doorbell. Gerry came to the door and was surprised to see the identity of his caller.

"I hope I'm not interrupting anything important," Richard began, noting Gerry's paint-flecked jeans."

"Nothing that can't wait. Come in." He opened the door wide. "Can I get you a coffee or something?"

No thanks. I've not long had breakfast. I can see that you have already started your work, so I'll be as brief as possible. It's just that something big has happened and I thought that you should hear about it from the horse's mouth."

"Oh! Sounds ominous. We had best go through to the sitting room."

He led Richard through to the room with the collection of family portraits that he had seen before with Jenny.

"Grab a pew and tell me what is bothering you."

"It's not exactly bothering me, quite the contrary in fact. It's just that I thought you should hear about what's been happening directly from me."

"Right. Fire away. What's the big news?"

Richard looked at him with a grin.

"I've been fired."

Gerry looked at him in astonishment.

"You've what?"

"I have been fired, with effect from five pm yesterday."

"Good lord!"

He looked at Richard askance.

"You're not having me on, are you?"

"No straight up. I am now unemployed."

Gerry looked at him with incomprehension initially. The look gradually darkened as Richard provided him with a detailed account of what had taken place at the very moment Gerry had been leaving the Rayleton building.

"Well, I have to hand it to your uncle. As bastards go, he is in the first rank. Although I must say, you seem to be taking it in your stride. You seem almost pleased."

"Oh, I am. I'm not sure whether it is because he is no longer my uncle or because it means an end to being used as a method of perpetuating the family line at the head of the bank. Either way suits me fine. I had been giving a lot of thought to how I could manage to extricate myself and now, at the drop of a hat, he's done it for me. Not only that, he's paying me until the end of the year."

Gerry smiled with him.

"Thank you for letting me know. It will be interesting on

Monday morning to hear what cock and bull story Charles will spin to John and myself."

He sighed and shook his head in mock sadness.

"Right then. What was the other matter you wanted to talk about?"

Richard looked directly at him for a few moments.

"Much as I am happy to be cut adrift from the bank, I'm still left with two problems. The obvious one – how am I going to earn a living – will sort itself out in time. The other is a more basic human problem – if Bill Rayleton was not my genetic father…"

"… then who was?"

Gerry finished the sentence for him.

"The only person who can help with that is my mother, but she has re-married and now lives in Australia. It is time I paid her a visit and met my step-father. This is not a matter I want to bring up by telephone, so I am planning to fly out there to discuss matters with her. I'm not sure how long I shall be away. It will probably be for a week-or-two. Who knows."

"So, you would like me to mind the shop while you are away."

"Yes. Something like that. There should not be any problems with my

employment severance, but I would like you to handle my shareholding disposal if it becomes necessary."

Gerry nodded in agreement.

"No problem. However, I shall need some form of written authority to act

on your behalf in your absence. It may not prove necessary, but one never knows with this type of situation."

As he finished speaking, he rose to his feet.

Richard stood to join him and they solemnly shook hands.

"Thank you, Gerry."

He turned to make his way back to the hallway."

"I'm driving down to Hamble now to see if the Maitlands can shed any light on my parentage. Lou and my mother were good friends in those days. Who knows? Enjoy the gossip on Monday. Now I'll leave you to get back to your painting."

Gerry had followed him into the hall.

"I'm putting the finishing touches to Jenny's grandpa and his horse. Would you like to see it?"

"Thanks, but no. It's Jenny's picture. I think that she should be the first to see it."

Gerry looked at him questioningly.

"Is everything all right with you two?"

Richard shrugged.

"I don't know. The evidence that she had uncovered had convinced her that she belonged to the Weybourne – now calling themselves Rayleton – family. The DNA tests were intended to verify this. Until we knew definitely one way or the other, she thought that we should stay away from each other. The last I heard of her was that she had gone back to the States while she waited for the lease on her Jersey property to expire. That was her original intention, I don't know if that is still the plan or whether she would like us to get back together."

"Well, your DNA results put you back to square one."

Gerry gave him a long, studied look.

"Would you like to get back together, now that you know you are not related?"

"I think so, eventually, but not until I have sorted out who I really am."

"I can understand how unsettling all this is for you."

He had opened the door as he spoke.

"Don't leave it too long. Remember things don't just happen. Someone has to make the first move."

· · ·

It was early afternoon before he finally drove into the Hamble boatyard. As he climbed out of the car he cast his eyes around. The yard seemed strangely quiet with no signs of activity. He had not phoned ahead and for a moment he thought that he might have made a wasted journey but, as he approached the cottage door, Lou emerged to greet him. After the customary hug she ushered him into the kitchen and prepared to make a cup of tea.

"I thought for a moment that no one was here," Richard commented as she filled the kettle, "It's all so quiet."

"Ben has taken Rob to a football match in Southampton."

"I didn't know Rob liked football."

"Well, I think it is mainly about building bridges."

"Oh, I see. Anyway, it is you that I came down to see. There is something private that I wanted to talk to you about. So, it has worked out quite well."

Lou looked at him puzzled.

"I thought that you were not your normal self, like you had something on your mind."

Richard attempted a smile.

"That's about the strength of it."

"Just give me a couple of minutes to make the tea, and then you can tell me what it is that is on your mind."

She methodically made two mugs of tea, brought them to the table and sat down opposite him.

"Right. Fire away."

Richard was unsure what to say and groped for a suitable starting point. In the end he settled on a meaningless generality.

"Things have been happening."

He noted the long questioning look that greeted this first offering.

"What sort of things?"

"Pleasantly unpleasant things. It's about work."

"I'm still not with you. Are you thinking of quitting and want my advice?"

"No. I've already left."

"You have quit your job?"

"No. I think the correct term is that I have been summarily dismissed."

Lou's face registered shock.

"You've what? When and for what reason?"

"Yesterday afternoon I was summoned to the General Manager's office at four-thirty and told to clear my desk."

Lou shook her head in disbelief.

"I thought that you were well set up there with your uncle. Was any reason given?"

"It's all to do with the DNA analyses that we had done to see if Jenny was descended from a branch of the Rayleton family. We had asked cousin Sally to join us in the tests as a cross-reference. On Thursday she had received the results of her test and also the cross-references to Jenny and myself and had shown them to her parents."

"And on Friday afternoon you were dismissed. I don't understand."

"What the cross-referencing showed was that Jenny's genetic make-up was very similar to Sally's, proving that she was a Rayleton."

"Oh, my goodness!"

She suddenly stopped, aware that she had only heard half of the story.

"So why were you sent packing at such short notice?"

"Well, apparently the cross-referencing showed that my genetic make-up bore little if any relationship to that of the two girls."

Lou thought about the matter for a moment.

"You must have guessed that there would be some sort of reaction from your uncle?"

Richard shook his head.

"No. I still haven't received my copy of the results. It all came as a complete shock. Oh, and from now on, I would prefer you to not refer to him as my uncle."

Lou sat taking everything in.

"Well, if that doesn't take the biscuit."

She sat back in her chair and looked directly at Richard.

"You don't appear to be put out by any of this."

Richard smiled back at her.

"If you remember, I described yesterday as pleasantly unpleasant. At the time, I actually felt more sorry for Charles Denning having to do Henry Rayleton's dirty work for him. The consequences could not have pleased me more. For some considerable time, I have been thinking how I might to extricate myself from Rayleton Securities. Now in one single moment he has done the job for me."

"So, what did you want to discuss…?"

She left her sentence unfinished as she realised the hidden import of what Richard had just told her.

"Of course. I get it now. If Bill Rayleton was not your biological father, you need to find out who is. That is what you have spent the last fifteen minutes trying to get around to. Can I shed any light on who the missing sperm donor might be?"

Richard, relieved, nodded in agreement.

"That's about the strength of it."

Lou smiled ruefully.

"Sadly, the answer is not a lot. I didn't know your mother until we moved into next-door married quarters. We became good friends after that."

"Did she ever say anything that might shed light on any of this?"

"No. She always spoke of Bill as your father and she grieved when he died. I didn't see so much of her after you finally had to vacate the married quarters. After that we just met up for a chat occasionally."

Lou sat for a moment, casting her mind back over past years.

"The last time I saw her she told me she had met this Australian chap and was moving to Australia with him. I get a Christmas card every year and that's about it."

They sat in thought for a moment before Lou made a final comment.

"At the time I thought it strange. She had lived like a nun for several years after Bill died. Then out of the blue she announced that she had met someone and was moving to Australia. It all seemed very sudden. I don't know why, but I got the impression that she had known him years earlier."

"Female intuition?"

"Perhaps. Who knows."

They continued chatting at the kitchen table until the sound of voices heralded the return of Rob and his father.

Lou made a large pot of tea while Richard gave the newcomers a second recital of the events of the previous afternoon.

"Well I'm damned," Ben exclaimed. "Rayleton didn't waste any time."

Richard nodded in agreement.

"He has this thing about family pedigree. I'm pleased to be shot of it."

"So, what now?"

"He's off to Australia to see if he can dig out anything which might point to who his biological father might be." Lou chipped in.

"Of course. You're a gentleman of leisure now."

Ben finished his tea and rose to his feet.

"Unlike some of us, who have to earn a living. There's something I need to do before evening."

He went out to the yard. Lou began to collect the empty mugs leaving Richard and Rob at the table.

"There's something I want to discuss with you. Let's go outside." Rob said quietly.

They went out into the yard, largely empty at this point in the season, and strolled across to where *Sea Urchin* had once been moored.

"It looks empty without her," Richard commented as if reading Rob'sthoughts.

"Mm. It's what I wanted to talk to you about. I know this is all *sub judice* but you are in the middle of it all and I thought that you should know. That is why I thought it would be better if we discussed things in private."

Richard nodded in agreement.

"The uni's findings were pretty damning. There was scarcely a statistic in their measurements that matched those registered. When Dick Jennings ran them through the department's computer and carried out various stress tests, it showed an almost twenty per cent drop in what could be called seaworthiness."

Richard drew in his breath at Rob's last words.

"Exactly. She was a fair-weather boat. Any sizeable storm would have caused problems and poor Alex caught a beauty."

"Was my boat the only one?"

"No. Originally, I suspect Baxter was looking for ways of reducing construction costs, but then they noticed that the weight-saving improved speed. That became their big selling point. So, it seems it became standard practice. Once the police started to make enquiries, Baxter's workers began to sing like canaries, even the foreman. He knew exactly what was going on. All in all, I would say our beloved neighbour will find himself well and truly up a well-known creek without a paddle."

"Have the police brought charges?"

"Not as yet, they are still compiling evidence, but I was

told that they are looking at fraud, false accounting and manslaughter for starters."

Richard drew in his breath for a second time. Rob looked hard at his friend.

"It's not just your boat and Alex, is it?"

"No. It will impact directly on the bank. Henry Rayleton has made a major mistake pushing bonds secured on Baxter's operations and it has resulted in the loss of important client accounts. That is just between us and must go no further."

"Why the angst? You don't work for them anymore."

"No, but I am still a significant shareholder."

They strolled back across the yard.

"There is something else. What I was wanted to ask you is, could you drive me into Southampton on Monday morning? I'm going to ask Ben if I can leave my car here while I am away in Australia. It will be at your disposal to use any time you need it."

"Are you planning a long stay?"

"Who knows. I'm a free man these days."

"And Jenny?"

"I've no idea."

"Do I sense that you are pissed off with her?"

"I suppose I am. Oh! Everything is a bloody mess. It will be good to get away from it all."

It was early afternoon on Monday when Richard arrived back at the Richmond flat. He had scarcely set down his weekend bag when there was a ring on his doorbell. When he opened the door, he found that his visitor was Mrs. Cousins, a neighbour from one of the ground floor flats. She smiled at him holding out two envelopes.

"I've been looking out for you. I've been away on a cruise with friends. These are yours. I found them in my post box when I returned home on Saturday. It must have been a new postman."

They chatted briefly about her trip for a few minutes before she returned downstairs. Richard closed the door as she disappeared and glanced at the two envelopes that she had handed to him. The upper one was the immediately recognisable envelope of a bank statement. The other was a large plain envelope. When he opened it, he found the expected copy of the DNA analysis results. He glanced briefly at the findings of the comparison with the DNA of both Jenny and Sally. It confirmed what he had already learned, that Jenny was undoubtedly related to Sally and that he was related to neither of them. He scanned the sheets detailing his own personal analysis and was about to return the papers to the envelope when a sentence caught his attention. It simply stated that a significant element of his genetic make-up was of a type most commonly found in areas of Gaelic settlement. The most likely explanation of this, he mused, was that his genetic father was of Irish descent.

22

It took a few moments for Jenny to fully clear her head and blink away the last vestiges of sleep. Around her she saw the familiar furnishings of the bedroom that she had occupied since her grandfather's death. Her ears picked up the sounds of Martha already busy in her kitchen and from outside the old familiar noises of the farm drifted in. Momentarily, as she lay taking stock of the new day, it seemed to her that time had stood still and nothing had changed.

As she dressed, she smiled ruefully to herself. Time, she reflected, had not stood still after all, and things had changed. Worse still, she had still to learn when and what final form those changes would take. She sighed inwardly at the thought. Today promised to be yet another in a series of days, spent waiting for news from the world outside the farm, a world which she would only be able to re-enter when all of the current uncertainties had been reconciled.

When she entered the kitchen, she found that in another matter she had been mistaken. Martha was not engaged in her usual breakfast-time activities, but was dressed for outside work.

"You will have to get your own breakfast this morning, honey. I have to feed the poultry."

"Where's Hal?" Jenny questioned, surprised by the change in the normal schedule.

"He's in bed. It seems he tripped over something in the barn yesterday and came down heavily on the stone floor. His left leg is badly swollen and very painful. He can't walk."

"Has he broken it?"

"Can't tell yet, but it looks as if he has. I'll have to take him into town to get it looked at."

She sighed and shook her head.

"As you can imagine he's not in the best of spirits. Like all men, he don't take easily to being out of action, especially now at the end of the month."

Jenny pricked up her ears at the last comment.

"What's special about the end of the month?"

Martha paused as she was about to go outside.

"Mortgage payment's due. Now we won't be able to make it."

With that she disappeared outside, leaving Jenny to ponder on what she had just heard.

It was a while later, when Martha had done her work outside and had checked on Hal that she sat down with Jenny for a mid-morning coffee. Jenny lost no time in returning to their earlier conversation.

"You mentioned a mortgage payment as you went outside. I didn't realise that you still had a mortgage."

Martha gave a sigh.

"Yes. Unfortunately, we have. We never intended this. It was supposed to have been paid off by now, but that is the way things are for small farms like this. We have struggled for some time now. Instead of paying off the loan, in recent years we have had to increase it. Your grandpa was in the same position."

Jenny nodded in sympathy.

"Hal worries how we are going to keep a roof over our heads. He'll worry even more now."

She wiped away a tear that had trickled from the corner of her eye.

"Yet you looked after me after Grandma died and have fed and housed me since Grandpa passed away."

"Well, someone had to."

Jenny shook her head.

"Maybe then, but not now. Things have changed. I have money now and I am not going to sit on it while you and Hal worry yourselves into an early grave."

Martha smiled sadly.

"Thank you Honey. That was a lovely thought, but I don't think Hal would be happy to take money from you."

"OK. Then I will lend him the money. I'll become his banker, only I'll not charge any interest or demand any repayment."

Martha's tears now flowed freely as Jenny clasped her hands across the table.

"Just think. You will be able to drop some of the heavy work and just do whatever you are comfortable with. Anything you chose to do would be for yourselves. You would no longer be working for the bank."

Martha wiped away her tears and sniffed deeply.

"We had not said anything to you, but we had been thinking of leaving the farm, or whatever was left, to you when we have gone. So, what you are saying would make sense."

"Good. That's all settled. I'll contact my Jersey bank to transfer whatever cash is needed into my current account and I'll help with paying the monthly interest until the mortgage can be closed."

· · ·

It was late afternoon before Martha drove back into the yard from town and helped Hal, his left leg now encased in plaster, out of the truck. Jenny hurried to help as soon as she saw them.

"How did you get on?"

Martha nodded towards the plaster cast around Hal's left leg.

"It was much as we thought. His leg is fractured in two places. He'll be out of action for several weeks. Jenny moved to help support him, but Martha had produced a lightweight crutch from the vehicle. Waving all offers of help aside, Hal placed the crutch under his left shoulder and with Martha in close attendance and the encased leg held away from the ground, began to painfully hobble up the steps of the porch and into the house. As soon as they were on level flooring, Martha called over her shoulder to Jenny.

"Honey, I forgot to stop at the mailbox on the way back. Would you go and check if there is any mail?"

"Will do."

It took only a moment for Jenny to collect the mailbox key from its peg in the kitchen and to head across the yard. It was a pleasant stroll along the farm track to where their mailbox was situated alongside the road. Mechanically she unlocked the box and removed the three letters that she found inside. It was only after she had relocked the box that she glanced at the letters. The first two were obviously commercial mail for Hal from agricultural suppliers, but her heart momentarily missed a beat when she realised that the third larger envelope was addressed to herself. She took a deep breath and turned to head back to the house.

It was no longer the same leisurely walk enjoying the evening sunshine she had made only minutes earlier. Now it was a tense hurried return. Thoughts which had lain dormant since she had left England came crowding back in a strange jumbled mass. By the time she reached the house, the hand holding the letters was trembling.

Martha was coming out to the porch as Jenny mounted the steps from the yard.

"I've put Hal back into bed. Hopefully he'll get some sleep."

Her voice tailed off as the strange look on Jenny's face, part excitement part anxiety, finally registered with her.

"This is it. It's a letter from England. It must be from Sally."

"Well, aren't you going to open it. There's no point in standing there guessing what it might say," Martha commented with her usual common sense.

Jenny handed the two business letters to Martha. Then, taking another deep breath, she tore open the envelope of the other. Inside was the briefest of notes from Sally and her copy of the DNA analysis results.

She ran through Sally's note in seconds and then turned quickly to the printed letter. Her face broke into an immediate beaming smile.

"I'm a Rayleton. I knew it." She gasped to Martha before returning to the remainder of the report.

Martha saw her initial smile change first to a frown and then a look of consternation.

"What does it say? What is the matter?"

Jenny said nothing but simply handed her the report.

Martha read the document through slowly and carefully and then handed it back to Jenny.

"Well. Doesn't that just beat everything, although I didn't understand the bit at the end."

"Me neither, but it doesn't matter. The main thing is that I have discovered my ancestry. Those old letters stored at the bank in Jersey will be even more precious now."

"I'd like you to tell me about them sometime in more detail, but right now you have other things to think on. This news is two-sided. It shows, as you believed, that you are descended from that landed family that changed its name. I can't remember what the original name was."

"Weybourne."

"That was it. Weybourne. So, you are descended from that family. That's the upside. Now you have to consider the downside. Your sweetheart, Richard, thought he belonged to that same family, but this report shows that he couldn't have done. So where does that leave him?"

Jenny thought for a moment before answering.

"In the position I was in when I first read those old letters."

"Exactly. You have found out who you are: he has found out who he ain't."

"Oh Martha! Thank goodness I have your common sense to guide me. I have been very selfish, thinking only of myself."

"Now don't you go about beating yourself up. You only read about this a few minutes ago. You have not had time to thoroughly weigh things up."

"You have had the same time."

"Yes, but I am not personally involved and any emotions I have are directed solely to whatever will make you happy."

Jenny threw her arms around Martha.

"I'm so lucky to have you to rely on."

Martha gently disengaged herself from the embrace.

"I feel the same about you, but that has nothing to do with the matter in hand. So, let's look at the basics of the situation, which are this. Firstly, do you truly love Richard?"

"Yes. Absolutely. I know it was me that said we should stay apart until this genetic matter was settled, but that was because I thought there was a strong chance that the analysis would I was part of that Rayleton family. I didn't think for a second that he might not be. Keeping apart seemed to be the right and only thing to do until we knew. I did not stop loving him. Moving away from him was the hardest thing I have ever done."

"I know. Doing the right thing isn't always easy. Leaving that aside, my second question is simply this. Do you think he loves you?"

"Yes. I don't just think it. I believe it."

"Good! That is all that matters. You have gone through a difficult spell, but the hard things, your Grandpa's passing and having to leave your old home, came at the beginning. It will be the same for Richard. This information rips apart the life he's grown up with and if what you have told me about this bank he works at is true, then I would not be surprised if there ain't fall-out there still to come. He helped you through your difficult period. Now you must do the same for him."

"But how do I do that?"

"Simply by being patient and carrying on loving him. It has always seemed to me that if two people truly love each other they will end up together. In the meantime, it helps if you find something to occupy your time, which reminds me, today's eggs haven't yet been collected."

This chore, together with a number of others, which included what had been Hal's customary walk to check the mailbox, became settled as part of her regular schedule, as they adapted to Hal's incapacity. Hal, for his part, soon tired of lying in bed. Within days he had taken to spending each day sitting on the porch couch with his injured leg stretched along the seat, a position from which he could witness the everyday movements of the two women as they went about their tasks and where necessary offer directions and advice.

It was at the end of the second week of this regime that Jenny received a second letter. Unlike Hal, her habit was to make the walk to the mailbox in the evening, when the heat of the day had begun to ease. Other than the forwarded DNA analysis results, she was not expecting to receive any more personal mail from England. It was as she strolled back to the house that she remembered that she had given her address to Gerry on the evening she and Richard had visited his riverside home. With so much happening in her life, she had not given any thought to Gerry's offer to paint a portrait of her Grandpa.

Once back on the porch she handed the farm mail to Hal and hurried to her room. The letter, as she had guessed, proved to be from Gerry. Inside the A3-sized envelope she found two carefully folded sheets. The first was a simple hand-written note. After the customary greeting, it simply stated that he had completed the first outline stages of the portrait and would proceed with the detailed finishing stages after receiving her approval. To this end an email address had been appended. As there was no evidence that he had used a computer, she guessed that this was probably his London office address.

When she turned to the second sheet she was puzzled at first by the numbers scrawled on the back, until she realised that these related to the picture's actual dimensions. Once she had opened the folded sheet, she could see that he had taken a photograph of the painting and had then sent her a photocopy of the photograph. Even with third-hand photocopying, the picture made her gasp. By small, subtle alterations he had brought the familiar old photograph of her Grandpa to life. Gone was the stiff freezing of the subject that photographs tend to display. In its stead was a picture of the close affinity of man and horse brought to life. She could only imagine what the effect of the full-sized finished picture would be. As she sat on the edge of her bed looking at the copied picture, tears began to trickle down her face.

In time, other thoughts drifted into her head. She found herself comparing the care and thoughtfulness that Gerry had shown over the portrait with the brief almost cold note from Sally that had been enclosed with her copy of the DNA analysis. She had not picked up on this when she had received that letter, perhaps because she had been so focussed on the DNA results and their implications. It had taken the words and actions of a person whom she had only met on that one occasion to throw, what she now saw as coldness, into relief.

Looking back to the days that she had spent at Sally's stable apartment on the Rayleton estate, she could not remember any traces of such indifference. She ran back in her mind each of the days she had spent there and all through was the same feeling of being very much at home with each other. She was at a loss to explain the change. The only difference between then and now was that the DNA analysis had shown that they were related. It was then that it dawned on her. When she was staying on the estate she was welcomed as someone used to horses, who could talk from experience and who could at times be called on to lend a hand. In all probability, no one at Rayleton could believe that a strange girl from America could possibly be a member of their wider family.

It seemed an improbable theory and yet, the more she thought about it, the more likely it seemed. What was it about her being proven to be a Rayleton that could produce such a change. She thought about that first visit she had made to the house with Richard. She had missed the group viewing of Sir Henry's portrait and Sally had taken her later to see the new portrait, resplendent in its position at the head of the main staircase, looking down on the other holders of the baronetcy. She had also been shown the portrait of the man who had built the family's fortune and forged the political connections that had resulted in the award of the title. That had been a smaller picture hung away from the others in an obscure corner of the landing.

Was the new coolness from Sally that she sensed, connected to this? It certainly seemed that way, but why after more than two hundred years? The staircase's family portrait arrangement was the key. There in full splendour was the family's prized title and social status displayed. The portrait of the real founder of the family's position was tucked away in a quiet corner. The portraits around the main staircase were solely of those men that had held the title of Baronet, and yet, each and every one of them had simply inherited it. More to the point they were all members of a secondary branch of the family.

She stopped, as the realisation of the full implications of all this suddenly came to her. If the existence of that little boy, taken by his grandfather to America after the death of both his parents in the Channel Islands, had been known about, then he and his descendants up to and including her Grandpa and not any of the group featured around Rayleton's grand staircase, would have carried the title. They would not even have lived in the house, for he was the sole survivor of the senior branch of the Rayleton family.

She began to re-run over the whole train of thought, cross-checking every factor in her mind, when a further thought struck her. Martha had advised her to not think solely of herself. Richard was caught up in all of this. Now he had been shown to be not even a member of the junior branch of the family. What effect would all of this have on his position at the Rayleton family business? She made a mental note to take this up with Gerry when she answered his letter. She shook her head sorrowfully. The awful mess continued, only now it had taken a different form. Not for the first time, she rued her decision that they should separate. If only Richard would contact her.

It was some time before she felt settled enough to take the photocopy of Gerry's work through to the porch to show Martha and Hal.

23

Richard had not taken any chances. When he had booked his flight to Sydney, he had noted that the scheduled flying time was less than the time he had spent at sea when he had made his double channel crossing to pick up *Sea Urchin*. Although tiring, that had been tremendous fun and he had been fully occupied with handling the boat and entertained by the vagaries of wind and sea. This journey would be very different. There would be little in the way of movement and he would be enclosed in an airtight aircraft compartment. There would be opportunity for discourse with fellow passengers, but experience had taught him that this was something that required a degree of circumspection. As a result, his shoulder bag was filled with a variety of snacks, reading matter and drawing materials. These he hoped would be sufficient to occupy the long hours that lay ahead.

In the event it had worked out better than he had dared hope. He had been fortunate in having been allocated an aisle seat that allowed a little more shoulder room and scope to stretch his legs. Alongside him, two diminutive young women had maintained a non-stop conversation in a language which he did not recognise, but which from their appearance he assumed was Malayan. They had left the flight at Singapore, still talking, as they queued to disembark.

For the second leg of the flight, a single middle-aged male had taken the vacated window seat, the mid-row seat remained empty. With no one to talk to, Richard had spent the first leg reading the mystery story he had bought at the airport bookshop and sleeping. Now with more space he felt free enough to take out the drawing pad and pencils he had brought with him and begin sketching. He had not made any conscious decision on what he was going to draw. He simply began making marks on paper. What began to take shape was not the boredom sketches of his years at the bank, but a serious preliminary drawing of the cockpit and cabin roof of a yacht. Nor was it the cockpit of the small yachts that had formed the bulk of his sailing experience in the past. This would be the nerve centre of a larger craft that could be used for long-distance sailing rather than short-term fun. It was his sketching that drew him into conversation with his new fellow-passenger.

"Do you sail?"

The man in the window seat leaned towards him as he spoke. His accent was unmistakeably Australian.

"Yes, I do. Or should I say, did."

"Why the change?"

"I don't have a boat at the moment. I lost it in a storm."

"What happened? You obviously got out in one piece."

"I wasn't sailing her at the time."

Richard explained to his new companion about the inter-bank yacht race and the circumstances that had led to Alex's death.

The Australian shook his head sadly.

"That was rough. It seems that it could so easily have been you.

Richard nodded in agreement.

"I keep seeing him on that last day in the office before the race. He was so excited. It was his first big race and he thought that I was doing him a favour, lending him my boat at the last minute."

The Australian looked directly into his face.

"That's life. You weren't to know, so don't blame yourself."

"I don't. I have since heard that the company that built the boat had been indulging in sharp practices. The police are currently carrying out investigations that may result in fraud and manslaughter charges being brought against them."

"The rotten bastards!"

He thought for a few moments before continuing.

"You say your pal was excited about the race. So, think of it this way. On that last day, he was having the time of his life."

Richard thought for a few moments about what his fellow traveller had just said.

"Thanks. That's a good way of looking at it."

The Australian craned his neck to look at Richard's drawing pad.

"So, why the boat sketching? Is it some form of therapy?"

Richard smiled.

"In a way. I always sketch when I'm bored."

The Australian took a further look at Richard's drawing.

"Very impressive. You obviously have something in mind and a long-distance flight is the perfect place to sort out your ideas. What it is also good for is to have a sleep, which is what I'm going to do now."

With that he yawned deeply, settled back in his seat, closed his eyes and slept for the remainder of the journey, leaving Richard to continue his sketching.

After the long trek from London, the flight that was bearing him to Hobart seemed nothing. He was in good spirits at the prospect of seeing his mother again and meeting her new partner. It was only as the plane was making its final descent that the thought struck him. He had not contacted her about visiting her. She might not be at home. Oh well, he thought, I'll be using a hire car. If she is not at home I can wait in the car until she returns.

Home he discovered to be a bungalow in a prosperous neighbourhood in which every property stood alone in its own sizeable plot. The dwelling stood on a low ridge which sloped away at the back and on one side. Use had been made of this in the provision of a driveway that curved down to a garage built into the slope beneath the living accommodation. He turned into the driveway and parked in one of spaces provided at the end. He then walked up a paved footpath which curved through carefully tended flowering shrubs to join the direct footpath from the roadside to a front door flanked by plant tubs and wall baskets filled with a variety of colourful plants. It all seemed a far cry from the naval married quarters that he had grown up in.

He stood for a few moments taking it all in before pressing the doorbell. He waited. There was no response, so after waiting a few moments more, he pressed the doorbell button a second time. As before there was no response. He hesitated, undecided as to what to do next, but, as he did so, he became aware that a car had pulled up outside the house. The figure of a lady, her face obscured by the foliage of the potted plant that she was holding, struggled out of the car and exchanged parting comments with the driver. Then she watched briefly as the car drove away before turning into the front path. It was only then that Richard realised it was his mother.

It had been several years since he had last seen her. She had changed in those intervening years. Those last months of his father's life had been difficult with the strain of caring. Later, after they had quit the married quarters and had to pay full commercial rents and outgoings, money was tight. His mother had always seemed strained and tired. This new mother walking down the path towards him seemed a different person. The climate obviously suited her, for her face and bared arms were tanned a golden brown. Her dress was well-chosen and chic without appearing frivolous. Even behind the barrier of greenery she was carrying he could see that her fair hair, which she had formerly kept long, had been changed to a new short style which lifted her face and made her look younger.

She was halfway down the path before she recognised him. Setting down the potted plant she screamed out his name before rushing to fling her arms around him.

"Richie! What are you doing here? Oh! It is so lovely to see you."

She gave him a long kiss on his cheek.

"Why didn't you let me know you were coming? It's such a long way to come for a visit, but never mind that, let's get inside and I'll get you something to drink."

Taking a key from her handbag she unlocked the front door. Richard retrieved the discarded potted plant and followed her inside. Once she had closed the front door behind them, she took the pot from him and deposited it outside, before returning to hold him at arm's length and giving him a close inspection.

"You look tired."

"I feel tired, but that's not surprising after three days of travel."

"Maybe, but I sense something else. Has something happened?"

Richard smiled to himself, thinking how hard it was to hide anything from one's mother.

"There have been a few minor issues. I'll tell you about everything later after the drink you promised. Right now, I would love a cup of tea."

He had begun to look around him, but paused.

"You do have tea, I hope?"

His mother gave him look of pretend annoyance.

"Yes. We do have tea and bottled milk and running water. For poor colonials, we are becoming quite civilised."

With that parting shot she disappeared into the kitchen, leaving Richard to take stock of his surroundings.

The bungalow appeared to be quite spacious. The entrance hall where he was standing had multiple closed doors on either side, which he guessed must be either bedrooms or bathroom. At the end was the door his mother had used, presumably the kitchen. He settled on the half-open door at the end of the hall and found himself as he expected in a large sitting room furnished with comfortable-looking easy chairs and settee. Sunlight poured in through the full-length glass of sliding doors. He moved the door catch to open and stepped out on to a balcony that ran the full length of the bungalow. He looked down on the carefully manicured garden below and beyond to the rocky headland of the coast curving away to his right.

He was still standing there admiring the beauty of the scene when his mother emerged from a door opening directly from the kitchen. She was bearing a tea tray which she put down on a patio table before joining him at the balcony rail.

"It's lovely, isn't it," she remarked simply.

Richard nodded his head in agreement.

"Very much so. I hope no developer comes along and spoils it."

His mother smiled.

"There is no chance of that happening, unless we do the developing."

Richard looked at her questioningly.

"You mean you own it. All of it?"

"Yes, well Matt does. It's been owned by his family for generations. It was a smallholding in those days. Matt's father had the old cottage demolished and built this house and the others around us. You will have noticed that they all have large plots which means it doesn't feel too crowded."

Richard nodded appreciatively as the unmentioned consequences of this sank in. Beside him his mother was directing him towards the left.

"You can't quite see it, but if you follow the road outside downhill, there is a sizeable creek. That's where he keeps his boat."

Richard's ears pricked up at the mention of boating.

"An old friend from his boyhood has a small boatyard there. Matt keeps his boat there."

"What sort of boat?"

"It's a fairly large sailing boat that he bought during his last leave period. It had been a bit neglected, so Dan is bringing it up to scratch for him, ready for the big day."

"What big day?"

His mother moved back to the table where she had left the tea tray.

"Come and have your tea. There is something we have to discuss."

Richard did as he been bid and took a seat at the patio table.

"It has been such a lovely surprise having you here, but you have come at an awkward time."

She noted the startled look on her son's face.

"It's nothing for you to be concerned about. The big day I mentioned is the day after tomorrow. That is the day set for Matt's retirement from the Navy."

"I'm not with you. He's not of retirement age, is he?"

"Well, he could have carried on, but it would have meant being desk-bound in an office. He's always been a seagoing officer and that that didn't appeal to him."

"So that is where the sailing boat comes in."

"Yes. We are lucky here. There are so many lovely places that we shall be able to explore together."

"So I'm in the way. Is that what you are trying to say?"

"No. I'm so glad that you have come today. If you had turned up tomorrow, I would not have been here. After breakfast in the morning I shall be driving to the airport. Then I will be flying to Sydney. We have booked a suite at a swank hotel and Matt will join me there after his ship's officers have given him a send-off."

She shook her head at the thought of it.

"God knows what state he will be in afterwards, but if he needs a lie-in on Saturday morning that's fine by me. He's promised that Saturday will be my day, and I intend to hit the shops with or without him."

"When are you planning to get back here?"

"Probably late on Tuesday."

"And will it be okay if I stay here?"

"Of course. You can stay as long as you like. As I said, it's just awkward timing."

Richard nodded in agreement and, after a pause, cleared his throat.

"There is something I need to discuss with you."

"I hope it will not take long."

"I don't know. It could do."

His mother looked at him hopefully.

"Can it wait until I get back? I have not done my packing yet and then I shall have sort out what I'm going to give you to eat."

"OK. On the scale of things concerned, another few days is not going to matter."

Puzzled by this last comment, she left him on the balcony and went into her bedroom to begin her packing.

Left to his own devices, Richard finished his tea and then strolled into the sitting room. Looking round with time on his hands, he was drawn to the bookshelves that ran along one of the room's shorter side walls. It seemed to have been deliber-ately constructed in two halves. Closer inspection revealed that this division also applied to the contents of the shelves. One half was filled with a variety of books related to the sea and naval affairs. As his eyes ran along the shelves he noted volumes on purely technical issues together with a large group on navigation covering winds, tides, ocean currents and ship handling. Finally, there was a section on naval history covering all major encounters and actions up to and including the Falklands war. After all of this technical matter, the contents of the other half came as surprise. The upper shelves contained numerous volumes by noted post-war writers of literary fiction. He guessed that these were probably his mother's, a guess confirmed by the name Evelyn Rayleton written on the fly leaf of one he selected at random. Below these was a range of volumes that appeared to be of English poetry. The scope was quite comprehensive, covering every era. He was still idling over these when his mother came into the room.

Richard looked up as she came in.

"A strange contrast between the two halves of the shelves," he remarked.

His mother looked at the book he was still holding.

"The novels are mine. The poetry books belonged to Matt's mother. She taught English literature. Help yourself."

Left to his own devices on the following day after his mother had left for the airport, Richard was drawn again to the book-shelves. At another time perhaps, a number of the naval battles might have interested him, but now was not the time. He was again feeling the same strange restlessness that he had experienced on the long flight from London, but could not pinpoint why he felt this way. Thinking of the flight reminded him of the sketching he had done then and he went to his room and looked for it in his travel bag.

Looking at the drawing again two days later, the design

puzzled him. It was unlike anything he had done before. What subconscious urge had driven him to do it. Equally strange was the fact that his mother's new partner had acquired a yacht of similar dimensions for seagoing exploration with his wife. Was it the same subconscious idea that had produced the sketch? Inevitably his thoughts turned to Jenny. Could it be that he had he been planning a future much like the one that Matt and his mother were embarking on. He stopped himself angrily at that point. Memories were being raised that were all too painfully raw. He decided that he needed to do something that would keep him occupied for some time. He decided that he would fill his morning by walking down to find the creek that his mother had spoken of and take a look at Matt's boat.

Finding the way to the creek was simple. From the front of the house the road curved gently downwards to the left for some way before passing a small scattering of dwellings and then reaching the water's edge. A little way beyond it was the house and workshop of Matt's friend Dan. At this point, behind a low boundary fence, a slipway and stone quay had been built. Against this Matt's boat and two smaller ones were moored.

There was no sign of activity, so Richard made his way to the house. Repeated raps on the door producing no response, he walked across the yard to the workshop. The building looked old and tired, with rust already well entrenched on its corrugated roof sheets. The door had obviously received little attention since the day it was built and hung awkwardly open. Richard put his head around the door and called loudly.

"Hello. Anyone about."

Noises of movement were made and a man appeared at the door. He was of medium height and had obviously at one time been muscular and strong. Since then the years had taken their toll and now in middle age his face and arms looked flabby and his stomach had sagged into a fat paunch that sagged over a low-slung leather belt. A three-day growth of beard did nothing to alleviate his generally unkempt appearance.

Richard smiled as he greeted him.

"Hi. I'm looking for Dan Smithers."

The man looked at him, his face giving nothing away.

"And who might you be?"

"I'm Richard Rayleton. I'm visiting my mother. She's married to Matt Keogh."

Smithers visibly relaxed at the mention of Matt's name.

"Ah, that's the connection. I could tell you were from England. Matt been telling you about his new boat?"

Richard made a rueful grin.

"Actually, I've not met him yet. He and Mum met up and got married without saying anything. I was away at college at the time."

"That's typical of him. He's not one to hang around. When he decides on summat, he just does it. There's no waiting around with Matt."

He took a reflective pause before continuing.

"So, Richard you said your name was, what can I do for you?"

"I just wanted to ask if it was OK if I had a look at Matt's boat."

"Of course. Matt and me go way back. Any..." he paused thinking for the right word, "I was going to say friend but I can't call you that if you ain't met him."

"Technically I'm his stepson."

Smithers laughed.

"Of course, that's it. Now where was I. Any stepson of Matt is welcome here. So just help yourself. You can go aboard if you want to."

"No. I'll leave that until Matt is here, but thanks all the same."

He turned to stroll back across the yard to where the boat was moored, conscious all the time that he was being watched. It was not a case of being watched distrustfully. The look on Dan's face, that he had briefly glimpsed as he turned away, had been something altogether different. It had been the sort of quizzical look of someone puzzled about something.

Later, as he walked back up the road to the bungalow, he reflected on his visit to the creek. Things had not been as he had expected. There had been none of the size and organization of the marinas that he was accustomed to. It had all been much more homespun. The creek-side moorings seemed to be incidental. Dan's oily hands suggested that his main source of income was from servicing or repairing combustion engines. His thoughts returned to the questioning look on Dan's face as he had walked over to examine Matt's yacht at closer hand. It was intriguing, perhaps even a little unsettling.

Leaving his impressions of Matt's old friend aside, he turned his thoughts to the boat he had just seen. It was certainly not a simple pleasure craft, but something much larger than the yachts that he was familiar with sailing. It was of a type that he had seen in yachting magazines that were aimed at longer distance cruising and exploring. Powered by both sails and engine, it would be able to handle whatever conditions mother nature served up. Given their position on the southern coast of Tasmania, it was a good choice. The situation of its cockpit almost at midships and the positions of its numerous portholes, suggested that the design had been influenced by the aim of providing not only the usual day cabin accommodation but also a comfortable master cabin in the after part of the hull. This would provide many of the comforts of home life within a seagoing format. It seemed the ideal choice for what his mother had suggested she and Matt were planning to do once he had taken retirement. He realised with a jolt that this would be taking place within a few hours.

The walk down to the creek had gone some way to removing the restlessness he had experienced over the past few days. In its stead, there was now something different. Again, he was reminded of that questioning look on Dan's face. He smiled to himself as he realised that it was probably a mild apprehension at the thought of meeting his new step-father. That was silly he told himself. One had only to look at how his mother had changed, how positive and happy she looked, to sense that there should be no problems there.

The walk had settled one thing, however. He had made a limited study of the cockpit of Matt's moored yacht from the quayside. The sketch of a yacht cockpit he had made during the flight two days earlier bore little resemblance to the real thing. It had been purely imaginary. So, what had he been imagining he asked himself. The more he thought about it, the more the realisation grew that his subconscious mind had been thinking of a yacht that he and Jenny might use for their explorations. It was then, all at once, that it hit him. He felt that awful emptiness of missing her. He wanted desperately to be with her again, but she was back in America, more than ten thousand miles away. Gerry's parting advice, to not leave things hanging for too long, came back to him. It was up to him to bridge that gap. The only question was how could he do this.

He made himself a snack lunch while he thought things through. It proved to be only a temporary diversion. After-wards, still looking for diversions to fill his time, he had cast his eyes over the range of books in the sitting-room shelves, hoping to find something that appealed to his taste. It was as he scanned the books left by Matt's mother, that the realisa-tion came to him. Whether in verse or prose, they were largely works of fiction, but all were based on real or imagined human emotions. The writers were expressing these in written words. In the past, whenever he had felt bored or at a loose end, he had always turned to his sketch pad. In his present circumstances, that would be a simple waste of time. What he needed to do was to examine his feelings, make note of them and then transmit all of this to Jenny.

The more he thought about it, the more he began to feel that he was on to something. He felt an immediate sense of relief. It was good to be doing something positive. This would be real bridge building. Moreover, he decided almost at once that it should be in an unconventional form. That, he knew, would appeal to her most. He spent the next two days roughing out and amending his ideas until he had formats that he thought were good enough.

On the final morning, he drove into the city in search of a stationery store where he purchased quality A4 notepaper and envelopes and fibre tipped pens. That done, he asked passing pedestrians for directions to the nearest post office. Outside the office he had been directed to, were two round topped mail boxes. He smiled when he saw the same red colour had been used for the boxes as at home in England, although the design of the boxes had moved away from the British originals of colonial days. He had noticed such a box in the outer suburbs on the way into town and posting the letters he was planning would be a simple matter.

Later that evening, soon after he had returned to the bungalow, the telephone rang. It proved to be his mother ringing to check that everything was all right and to inform him that they were staying on for an extra day or so. He was quite cheerful when he finally went to bed. The extra time before his mother's return ought to be sufficient for him to write and post the first of the letters that he was planning, without having to explain everything to her until he was ready.

The next two days were spent in a continuous process of

writing and re-writing until finally he was satisfied. On the afternoon of the second day, each transcript was carefully written out as neatly as he could manage each on a separate sheet of the notepaper he had bought. That done, the second and third sheets were placed in a folder until he was ready to use them. Then, taking the first of the finished copies, he carefully folded it and slipped it into one of the envelopes that he had already addressed and the required postage stamps affixed.

There was no deadline to meet, but nevertheless a sense of urgency had begun to develop which would not subside until he had posted the first of the letters he had planned.

It took only minutes to drive into the Hobart suburbs to locate the post box he remembered seeing on his earlier visit. As he closed the tray of the box and heard the sound of his letter falling into its depths he could not help giving a sigh of relief. He had taken the first step.

He drove back to the bungalow lost in thought. There was no accepted textbook method on how to rebuild bridges that have been broken or of rekindling old fires he mused. The method he had adopted was somewhat unusual. Only time would tell if it had the desired effect.

He was still in reflective mood as he turned into the bungalow's driveway, but this was quickly dispelled by the sight of his mother's car parked in front of the garage. It was time to meet the owner of the house, who was also technically his stepfather. He did not hang around, but strode quickly up the path to the front door. His mother had obviously noted his arrival for she was standing alongside the open door waiting to greet him. She gave him a hug as he entered.

"Come and meet Matt. He's been looking forward to meeting you."

"Same here. It's been strange living in someone's house when you haven't yet met them. It leaves you wondering what they are like."

"Well, I hope that I come up to scratch. Hi, I'm Matt."

Richard took the hand outstretched to him and returned the same firm handshake.

"Hi. I've been wondering how we would do this, but it has just seemed to happen."

As he spoke, he took a steady look at his new stepfather. He himself had always been considered tallish and well-proportioned, but Matt was a good inch taller and with the same strong physique.

Eve moved around them as they completed their greeting.

"I'll leave you two to get to know each other while I make a pot of tea."

Matt waved an arm in the direction of the sitting room.

"Go on through. I hope tea will suit you. Alcohol is of no use in this heat."

He laughed at himself as soon as he had made the remark.

"I was forgetting that you are from England."

Richard laughed with him. He was already feeling at ease as he sensed a genuine feeling of welcome. He could now see what had attracted his mother. It went a long way to explaining the glow of happiness radiating from her that he had noted since his first arrival.

Later, after they had eaten, Eve served coffee in the sitting-room. All three felt relaxed and conversation momentarily lapsed as they sampled the coffee. It was at this point that Eve recalled the brief conversation she had had with Richard when he had first unexpectedly turned up at the bungalow.

"What was it you wanted to ask me about when you first arrived?"

Richard glanced uneasily across at Matt, fazed at the sudden posing of the question.

"Not now. We can leave it until tomorrow."

Eve had noticed the involuntary glance at Matt.

"There are no secrets between Matt and me. You can talk openly."

Reluctantly Richard began his reply.

"I think it will help if I tell you the background first."

With that, he launched into his story of how Jenny had turned up in his Jersey office, how they had fallen in love and how, piece by piece, the history behind her surprise inheritance had been traced up to the decision to undertake DNA analysis.

Eve and Matt sat enthralled by his account.

"Well. I thought I had an interesting career," Matt commented.

Eve's mind was elsewhere, thinking already about the implications of what he had been recounting.

"Let me get this straight. The analysis was to establish whether or not Jenny was genetically a Rayleton.

"That's right."

"And was she?"

"Oh yes. There was a very strong correlation between her genetic make-up and that of cousin Sally's."

Matt shook his head.

"I'm sorry. You have lost me. Is that good or bad?"

"Very good for Jenny. Perhaps not so good for Sally and her father, as it shows that their branch of the family ought not to have inherited the estate and baronetcy."

"So where does that leave you?" Matt enquired.

"Wait." Eve intervened. "I think that there's something else you haven't told us."

Richard nodded before answering.

"What the DNA results also showed was that there was no correlation whatsoever between my DNA and that of the two girls."

Eve gasped and sat without speaking, the fingers of her right hand resting on her lip.

"So, that means that you are not a Rayleton," Matt mused. "I bet that went down well in certain quarters."

"Oh yes. My copy of the results had been mistakenly delivered to a neighbour's post box and she was away on holiday at the time. 'Uncle' Henry had learned about the DNA results before I did. The first I knew about it was when I was called into the MD's office late on a Friday afternoon and given my notice."

"Henry sacked you!" Eve echoed.

"Mm. As from 5pm that Friday, but I'll continue to get my salary until the end of the year."

"This doesn't surprise me. I have never liked that man."

"You don't seem too upset about it." Matt chipped in.

"No. I never warmed to him at personal level and I was developing an increasing dislike of the job. So, all in all, I'm not in the least displeased."

He was aware of his mother looking at him with a sad loving expression.

"And now you want to know if I can help you to trace who your father might be. That's why you have travelled all this way to see me without notice."

Richard nodded his head.

"I thought it best to do it face to face, rather than telephoning."

She moved over to his armchair and, sitting on one of the arms, slipped an arm around his shoulders.

"It's lovely seeing you like this and I can see how unsettling this must have been for you."

"So, can you point me in the right direction to begin my search?"

There was a note of almost gaiety in her voice as she answered.

"There is no need for any search. He's already here in this room."

"You mean…"

"Yes. Matt is your father."

Richard looked at her in astonishment.

"How can you be so sure of that?"

"Quite easily. I've only ever had physical relationships with two men. If Bill Rayleton was not your father, then that only leaves Matt."

Sleep did not come easily when Richard finally went to bed. So much had happened in such a short space of time. His head needed time to process the details and implications of it all. Foremost in his mind was the look of first astonishment and then pure delight that had crossed Matt's face as Eve had made her shock announcement. Both he and Richard had risen to their feet as if impelled by a single thought. They had met in the centre of the room. Matt had placed his hands on each of Richard's shoulders and studied his face. Then he had simply said 'welcome home son' and they had embraced. Eve had watched them with tears streaming down her face. It had been an occasion like no other.

He had not been able to make any sense of things at first, until after a flurry of reminiscences from each of his parents, with each adding details and minor corrections, the story gradually emerged. For some time, Eve had been dating Bill Rayleton when he was in port. It had been during one of the periods when he was at sea that she was asked by a friend to make up a foursome as partner for a visiting Australian naval officer. There had been an instant rapport between her and the visitor and after he had escorted her home to her flat, they had spent the night together. As he left early the next morning, arrangements were made to meet again that evening. That second meeting never happened. Instead, as Matt recalled, on reporting in for duty he was informed that the commander of an Australian frigate had suffered an accident and that he would be flown immediately to Singapore to take over the ship. With that, he had been bundled into a car and driven to board a transport plane at the nearest RAF base. He had not even had time for breakfast, he remembered ruefully.

I had been stood up, or so I thought, Eve added. I only found out much later what had happened. By then, Bill was back in port and we resumed dating. When I found that I was pregnant, we decided to get married. All along both Bill and I thought you were our child. It came as something of a shock when you spoke about your DNA analysis. The rest you know.

It had been years later when Matt had been sent back to England on a liaison posting that he had finally made contact. Bill Rayleton had died some years earlier, and with nothing in their way, this time there had been no hesitation. They had immediately married and when Matt had to return to Australia at the end of the liaison posting, she had soon followed him.

It was at that point that Richard had retrieved his DNA analysis details from his bedroom and showing it to them, had asked if they had any idea what was meant by the reference to Gaelic influences. His father had chuckled. Keogh is an Irish name, he had explained. During the 'troubles' hundreds of Irishmen were transported to Australia.

That had resonated with him. His own love of sailing was an obvious link with his father, but the knowledge that one of his parental ancestors had been involved in protest movements in the past went some way to explaining his own antipathy to establishment hierarchies and their influences back home in the present-day United Kingdom.

Imperceptibly he slowly drifted into a sleep filled with dreams of his mother and new-found father in their sailing boat, cruising through rolling waves in tropical sunshine. Slowly the dreams morphed into different scenes until they centred on a new sailing boat with himself at the helm and alongside him, a tanned and happy Jenny clinging to a halyard, her hair streaming in the breeze.

As so often happens after a delayed sleep, the clock was advancing towards mid-morning when Richard finally awoke the following morning. Once dressed he went in search of breakfast. His mother was in the kitchen, but there was no sign of his father.

"Where's Dad?" he asked as if this was the most normal thing in the world.

His mother noted the words with pleasure, but made no comment on that score.

"Oh. He still gets up at his usual navy time. He went out after he'd had breakfast. He's anxious to see how the boat is shaping up."

"It looked pretty well finished as far as I could see."

He paused momentarily before continuing.

"I did not say anything last night. There was so much happening. It was curious. I had walked down to the boat-yard and went to find Dan to ask permission to look around.

"There was no problem, was there?"

"No. None at all. As soon as I mentioned Matt's, sorry, Dad's name he was very affable. It was what he didn't say that I found curious. As I moved away to go over to where the boat was moored, he just stood there giving me puzzled looks."

Eve smiled.

"Don't forget that he and your father go back a long way. We all change imperceptibly as the years go by. Perhaps there was something about you that reminded him of your father at the time they were young."

"Maybe you are right. What we can be sure of, is that there will be a bit of leg-pulling from Dan when I go down to the yard later."

He was aware that his mother was looking at him steadily. Finally, she spoke.

"Now that you have slept on it, are you OK about all this?"

"I could not be happier. I didn't really know the man I once thought of as my father. This time round it's different. I can't explain it, it just feels right. It's as if I've known him for a lot longer than half of a day."

Eve smiled with relief.

"That's good, but you still have a lot of catching-up to do."

"I know. I'll make a start by joining him in Dan's yard, but first I need to get acquainted with a large mug of coffee and a couple of thick slices of toast."

It was over half-an-hour later that Richard walked into the boatyard. Dan was working on the quayside alongside the boat, but there was no sign of his father He must have been inside the boat as when he neared the boat Dan called out in a deliberately loud voice.

"Your stepson has just turned up Matt."

Having had his fun, he ambled off and appeared a few minutes later bearing three cans of beer. He then joined Richard and his father in the cockpit of the boat and handed a beer to each of them. Then he pulled the ring to open the can and when the other two had done the same, he raised his and offered a toast.

"Here's to families and the ships they sail in."

"Families and the ships they sail in," was echoed.

Having taken a long drink from the can, Dan turned to his old friend.

"What beats me, is how you couldn't see it. He's got you written all over him."

They chatted briefly while they drank the remainder of the beer in their cans before the two older men returned to work. There was little room for all three of them to work in the cockpit, so Richard only stayed long enough to help with the laborious work of hauling the sails from one of Dan's outbuildings, where they had been stored during the refit, and heaving them aboard the boat. That done, he left the other two to carry out the technical work of rigging the yards and making the fixing and trial raising of the sails in preparation for the sea trial they had planned for the following day.

As he made his way back up the road to the bungalow, he reflected on what he had just witnessed. It had been interesting to see his father in company with his boyhood friend. Amid the banter and humour of their exchanges, Richard noted a definite deference to Dan on technical matters. Matt might be the expert on seamanship and navigation, with until recently, high rank in the Royal Australian Navy, but when it came to the physical aspects of boats and their electric and mechanical equipment, there Dan was the acknowledged expert.

There was no sign of his mother when he let himself into the bungalow and he remembered that she had spoken of needing to do food shopping. Her absence provided the opportunity to address and stamp his second letter to Jenny without needing to field any questions. That done he drove into town to post his letter.

24

With Hal incapacitated, Jenny found herself fully occupied in taking over much of the work that he would have formerly done. She had not found it in any way challenging, as, apart from the absence of horses, it was very similar to what she had been used to while her Grandpa was alive. However, other than a small amount of cycling in Jersey, she had done little manual work for some months and, initially, she found the return to it tiring. She said nothing of this to Martha and was pleased that within a couple of weeks she was finding that she was getting back into the old rhythm of farm life. With more activities to fill her days, time seemed to pass more quickly and the weeks imperceptibly slipped away. At the same time Hal had begun to come to terms with his immobility and general incapacity. The impatience and general bad temper that he had shown in the first few days following his accident had gradually softened. Now he was content to offer helpful comment and advice from his position on the porch settee, with only the occasional muttered comment under his breath.

In due course Jenny received notification that the requested transfer of funds into her current account had been carried out. At that point the idea was put to Hal that she should fund the pay-off of the farm's mortgage. His first reaction had been an emphatic rejection. The debt was his, he exclaimed and it was his responsibility to repay it. It was exactly the reaction Martha had expected. Knowing her husband, she could see that he probably saw it as an affront to his manhood and patiently proceeded to wear down his initial reluctance by playing on his strong antipathy to banks in general and the increasing burden of their mortgage interest payments. Eventually, she got him to see that, as they intended to leave the farm to Jenny, it was in her interest that they did not fritter away any more money on unnecessary bank interest payments. Jenny had then transferred a sum a little larger than required into their joint account and they had arranged for the closure of the mortgage account. Now, bearing a cheque made out and signed by both account holders, Jenny and Martha had driven into town and effected the final payment.

On their return, as Jenny turned into the farm's entrance, Martha asked her to stop so that she could collect whatever mail was in the mail box. She returned to the pickup truck bearing a small bundle of letters that she did not give so much as a glance, as her mind was set on reporting to Hal on the morning's events. The mail was simply set down on the low porch table while she made her report.

"Don't you feel better without that load of debt bearing down on you?" she said to him. "In the morning you will realize that it makes a whole new world. I know that I do already."

She turned to speak to Jenny, but she had gone directly to her room to change. When she returned to the porch some minutes later, Martha was surprised to see her in her work shirt and jeans. Jenny noted the look on her face.

"The mortgage might be paid off, but there is still a farm to run."

Martha sighed.

"You are right enough there, Honey."

As she spoke, she reached for the mail she had just collected.

"And no doubt there will be more bills here to pay …Oh. There's a letter for you Honey. It's got a different sort of stamp on it."

Jenny took the proffered letter and studied the stamp.

"It's from Australia," she said.

Then quietly she returned to her bedroom and closed the door.

For several minutes she sat on the edge of her bed, steeling herself to open the letter. What would it say, she wondered? Would it be good news or bad? Did he still love her, or was he writing to tell her to get lost? Finally, she became impatient with herself, telling herself to stop being silly. Whatever the letter had to say would not be changed by delay. In a sudden quick move, she slit open the letter and drew out a single large sheet of notepaper. It bore no address, date or signature. Only half of the sheet was taken up by lines of simple ordered handwriting. As she scanned the script, she realised that she was reading a poem.

Love's Bane

Before we loved I little knew of life
Bright robed in multi-hued variety.
Day followed dreary day in sterile strife
Mired deep in sombre grey sobriety.
What change from this sweet love then softly
     wrought
A sun now shone whate'er the day outside
New riches fed emotions long untaught
A beauty grew within I feared had died.

Yet now against this splendour breaks a fear
An aching emptiness when you're not there
The dread that you will fail to re-appear
And leave me hostage to that old despair.
Love wears both guises – passion's cruel bane –
Hearts that know rapture also feel its pain.

Having read it through quickly, she read it through a second time, but this time slowly and carefully, noting the overall structure and rhyming pattern. Although unsigned, it was undoubtedly from Richard and he had written her a sonnet. She sat silently for some time with tears slowly trickling down her cheeks. She could feel, in a very real sense, the unhappiness and doubt that he had felt when penning this verse. In that perverse irony that life can sometimes produce, she saw that this was exactly what she herself was feeling.

She read the poem a final time looking for any clue that might ease her own thoughts. It said nothing more. The emotions it spoke of were ongoing. That in itself said something, she told herself. If there was no conclusion, then hope remained.

She remained in her room a while longer, then spent a few minutes in the bathroom washing her face before returning to the porch. She did not feel composed enough to face the inevitable enquiry about her letter from Australia. So, putting on a brave face, she made a cheerful comment about being behind with her work and, stepping quickly down to the yard, made her way to the chicken sheds.

The work she was now doing was largely what Hal usually handled. None of it was new to her, but with egg, milk and horticultural production involved, the work was relentless. Martha joined in whenever possible, fitting in this work around running the home. No doubt Hal would continue to fret, but, for the time being, the farm was operational. As they moved into autumn the weather remained good, as it usually did at this time of the year. The problem was that this would not continue indefinitely. Hal had chosen to grow spring wheat and as a result the main acreage at the back end of the farm had developed a rich golden hue. The wheat was ready for harvesting. She made a mental note to check with Hal what he intended to do about this. With luck, she thought, such a course of action would also divert Martha's mind away from the letter from Australia.

She brought up the subject of harvesting as they ate their evening meal. Hal shook his head when she had scarcely started on her observations.

"There's no need for you to worry. You will not have to do anything about that side of things. We always have contractors in to do all that."

"So, when are they coming? Have you remembered to book them?" Martha chipped in. "I wouldn't put it past you to have forgotten all about it."

"Of course, I've remembered to book them. I may not be fully mobile, but my mind works just fine."

Martha was not going to let things rest.

"So, when are they coming?"

Hal thought through the dates before answering.

"I make it the day after tomorrow."

"And when were you planning to tell me this. You know I always like to lay in some beer and vittles for the crew. We were in town this morning. Now I'll have to go back into town in the morning."

Jenny smiled to herself at the latest in the customary daily exchanges between the two. It was a game played between them with no real rancour. On this occasion, victory in their marital spat went uncelebrated. Martha now had something more pressing to occupy her mind. For the time being, it also meant that she would forget about Jenny's letter with its Australian stamp and postmark.

Grain harvesting was something new to Jenny. She had seen the machines at work from afar, but her grandpa had never bothered to grow cereals, relying instead on Hal to supply him with grain and straw. It promised to be interesting.

On the morning of the harvesting she was awoken by the sound of heavy engines. This was followed by the voice of one of the crew speaking with Hal. Slipping on a gown, she found a curtained window that gave a partial view of the yard. Peeping out, she could see the length of the complete, self-contained harvesting unit stretching back from the yard towards the road. At its head, it's engine still running, was a huge truck. Towed behind was first a long low-load trailer bearing a massive combine harvester and behind that a second smaller trailer carrying a standard sized tractor. Behind all of this was a second smaller truck pulling another low trailer bearing the harvester's long cutting head and a high-sided wheeled hopper for receiving the threshed grain.

The convoy had come to a halt in the final stage of the track from the road. As she watched the other members of the crew set to work. The second trailer was detached and the master truck then manoeuvred in the yard to allow for the harvester unit to be carefully driven down ramps to stand free on its wheels. Jenny watched it all, amazed at the speed and professionalism of the crew. It seemed that in a matter of minutes the harvester's cutting head had been attached, the tractor driven off its trailer, and then coupled to the hopper trailer, ready to follow the now fully operational harvester into the field. When Jenny finally emerged from her bedroom to take breakfast in the kitchen, the sounds of work in progress was already drifting across from the wheat acreage.

Mornings were normally taken up collecting eggs and

feeding the hens and other stock. With Martha and Hal preoccupied with the harvesting, she thought that this afternoon would be the best time to make the trip into town for a much-needed solo shopping expedition. Once her morning work had been completed, she returned to the kitchen. Martha was already preparing the food she had purchased for the harvesting crew's short lunch break. She asked if there was anything else that needed doing, otherwise she would take a trip into town for some things that she needed. Hal was happy to see her go.

"It's not a normal sort of day." He commented. "I guess that they'll be all done by early evening at the latest. Then tomorrow we can get back to normal."

As she headed to the farm's pick-up truck Martha called after her.

"Don't forget the mailbox."

She retraced her steps to where Martha stood at the foot of the porch holding out the mailbox key. When she reached the end of the farm track, she made a point of stopping to unlock the mailbox on the outward journey, while it was fresh in her mind. For once there was none of the commercial mail that seemed to arrive daily. There was only one item. Her heart gave a small tremor as she recognised the familiar shape of the envelope and the distinctive Australian stamps. She returned to the truck and placed it beside her on the seat. Her original plan had been to get a snack lunch and follow this with a little time browsing in the stores and after that to find somewhere to settle with the new novel that she had bought on her last visit. Now, she thought, here is something else. As she drove into town, she knew that this new letter would take precedence over all else. Would this one be as surprising as the first? More importantly, what would this one have to say?

She drove to a spot she knew on the edge of town, where people parked while they exercised their dogs. She parked facing the river and reached across for her letter. This time there was no hesitation or finesse as she tore open the envelope. It contained two sheets of the same notepaper and as before written in the same way with no name or address.

Continuum

Look for me when first awaking
Warmed and sleep-strewn with the dawn.
I am the gleaming sun new risen
That gilds the widening heavens
With artists palette opulent and rare.

Taste soft my kiss at early morn
When earth frost-fettered lies in thrall.
I am the snowflake gently swirling
Amid your rhymey exhalations
To moisten sweetly contoured lips pursed fair.

Reach out for me that I might touch
Your hand so small and silken formed.
I am the springtime breeze new risen
That pirouettes so playfully
And trails caressing fingers through your hair.

Breathe in my being ready perfumed
As lovers waiting evening tryst.
I am the heady scents of summer
That linger late as shadows fall
And fragrant drift upon the bee-blessed air.

Hark to me, my sigh is for you
As autumn's bounty bids adieu.
I am the orphan leaves late fallen
That rattle-rustle round your feet
And whisper sad beneath the branches bare.

Dream fond of me at day's last hour
When weary limbs sink into rest.
I am the drowsiness descending
To bear you gently hence and
Interlace your lashes with sweet care.

Know this of me, whate'er befalls
Though senses disavow such truth.
My love accepts no separation
And seeks your soul's society
Always, in all doing and everywhere.

She paused for a moment, her chest was tight. She felt unable to breathe. Then slowly, taking in each word, she read it again. As she reached the last word she breathed out. The hand holding the sheets fell to her lap and she just sat. Tears rolled gently down her cheeks. She had her answer. Despite everything that had happened, he still loved her.

It was obvious to the two women that Hal had enjoyed the bustle of the harvesting, despite being unable to participate in his customary way. After they had finished their evening meal, he was insistent on one of them helping him to inspect the larger barn where the reaped corn had been placed into storage. As Martha had clearing up and dish washing to do, the task fell to Jenny. Hal was now more accustomed to hobbling with his crutch, but it was a slow and awkward walk down from the porch and across the yard. He spent a little time examining the corn before declaring himself satisfied. That done, he wanted to be driven down to the now stripped corn field. The truck had only the front seat to offer with little room for his stiff encased leg. The back seat of a car would have been a better option, but the pick-up truck was the farm's only vehicle.

Jenny drove slowly and as carefully as possible, but she could not completely avoid all of the bumping and swaying that the negotiating of farm tracks involved. Once they reached the cleared area, she stopped the truck so that he could take a long look around. There was little to remind them of how the field had looked in the days before the harvesters had done their work. What had then been a sea of waist high, golden corn had been reduced to a lifeless expanse of stubble. There was a scattering of broken corn stalks, but the bulk of this straw had been drawn in by the team's baling machine and dropped off in irregular rows of bound bales.

Hal sat looking around him.

"I'd say they have done a good tidy job," he finally said.

"What about the straw bales?" Jenny asked. "Didn't you want those collected and stacked l?"

"I had not thought about that." Hal said. "You don't need fancy equipment for that, so I usually do that myself. Besides," he added with a chuckle. "It saves a whole lot of dollars."

Jenny gave him a sad look.

"Well, you'll not be in any shape to be doing anything for a while yet."

Hal looked at the expanse of fading blue sky.

"They'll be all right lying there till then. This weather should hold for a few more weeks I reckon."

They sat silently for a few minutes while Jenny debated

inwardly whether or not to say what was on her mind. Finally, she made up her mind to go ahead.

"In a way, you should look at your present injury as a pointer to what it will be like for you in a few more years. You did not have any problems with the harvesting itself because you had contractors to do the work, but right now you can't handle the lifting and stacking work. You're not as old as Grandpa was, but think of what it will be like when you start to get older. Looking ahead, now the farm mortgage is paid off, you only need to earn enough to live off. You could drop all the heavier work and just do the lighter operations. "

Hal looked at her with a smile playing round his lips.

"What are you saying, that I've got one foot in the grave?"

Jenny smiled back, relieved that he had not taken offence.

"In one sense we all have. No. What I meant was that there is more to life than work. Become a free man. Cut out what is heavy or ties you down. Go places, take a holiday while you can."

"I can see what you mean. I ain't yet got used to the idea of having no mortgage, but I'll think about what you have just said. I know Martha would love to see the Grand Canyon and Niagara and places like that."

"Well, there you are. There's lots to think about, but right now we need to get back. Martha will be worrying that something has happened to you."

In one sense something had happened to him. The hobbling and jolting of the truck had combined to tire him sufficiently to go to the bedroom to lie down as soon as they were back in the house.

"There he's gone and tired himself." Martha said, as soon as he had left the porch. "I knew this would happen. We could have strolled down to take a look at things for him, but he always has to see for himself."

"Never mind," Jenny was quick to comment. "It gives us

the chance to talk, and there is something I would like to show you."

With that, she quickly walked to her room. Moments later she retuned bearing the two letters she had received from Australia. Without any explanation she handed the papers to Martha.

"These are the two letters I got from Australia."

"Two?" Martha queried as she received the proffered documents. I thought that you only got one?"

"The second one came the day the harvesters were here."

Martha looked at the first one and stopped.

"This is some sort of poem," she said puzzled.

"They both are." Jenny replied.

"What am I supposed to be looking for?" the still puzzled Martha asked.

"The first one is a sonnet, so it has a strict pattern of line lengths and rhymes. Don't worry about that, just read each one carefully and tell me what you think it says."

Martha read each poem as bidden.

"Well the second one seems easy enough. He loves you. I think I've got that right?"

She returned to the first one and re-read it.

"This one is more complex, but I think I get it now. He's saying that the world brightens up when you fall in love, and then when a patch of cloud comes over it makes things cold and dark again for a while. That's how love is. You can't expect the sun to shine every day."

"Yep. That's a good way of expressing it."

"And you still love him?"

"I never stopped, but back then there was this possibility that we were related. I think he felt very hurt and confused when I told him that we would have to stop seeing each other. I know I did and it must have been so much worse for him, especially after the results came through and he no longer knew who his father was."

"So, what do you think he's saying?"

Exactly what you described. I think that in the first poem he is explaining how love brightened his life until problems intervened. Then in the final section he has come to terms with this and sees that this is how love goes. The second poem simply confirms how much he still loves me."

Martha shook her head.

"I don't know. Things seemed so much simpler when I was a girl."

"It's not so very different now. People just travel more."

Martha thought for a moment.

"What's he doing in Australia?"

"I don't know for sure. His mother lives there. My guess is that he's gone to see if she can shed some light on his parentage."

"And you're sure this is from Richard."

"Oh yes! There's only Richard and Gerry the painter who have this address."

"Well, he's chosen a strange way of contacting you. Why doesn't he just write a simple letter?"

"I don't know. There was a gap that had to be closed. Maybe he was afraid that I might tell him that I was no longer interested. Maybe he just wanted to be romantic. What I do sense is that he chose to make it a one-way communication to avoid any chance of a negative response until he sees me face to face. If that is the case, one day soon he'll be turning up here."

25

It was some days before the shock and joy of discovering his true family began to assume accepted reality in Richard's mind. For those first few days he was in a form of dream time where he could scarcely believe what was happening around him. Fortunately, the presence of his mother provided an accepted base of reality on which to build. Time would provide more. For the moment he was happy to learn all he could about this significant new person in his life.

With the sea trials successfully completed, there was still much to do to bring the boat up to readiness. On successive days he and Matt drove into Hobart and purchased water tanks, radio equipment, navigational charts and a host of other items that would be needed to make the boat fully self-contained. It was an ideal way in which they could get to know each other. For Richard there was also the satisfaction of being accepted on equal terms and asked to make inputs into buying decisions.

On the last of these trips Eve had accompanied them to help select the porthole curtains for the sleeping cabins and all of the cooking utensils, cutlery and non-breakable crockery that would be required. All of the latter items, Richard noted, were purchased in sets of four. He brought up this point as they drove home.

"It seemed the most sensible thing to do," Eve replied, turning to face him in the rear seat. "Most of the crockery was in packs of four."

"In any case," Matt added over his shoulder from the driving seat, "we may at times have other people with us."

Richard nodded acceptance of the common sense of this, but already his mind was thinking along other lines. At the moment he was the most likely 'other person'. Were they thinking of his joining them?

Within a few moments Matt had confirmed what Richard had been surmising.

"We are planning to explore the east coast, maybe as far north as Cairns, and then spend time enjoying what the Great Barrier Reef has to offer. We were wondering if you would care to join us?" Matt ventured.

Immediately problems began assembling in Richard's mind. For the past few days his thoughts had been immersed in absorbing everything about his new family. Now here, for the first time in days, he was being reminded of Jenny. The trip to Australia had been planned as a fact-finding mission, best carried out face-to-face with his mother. He had never thought in terms of making a lengthy visit. From the beginning, it had been considered simply as an important, although not strictly necessary, precursor to a restoration of his relationship with Jenny. That very morning, he had separated briefly from his parents to post his final letter to her in America. In approximately a week's time she would be reading his final poem. If she interpreted it in the way he hoped, she would be expecting him to turn up in Pennsylvania.

It took only seconds for him to reach a decision.

"It's a lovely thought, but I can't. I'm in the middle of

sorting out things with Jenny and I really need to be in the USA in a week or so."

He noticed his mother's hand reach out and rest on his father's arm. Matt took the message.

"Oh. Right. I just thought that it would be good to sail together. Perhaps another time."

They completed the return to the bungalow in silence. Eve took all crockery items and utensils inside for washing and she and Matt spent the afternoon driving down to the yard and storing everything bought that morning in the boat. Richard elected to spend time sorting through all the travel options for his journey to meet up with Jenny.

It was later that evening, as they ate their evening meal, that Matt returned to the topic of their planned expedition.

"I've been thinking things over while we were down at the yard. Your mother and I missed out on many years together because of other circumstances interfering with our private lives. I can fully understand where your priorities lie, but I also think it is important at this point to strengthen our family links."

"Dad... ", Richard began to interject.

"Wait. Hear me out, and say what do you think of this? Your mother has a long-standing promise that I will take her to Melbourne for a shopping trip. I think we could incorporate that in our projected exploration of the eastern coast. You could come along with us as far as Melbourne and fly from there to the USA to meet up with Jenny. While you are doing that, your mother and I can complete our stay in Melbourne and then make leisurely progress round the coast to Sydney. Then, if it's thumbs up for you with Jenny, you have the option for both of you to join us in Sydney and enjoy the Barrier Reef with us. If it is thumbs down, then you can come on your own. It might then help take your mind off things."

"Both of us?"

"Why not? If the two of you want to make a go of things, we would like meet Jenny at some point soon."

Eve had initially reacted to Matt's return to the topic of Richard's future movements with worried looks across the table. Now she enthusiastically backed Matt's new suggestion.

"Oh Matt! I think that's a lovely idea."

Richard considered for a moment.

"I'll certainly take up the offer of the Melbourne part of the trip, but obviously I can't decide on the rest."

"Good. If there is a problem over costs of flying, I can cover that. I hope you will join us for the final leg. I think that it would be great for all of us."

It was not a new sensation for Richard, but a welcome one nevertheless. It simply felt good to be at sea again after a lapse of many weeks and to experience again the same feeling of being at one with the whole earth and all its various moods.

There were nevertheless some differences. The obvious one was that he was in a different type of craft to the light-weight yachts he had formerly known, designed for speed and the fun of racing. By contrast, Matt's yacht had been designed with the strength to handle all that deep-water ocean sailing might bring to bear. It was larger and heavier than any boat he had previously sailed, but that was itself a source of reassurance. He had found that she handled well and he had quickly settled into learning her ways.

The other difference was less easy to pinpoint, as it lay in himself. The young man he had once been had sailed for fun and excitement. Without perhaps his realising it at the time, Alex's death had closed the door on that era. The sight of the wreckage of his yacht in Penzance had brought a more adult recognition of the power of winds and waves. He was aware that the lives of his parents, sleeping below in the master cabin, had been entrusted to him. It was a measure of his developing maturity that he was in no way daunted by this. In time he would come to see it as the true beginning of deepening family relationships.

What had not changed was the experience of again sailing at night. With the onset of darkness came the change in human reactions. With visual perceptions no longer paramount, sound became of equal importance. The sounds of the sea and air and of the boat's reactions to these elements were soon learned. Subconsciously from then on, his ears were tuned to pick up differences in these sounds and evaluating them. As he stood at the wheel taking in all of this, another thought came to him. This was the first real journey that he had undertaken with both of his natural parents. That alone was the source of a strange new feeling of satisfaction. That feeling had begun when they had finally boarded the boat in Dan's boatyard, and with Dan to free their mooring ropes and wave them off, had set out on their family expedition.

There had been no hurry to their progress northward along Tasmania's eastern coast. In his youth Matt had learned his sailing skills along this stretch of coastline, but it was all new to Eve and Richard. At the end of their first day's sailing they had dropped anchor amidst the beauty of the bay at Saint Helens. That had been when feeling of being on holiday had begun to kick in and they had stayed a full day there, which Eve used to stock up with the plentiful fruit and vegetables that were on offer. Now, with the pleasures of their short stay in the northeast corner of the island behind them, they had set sail for Melbourne. Matt had stayed at the helm as they navigated the Banks Strait and then, when they were well into the open waters of the much greater Bass Strait, had laid a north-westerly course that would take them to Port Philip Bay and Melbourne. It was at this point, with the light rapidly fading that he had handed over to Richard and he and Eve had turned in for the night.

The first two days had been more like a holiday. Matt had deliberately treated it in this way, as he was anxious for Eve to relax, to get over any initial queasiness and find her sea legs. She seemed to have settled well, and they had set off on the lengthy crossing to the mainland. In a sense, this was where their journey began.

For Richard it had a deeper significance. This was the first leg of a journey that would take him across the Pacific and much of the USA. His last poem was already making the very same journey. If he had got his estimated times right, it would have been received before he turned up. That part he had been able to plan with reasonable accuracy. The reception he would receive was the only thing that lay outside his control. It would be good to lose the feeling of emptiness that had enveloped him since Jenny had said they must separate. Were her feelings for him still as they had been before their separation. Remembering how strong their love had been, he could not see any reason why there should be any change. Yet, even so, there was always the awful uncertainty of not knowing. Then he remembered the many years that his parents had spent apart. Real love lasts he told himself. Even so, at the same time he was realist enough to recognise the element of impatience in his feelings. Do not think about it, he told himself. Concentrate on your sailing and just be patient for a few more days.

Several thousand miles away in rural Pennsylvania Jenny had been feeling the same uncertainties. She was taking a short break from her farm work to have a mid-afternoon coffee. She was alone, as earlier Martha had driven Hal into town to have a further x-ray on his leg to check how well it was healing. With no one to talk to, her thoughts had returned to Richard.

Like him she was experiencing that same feeling of wanting time to move more quickly. She wanted something to happen, but, unlike him, she was not sure what it was that she was waiting for.

The uncertainties were made worse by the nagging recriminations she felt. Each day she asked herself why had she not listened to Richard. Why had she insisted on their separating? Without an address for him in Australia she had no way of letting him know how she felt. Was he now so scared of further rejection that he didn't include it in his letters?

Her thoughts were interrupted by the return of the car. She watched as Martha slowly emerged and then opened the rear door to help Hal out. He was still sporting the plaster casing on his leg, she noticed, as he hobbled to the porch steps. Martha left him holding the roof support post while she returned to the car for something she had left on the passenger seat. Jenny felt the normal urge to go to him to give support, but she held back knowing how fiercely independent they both were. Any offer of help would be swiftly brushed aside. As she watched, Martha returned to Hal waving a letter. Then they slowly mounted the steps and Hal with a thankful grunt settled on the porch couch.

"This is for you. It's from Australia. I recognise the stamps." Martha proudly announced, her cheerful expression changing to one of surprise as Jenny glanced at the letter she had been handed and placed it on the table.

"Ain't you going to open it?"

"In a moment. There are other things to deal with first. How is Hal's leg?"

"It's healing fine. The doc says the plaster can come off at the end of next week."

"About time," Hal grunted. "I can't wait to get back to normal."

"If you think you're getting back to work straight away

after your plaster is off, you can forget about it," Martha stated categorically. "It will be a couple of months before you can get back to anything like normal."

"A couple of months! I can't wait that long!"

"You can and you will. So, you can drop that sort of thinking."

Jenny smiled to herself at the pantomime. Hal had to make some pretence of being in charge of affairs, but in reality, both knew that it was Martha's views that normally decided matters. As if to reinforce that very point, she picked up Jenny's letter from the table and handed it to her. "There's no point in putting things off. Best open it."

Jenny took the offered letter and, slowly and carefully opening it, extracted the single sheet that it contained.

"It's another poem," she said and began reading it.

Homecoming

How shall you greet me, new returned?
Will eager footsteps tumble to my chime,
To haste a closeness glowing?
Or will self-conscious shyness rise
To bid you break this joy
And sip its pleasures quietly?
I know not.

What will your looks be then?
Will eyes that sparkle like a summer's morn
Lend lightness to your laughter?
Or will you hold that tender gaze,
Pale-framed with simple beauty,
In silent still solemnity?
I cannot tell.

How shall we love when I am come?
With hesitancy and the stumblings
Of a new beginning?
Or will two souls, so finely linked
Before this time apart,
Breathe soft again as one?
This last I know.

She breathed out slowly and read through the verses a second time. Then, without commenting, she handed the sheet to Martha.

Martha began to read. As she progressed beyond the first lines, Jenny heard her pronounced intake of a breath which was only finally released as she handed the sheet back.

There was a tear forming in the corners of her eyes as she did so.

"Honey, that is so beautiful."

Jenny simply nodded, sniffing as she did so, aware that her own tears were forming.

"You've got your answer," Martha gasped. "Now come here."

She opened her arms as she spoke and the two embraced with tears streaming down their faces.

Behind them they heard Hal moving on the couch.

"There's a strange automobile just pulled into the yard. It's probably another goddam sales rep."

Martha drew away from Jenny to get a better view of what Hal was reporting. The car had stopped. As she watched, the driver's door was slowly opened and a young man climbed out. She glanced to see how Jenny was reacting, but was surprised to see that Jenny was no longer alongside her, but had already run down the porch steps and was throwing herself into the arms of the newcomer.

. . .

The following morning it was Jenny who was the first to stir. For a few moments she remained in a half-asleep mode, slowly gathering her wits. She could remember their going to bed together the previous evening and lying talking well into the night. It was only when Richard stirred beside her that she remembered the momentous events of the previous afternoon. Still not trusting to fully believe her senses, she reached out to touch him for confirmation. It was enough to produce a response and a sleepy hand reached out to hold hers. Neither spoke. It was enough to simply be together.

It was Richard who finally broke the intimate silence.

"There's something that I've not told you."

"What's that," she murmured, still not fully awake.

"Mum and Dad would like to meet you."

"That's nice. I'd like to meet them one day too."

"That's not what they had in mind. They have invited us to join them for the second half of their Barrier Reef cruise."

Jenny turned to face him, suddenly fully awake.

"You mean a sea cruise?"

"Yes. Now that he is retired from the navy, Dad has bought a decent sized yacht. It's a proper sea-going boat and it's designed to carry up to six people, so there's plenty of room on board. In addition to sails, there is also has an engine. To add to that, Dad is also a top rate navigator."

"This is a bit sudden. I'll have to think about it. I hadn't even seen the sea before that first day in Jersey and I've not done any real sailing. The time in Jersey when you took me along the coast to see my property is the only time that I have sailed."

"It's exactly the same for Mum. She had never before been in a boat when we set out from Tasmania. I think that now that she has taken the plunge, she quite enjoys it."

He paused for a moment before adding an afterthought.

"Neither of us have jobs at the moment and it is still another five months before you can take possession of your property."

They lay in silence for a few minutes while she thought it through.

"OK. I'll give it a provisional maybe, but you have to do something for me in return."

"And what would that be?"

"I'm not saying, but we shall need to go into town first to get a few things."

As they ate breakfast Richard tried to draw out of her the nature of whatever it was she wanted him to do for her, but she remained resolute in her refusal to say anything. In the end he was happy to sit back while she drove them into town in the pick-up truck.

Since leaving England, almost all that Richard had experienced was large cities and their airports. He found it interesting to see an example of small-town America. Driving on the righthand side of the road and the size and style of vehicles and buildings were obvious differences, he mused. Once you look beyond these superficialities, however, you soon realised that small towns were the same the world over.

He was jolted from his thoughts by the realisation that they had stopped and Jenny was already getting out of the truck. He hurriedly joined her on the sidewalk and followed as she led him to a store where she stopped in front of a range of traditional blue jeans and asked for his waist measurement. Having selected a pair, she then led him to racks of thick work shirts where she asked him to select one in his size. That done the same pattern was repeated in the footwear section, where he was directed to select a pair of work boots. Then, after they had finally settled the bill for all these at the checkout, they returned to the pick-up. It was as Richard was piling their packages in the back of the truck that Jenny was struck by an afterthought and hurried back inside the store.

A few minutes later she returned to find Richard sitting patiently in the truck. She handed him a smaller package as she slipped into the driving seat alongside him. Richard looked into the paper bag and extracted a pair of coarse leather work gloves as Jenny gunned the engine into life. He was trying them on for size as Jenny swung the truck round in the wide street to make their way back out of town. He glanced across at her.

"What is it that gives me the impression that this task you have lined up involves manual labour?"

Jenny glanced across at him with a broad smile.

"You should be so lucky."

"Well, it would be nice to know exactly what it is that you have in store for me."

"All in good time. We shall be back at the farm in a few minutes. Then I will show you."

Richard could see that he would not move her from this position and sat patiently as they covered the short journey back to the farm. It was as they emerged from the farm track into the yard, that he realised that she was not parking the truck but had continued down the track into the fields. She continued until they reached the wide acreage of corn stubble and stopped the truck.

Richard looked across the undulating ground and its haphazard litter of straw bales.

"What am I looking for exactly?" he said.

Jenny treated him to an enigmatic smile.

"What you see."

For a moment Richard was nonplussed.

"All I can see is a field of stubble and straw bales … Oh! I get it. The straw bales."

"Exactly. Hal and Martha have always done this job them-selves. Martha drives the tractor and Hal does the humping. Next week he will be having the plaster off his leg. He's so pig headed at times that, if these bales are still here then,

Martha will not be able to stop him from getting out here before his leg is fully healed."

Richard nodded his understanding, but there was a smile playing around is face as he spoke.

"So, you want me to drive the tractor?"

"No chance, buddy. I'll be driving the tractor while you do the humping."

"Why the gloves then, where do they come in? That's only straw out there."

"It's because of the baler twine that holds the bale together. That is where you pick them up. Unless your hands are used to hard work, you would rub the skin on your fingers and palms in next to no time."

Having delivered that cheerful warning, she turned the car and drove slowly back to park in the yard.

"Leave your packages in the truck and remember to say nothing to Hal about any of this. We can make a start when he takes his snooze after lunch."

Their moves went according to plan and, as soon as Hal had disappeared into the bedroom, Richard slipped out to the truck and retrieved their morning's purchases. Within minutes he emerged from the other bedroom dressed as a typical farmhand and ready for action. Jenny gave him a once-over as he emerged.

"Everything fit?"

"Yes, although the boots are very stiff."

"The leather is new and you are not used to having anything tight round your ankles. At any rate, other than the newness of everything, you look the part."

Martha was standing watching.

"Are you sure that you want to go along with this?"

Richard nodded in reply.

"Well I'm very grateful to you and I'm sure Hal will be

eventually. He's been fretting about those bales since the harvesting. It's just a pity that we have to go to these lengths just to save stubborn old fools from themselves."

She followed as Richard and Jenny made their way to the yard.

"Remember you ain't used to this sort of work, Richard. The bales ain't heavy, but there's a lot of lifting and it's the lifting that tires you. So, take it steady."

"He'll be alright Martha. It's only a half day. That'll break him in nicely." Jenny added breezily.

"And the same goes for you, young lady, messing around with that tractor. You ain't done that for some time."

She was still mouthing advice as the passed out of earshot around the corner of the first barn where the tractor and flatbed trailer were kept. While Richard swung open the double doors, Jenny started the tractor and manoeuvred it into position ready for Richard to attach the trailer. Then, with a merry 'All aboard' to Richard, she began the short drive to the harvested corn fields where she halted alongside the first of the bales.

"This is where you get off and the real fun begins. Don't forget your gloves."

Richard slipped off the trailer as bidden and, taking hold of a strands of the baler twine in each hand, swung the bale up on to the trailer. Jenny looked over her shoulder from her perch on the tractor's driving seat.

"There's space for four rows down the length of the trailer. Now push that bale up to the front and across roughly to the centre, then set the next one alongside it and do that until you reach the tail end. After that you work a second row back up to the front."

"What happens then?"

"When the two rows on this side are done, I'll turn the tractor round and we work our way back up the field, picking up the second row of bales."

"Then what?"

"Then you jump aboard and we take them to the big storage barn and then…"

"Don't tell me. Then we take them off and stack them," Richard intervened.

"Got it in one. I knew we would make a farmer of you."

"It's not exactly rocket science and the bales are not as heavy as they look."

His words were lost, as Jenny was already moving on to the next bale, calling back over her shoulder as the tractor lurched forward.

"Just remember what Martha told you. Pace yourself."

By the time Jenny turned to tackle the second straggle of bales Richard was beginning to find a steady rhythm to the work, even so he was happy to hitch a ride as Jenny took the first load of bales to the storage barn for stacking. When the trailer had been unloaded they took a short breather before they returned to the stubble field. It was late afternoon, as they completed their fourth round-trip and Richard was beginning to feel weary. So he was relieved when Jenny suggested that it was time for a longer break.

They could see Hal sitting in his customary position on the porch as they crossed the yard. They approached the steps, each in their different way feeling unease at what reception they would receive from Hal. In the event he was in an unexpected good humour.

"I don't recall you asking permission to use my tractor," was his opening comment, the possibility that his words which might have been taken as a reprimand, belied by the humorous twinkle in his eyes.

"Nor," he continued, "do I expect guests at my house to do manual labour. However, as it is the first time, I'm prepared to overlook it."

Martha came out to the porch as he made this comment.

"Don't listen to the wicked old hypocrite. He's been fretting for days about that straw. He knows that he won't be up to handling it, but he's too proud to ask for anyone's help. He should be thanking his lucky stars that you two want to help us out like this."

Hal snorted at this interruption.

"Well, I must admit, it's a weight off my mind to see the straw being put into storage and I'm very grateful. I thank you both."

"There, that was easy, wasn't it? Now come on through to the kitchen. I've been baking, so just help yourselves."

The collecting and stacking of the straw bales continued for a further three days. After initial tiredness and the stiffness of his arms and shoulders in the first hour each day, Richard had been pleased at the way in which his body had responded to its first acquaintance with sustained physical labour for some time. By the final day he felt much fitter than when they had first begun the work and, despite the extra lifting involved as the barn steadily filled, he was handling the work without any noticeable strain.

With the end in sight they had indulged in the luxury of taking their mid-shift breather in the porch with a mug of fresh coffee. Hal was still taking his afternoon nap and Martha was busy in the kitchen. The rich smells of baking drifting out suggested that she was nearing the end of her work there.

"Smells good," Richard remarked.

"Mm. I think that Martha wants to give you a taste of some of the local specialities before you leave. I know that she's planning to serve up scrapple for dinner tonight."

"What's scrapple? I've never heard of it."

"It's a Pennsylvanian favourite – shredded pork and maybe buckwheat mixed and set in a loaf. We eat it in pan-fried thick slices with other items. I think she's planning potato fries. What do you call them in England?"

"Oh, chips. Now you are talking."

He rose to his feet and handed his empty mug to her.

"Time to get back to work. I'm beginning to feeling hungry already at the thought of it."

Later that afternoon, when the last bale had been set in its place and Jenny had parked the tractor and trailer in their customary places, they walked hand in hand together down the track to the stubble field. Neither of them spoke. At the end of the track they stopped and stood looking out over the cleared acres of stubble.

Richard was the first to break the silence.

"Job done."

"Yes, thanks to you. I am so grateful to you. I wanted to do something for them that would repay them for everything they have done for me over the years. This was all that I could think of, but you had to do all the hard work."

"It wasn't just me. We did it together."

They stood in silence for a few moments before Richard continued.

"On the plane as I crossed the Pacific, I was thinking of what I could do that would properly bring us back together again. The one thing that I didn't think of was four day's hard slog. Yet, I think that all this has really cemented things."

Jenny moved closer to him and slipped her arm round his waist.

"Absolutely. I think we shall always remember these last four days."

26

It had been a winter like no other. They had left Pennsylvania as the heat of the earlier weeks of autumn had begun to ease and the cooler air of approaching winter had made its first unwelcome appearance. When he had booked their plane tickets, Richard had calculated that they had a day in hand before taking the flight that would take them to Sydney and the rendezvous with his parents. He had decided, therefore, that they could spend that time in San Francisco. It meant a slightly longer flight on the second leg, but offsetting that was the opportunity to relax and spend time alone together.

For the early part of that day they had become archetypal tourists. They had ridden the cable cars, gazed across at Alcatraz as they strolled along the length of Fisherman's Wharf, and had spent time watching the seals in the harbour. Finally, after eating a takeaway snack from a quayside kiosk they had gone in search of a cab that would take them to the Golden Gate bridge.

The cab driver had obviously done this trip many times before. He had stopped briefly for them to look at the view of the Presidio and the bulk of the bridge rising above. It was at this point that he had leaned back in his seat to speak to them.

"Are you guys planning to walk across?" he had asked. "The views are terrific."

A crossing on foot was something that they had not expected, so they had happily directed their driver to drop them off at the northern end of the bridge. After paying their cab fare, they had looked for a cafe, but finding nothing, were about to make the return walk back to the southern end, when Jenny had noticed the statue. She had drawn Richard across to the solitary figure, cast in the modern natural style, of a young service man, complete with kitbag, taking a last wistful look at the city before leaving to face whatever the Pacific War had in store for him.

As Richard had moved across to join her, he had heard her drawing in a deep sniff. She had turned to him, tears already beginning to trickle down her face.

"Oh Richie! That is so beautiful. It's how Grandpa must have felt back in 1942. He was of the same sort of age."

They had stood for a while contemplating the statue before turning to make their way up to the bridge and join the steady stream of pedestrians making the crossing to the southern shore. It was as they had neared the mid-point that Jenny had broken the silence.

"I have not said anything to you, but I guess I have been a bit scared of what I was letting myself in for. You know, going so far, living on a boat for weeks on end."

"And meeting my family?" Richard queried.

"Yeah. That too."

She had paused as they stopped to look across the bay to the Oakland shoreline. As their cab driver had said the views were magnificent and their progress had been slow as they made frequent stops to gaze around in all directions.

"Seeing that statue back there and sensing the message the sculptor was trying to convey has meant a lot to me. Grandpa was facing far worse when he was shipped out."

Richard had slipped his arm around her shoulders.

"Don't worry about it. It's like the first night nerves actors get when a new play opens, or what children get when they start at a new school. It's probably what we shall both feel on the morning of our wedding day."

"And when might that be? I don't remember you asking."

"I have just been waiting for the right moment."

Even as he had said the words, he had realised that this was just such a moment, the reaction that followed had been unscripted. Withdrawing his arm, he had knelt on one knee, then taking her hand in his and oblivious of the steady trickle of people walking past them, had said what had been on his mind since leaving Australia.

"Months back, when you said that we needed to separate, it made me realise just how much you meant to me. There is no one else that I would want to spend the rest of my life with. So, Jenny Pearson, will you marry me?"

"Of course, I will. Nothing would make me happier."

She had drawn him back to his feet and they had kissed, aware for the first time that people, having stopped to witness this singular event, had now broken into applause.

They had flown to Sydney the following day and, as arranged, Eve and Matt were waiting for them as they emerged from the arrivals hall. It had been an early start for the travellers and they had been relieved when they were told that they would not be transferring immediately to the boat but staying the night in a central hotel.

Over dinner that evening Eve had asked Jenny what she had in the way of summer clothing, explaining that they were heading into the tropics and the weather would be getting progressively hotter. It had been decided, therefore, that the two of them would go shopping for sandals and lightweight clothing in the morning while Matt and Richard went in search of a few essentials for the boat.

Jenny had laughed at the mention of weather getting hotter as one travelled north.

"I haven't got used to this upside-down living."

"I felt much the same when I first came to live here," Eve had assured her. "Don't worry, you soon adjust."

The adjustment began the following morning when, after their first night on the boat, they had left the mooring in Bounty Bay and had headed north. Jenny had experienced an initial queasiness, but had soon thrown this off and settled into life afloat. The obvious difference with life ashore was the restricted space, but in all other respects the boat offered all the amenities of a modern apartment.

More importantly for Richard, Jenny had settled into an easy relationship with his parents. When he had remarked on this as they had turned in one evening, she had answered him simply.

"It's been really nice for me. My parents died while I was still a baby. So, I've never really had parents and all my experiences up until now have been of living with old people."

"Well, they like you very much."

"That's great. I like them. Now go to sleep."

That exchange had remained clear in Richard's memory. All else was a jumble of the sights and sounds they had experienced as they had slowly leap-frogged their way up the coast of New South Wales and Queensland, anchoring whenever a suitable bay presented itself and picking up basic foods and water at most of the small coastal towns they found.

Christmas Day had been celebrated in antipodean style on a beach near Cairns. It had been in a marked change from the many days spent amid coral reefs gazing at the seemingly endless panorama of tropical fish that had been their main occupation since their arrival in northern waters. It had seemed the obvious time for Jenny and Richard to break news of their engagement.

For all their splendours below water, the reefs themselves

were a major hazard that had required the most careful navigation. In many ways they were relieved when they had passed into the deeper waters south of the tropics line as they made the return journey. That relief had proved a mixed blessing. All four had become aware that each day's sailing brought them closer to Sydney and the inevitable parting. When that day arrived, Eve had made it clear that she would love them to stay on, with a view to their settling in Tasmania. She had probably known all along that this was a false hope. Over the past weeks there had been innumerable references to all the various matters that they would need to sort out when they were back in England, and they had eventually settled on promises that there would be lengthy visits in the future by both sides. Even then there had been tears when they had made their farewells at the airport ready to board their flight back to London.

An announcement from the cockpit broke into Richard's stream of reminiscences. In the seat beside him Jenny, her head resting against his shoulder, stirred from the sleep she had been enjoying for the past hour. She gave him a sleepy look and mumbled, "where are we?"

Richard reached for her hand and gave it a squeeze.

"Nearly there," he said. "We should be landing in about fifteen minutes."

"I'm sorry, Mr Thomas does not work here any more."

For a moment Richard stood nonplussed, then shrugged his shoulders before putting the phone back on its base. Jenny had been sitting watching him make the call.

"Problems?"

"Nothing major. It seems that Gerry no longer works at the bank."

"That's not a problem is it? In any case, you knew he was planning to quit."

"Yes, but I thought he was intending to leave after the end of the bank's financial year. There is still a week or two to go until then."

"Is that a problem?" Jenny enquired.

"None at all. He's probably at home. I just wonder what has happened to cause this change of plan."

"There's a simple way to find out."

Richard took the hint and, ringing Gerry's home number, was relieved to hear his voice answering the call.

"Gerry! Richard here."

"Richard. It's good to hear your voice. When did you get back?"

"We flew in yesterday. I just rang the bank to let you know that we were back, but it seems that you no longer work there."

"No. The bank and I parted company just after New Year."

"Amicably?"

"Let's just say that a lot has been happening while you have been away, but I won't go into that over the phone. Come around after six and have something to eat. I take it from your use of the 'we' pronoun that it will be for three?"

"Very much so. Jenny can't wait to see her Grandpa's portrait."

"Good show. See you this evening."

Richard put down the telephone and turned to Jenny.

"We have a dinner date this evening, but before then I need to catch up on some sleep."

The taxi they had called dropped them off at Gerry's house just as the delivery motor cycle was leaving. Gerry must have spotted it for he remained at the open door, carrier bags of delivered food at his feet, waiting to greet them.

"It's lovely to see you both again," he said as he embraced Jenny and shook hands with Richard. "Be careful not to step on anything, that could prove messy. I've settled on an Indian curry, so we should crack on with eating right away before it gets cold."

Picking up the carrier bags he made to follow them.

"We are dining in style in the kitchen. It's the door on the right."

They passed into an elegant modern dining-kitchen.

"Oh, this lovely!" Jenny exclaimed.

"Yes. Originally there was a dining room and a small galley kitchen. It was Lisa's idea to combine them. We managed to get it finished a few weeks before she died."

A momentary look of sadness crossed his face, before it was replaced with a beaming smile.

"Grab a seat."

He waved a hand towards the dining table, already laid for three people, and began to uncork a bottle of wine, which he then placed on the table. He then began to unpack the delivered food containers and bring them to the table.

"Pour the wine Rich, while I sort out the rest of this lot."

When he had completed all of the preparations, he took his own seat at the table. Then he took his glass of wine and raised it.

"What's the toast?" Richard asked, looking at their host.

"I would have thought that it was obvious," Gerry said. "There have been significant changes for all of us since we last met. So, I think the appropriate salute must be, 'here's to us and the future'."

They raised their glasses and chorused the words of the toast.

"I thought that we might keep off the heavy news until after dinner," Gerry suggested.

They nodded in agreement and there was a moment's silence.

"I have to say, you both look ferociously tanned. How did you manage that?"

Both of his guests answered together, Jenny emphasising sailing while Richard placed greater prominence on the days of labouring in Hal and Martha's fields.

Gerry laughed.

"Well you could not have been doing both at the same time. Which came first?"

They both looked at each other.

'Right then," said Gerry taking command of the situation. We can do it from my perspective. The last news I had of you was that you Jenny were already back in The USA and you Richard were planning to fly to Australia to confer with your mother about your parentage. So, how did that work out?"

"Much better than I had expected. Her husband was retiring from the navy two days after I got there and she had arranged to fly to Sydney to meet up with him. We only discussed the reason for my visit after they had returned. When I told them about that the DNA tests had shown that I was not Bill Rayleton's son, she stunned us both by saying that she had only known two men, thus if it wasn't Bill it must be Matt."

"That is 'known' as in the biblical usage?"

Richard nodded.

"And Matt is her second husband?"

Richard nodded again.

"How very convenient," Gerry commented. "Question is, how does that sit with you?"

"Apart from the fact that they live on the other side of the world, it's great. Dad is of Irish origin, which is what my DNA test had suggested. What can I say. It just feels right."

"That is wonderful news, but where do you reappear in the story?" Gerry said turning towards Jenny, "and how does Richard's farm labouring fit in?"

I had gone back to Martha and Hal's farm in Pennsylvania

where I'd been living before I first came to England, counting the days until I could take over my property in Jersey. Then after some weeks Hal broke his leg and I took over some of his work. Just before Richard turned up, Hal's contractors had harvested the wheat and we were left with a huge acreage of stubble littered with goodness knows how many straw bales which needed to be brought under cover before the winter weather set in."

"And that was when Sir Galahad came riding to the rescue?" Gerry asked with a chuckle.

"Not exactly. He sat riding on a trailer behind my tractor, but he did do all the heavy work of lifting, unloading and stacking the bales. It took four days."

"I'm impressed. It has obviously made a lasting impression on him."

"Yes. Not to take up farming," Richard chipped in.

"I'm still a bit confused," Gerry confessed. "You left London six months ago. Your harvesting work must have been done in the autumn of last year. Now it's nearly spring."

"We went to Australia."

"To meet Richard's parents?"

"Huh-huh," Jenny added, "and then we went cruising with them."

They described Matt's boat and life aboard it, and how they had journeyed up the Australian coast to the pleasures of seeing at first hand the sea life and corals of the Great Barrier Reef.

"It must have been quite an experience." Gerry commented when they had completed their account.

"It was." Jenny replied. "It is something that I'll remember for the rest of my life."

"There was another factor," Richard added. "I can only describe it as making us a family."

Gerry looked from one to the other of his guests.

"Do I detect there is something that you haven't told me?"

Richard nodded in agreement.

"Yes, there is. We got engaged on the way to Australia when we broke journey in San Francisco," Richard admitted.

"Did you now! Well my congratulations to you both."

"What he did not tell you," Jenny added, "was that he went down on one knee on the pedestrian sidewalk in the centre of the Golden Gate Bridge while people were streaming past."

"Ah!" Gerry responded. "That figures. That would be the Irish in him coming out."

He was still chuckling to himself as he rose to his feet and began clearing the table.

"Go on through to the sitting room while I stack this lot by the sink. There is something there for you to look at."

He could not help himself from following them into the hallway as they moved into the sitting room. There were a few moments of silence before he heard Jenny's long drawn out 'Ohh!' as she saw the portrait he had set up ready on an easel. Then she came running out in search of him and threw her arms around him before planting a kiss on his cheek.

"Thank you so much! It's beautiful!"

"I'm pleased you like it," Gerry said, as he followed her back into the sitting room, where she took up station in front of the easel and gazed at the picture.

"I don't just like it. I simply love it. Somehow you have brought Grandpa back to life. I keep expecting him to speak to me."

"He will, when he has lived with you for a while. Then he will remind you of his voice and any odd mannerisms and habits."

Richard looked at the portrait of Gerry's late wife Lisa mounted on the sitting room wall and understood fully what he was saying.

"Can I take it tonight?" Jenny asked.

"Better not. It is easy to damage a painting. I'll get it properly packaged and I'll bring it round to you tomorrow laid flat in the back of my estate car."

With that, he took the painting from the easel and set it facing against a bare wall, where there was little risk of damage, and moved the easel into the hall ready to take back upstairs to his studio.

This done he returned to the sitting room.

"Right then! Fun's over, it's time to get down to the serious stuff."

"You haven't said why you finished at the bank earlier than you planned."

"How much do you know?"

"Literally nothing." Richard replied. "We only returned to London yesterday evening. I rang the bank this morning, hoping to speak to you, and was told that you no longer worked there."

"That's all that was said?"

"Yes. Why do you ask? Is there some problem?"

"Good Lord, no." Gerry smiled broadly. "It's just that so much has happened, I wasn't sure where to begin."

"Why not try the beginning. That's always a good place."

Gerry ignored the jibe.

"No. I think I shall begin in the middle. Everything else hangs around that."

Jenny had been sitting quietly through this friendly sparring.

"I hope that this isn't going to be too complicated."

"Not at all," Gerry replied with a smile. "The central fact that I have referred to is that Rayleton Securities, as a company, no longer exists."

He paused to let this bald statement sink in. Jenny's face was a picture of incomprehension, but Richard seemed to be in a state of shock as Gerry continued.

"What we must do now is examine what led up to this. At

the time that you left the bank, Henry had pushed through his bond issue with Baxter Marine."

He paused, aware that Jenny was looking blank.

"A bond is a legally binding agreement by which a borrower is advanced money by a lender. It makes no difference whether the parties concerned are individuals, companies or governmental organisations. In return for the cash advance, the borrower pledges to pay interest on the loan at fixed dates and eventually to repay the loan at a predetermined date. Bonds are also the senior ranking form of debt and have first call in the event of an insolvency."

"Ah. I get it, but where does the bank fit in?"

"The bank acts as middleman. It arranges the loan and sells on part of the financing to other banks, insurance companies, pension funds and wealthy private investors. That is how it makes its money."

"What a boring way to earn a living!"

She turned to Richard as she spoke.

"Is that what you were doing when you worked there?"

"After I was brought back from Jersey, it's what I was being trained up to take on."

"Well I think that you are well rid of..."

She paused in mid-sentence as another thought crossed her mind and turned back to Gerry.

"Baxter Marine? Isn't that the outfit in Hamble who built Richard's boat?"

"The very same."

"Then why was the bank lending money to a jerk company like that?"

Gerry opened his arms and shrugged.

"That is what we would all like to know. It was Henry's big idea and he would not listen to anyone who disagreed with him. So, sales of the Baxter bonds began, but, before long, the upset of the yacht race storm set off whispers about the seaworthiness of the Baxter yachts taking part. Then rumours began to circulate about the police enquiry and soon existing bondholders were becoming angry and asking questions."

"That had begun before I left," Richard commented.

"In the weeks that followed your departure things got steadily worse," Gerry continued.

"Baxter's sales had begun to fall off and then, when he was arrested on multiple charges, they ceased altogether. It was at that point that the insurance company that was the leading bond holder foreclosed on them."

"I appear to have missed all the fun."

"Believe me, you were well out of it. After the collapse of Baxter Marine, whispers about Rayleton's own financial position began to circulate. The bank was in the first stages of a death spiral with a steady collapse of its customer base. Henry being Henry, dumped the whole problem on Charles' desk."

"The Portuguese shareholders must have been furious." Richard commented.

Jenny had been following Gerry's story with eyes steadily widening. "So how do you fit in to all this?"

"Richard had granted me power of attorney over his affairs while he was away and these developments became an obvious cause for concern. Charles had become aware of my position when the problem of dealing with the takeover bid from a consortium of South American interests, probably instigated by Banco Cardosa, landed on his desk. It seems that Rayleton had not taken over Cardosa, but had merged with them under a joint name."

"Did that mean that my Rayleton shares could not be bound by the old 'family only' rules?" Richard queried.

"That is what I assumed. It became important when the hostile takeover was launched. Henry's personal share-holding in the joint company was only slightly larger than

Cardosa's. Your shares, Richard, therefore held the balance of power."

Richard could see immediately where this was leading and began to laugh.

"You voted my shares with the Portuguese faction against Henry. Oh, I like it!"

"Got it in one." Gerry admitted.

"I approached the South American syndicate and told them that you would be prepared to sell your shares to them if the price was right. They took the hint and, after a bit of haggling, coughed up slightly more than I expected. So, my friend, you are completely clear of Rayleton and somewhat richer than you thought.

Gerry gave him a cheerful smile.

Jenny had been sitting quietly taking it all in.

"You must have known that your actions would have consequences."

"Yes, I was caught in a conflict of interests. Whatever I did would cause upset. I simply had to decide where my strongest loyalties lay."

"And you chose Richard."

"That's about the strength of it. Henry, of course, was absolutely incandescent when he heard. He came storming down to my office and sacked me on the spot."

"What's the state of play at the moment?" Richard asked.

"The new outfit is headquartered in Brazil. The London end of the business still operates, but has been drastically slimmed down and has been moved to a smaller building."

"And Henry?"

"As a way of saving face, he was given the opportunity to resign. I believe he is now tending his roses."

"What a mess." Jenny commented.

"It was of his own making." Richard countered. "To me, it always seemed that he liked all the perks of the top job, but didn't really understand the business."

"I would agree with you there," Gerry added. "Unfortunately, his foolishness has cost a lot of people their livelihoods."

"Yourself included," Jenny added.

Gerry smiled at her as she made this remark.

"I was planning to go in any case. Now I can concentrate on my painting."

27

It was late the following morning that the Richmond flat's doorbell rang. As expected, it proved to be Gerry delivering the now heavily packaged portrait.

"Come and give me a hand. The picture is a bit heavy with all the packaging and your stairs could be a challenge."

Together, they manoeuvred the bulky package up the two flights of stairs and laid it across the bed in the spare room.

"Jen not here?" Gerry queried.

"No, she's out shopping. She got in a bit of a panic when we had a call from my old office in St. Helier that they now held the keys to her property and she could collect them at any time that suited. Apparently, the tenants had handed in the keys a week or so early. So, we are going to Jersey earlier than expected. Jen can't wait to have a good look around inside her house."

"Exciting."

"Hmm. It's upsetting the timetable we had worked out. We were planning to go down to Hamble to spend the weekend with Ben and Lou Maitland, but we shall probably have to re-schedule everything."

While he had been listening to Richard, Gerry had been

fumbling in his coat pocket. His hand emerged clutching a large bunch of keys.

"Well if you are going to Hamble, you might find these useful."

"What are these for?"

"They are keys to a property. Some time back, you may remember me telling you about an American property investor nicknamed the 'grave dancer'. Well, while you were away, I used some of your cash to fund a bit of grave-dancing in your name."

Noticing the startled look on Richard's face he paused momentarily.

"Don't worry. It was only a few thousand pounds and, if anything had gone wrong, I would have reimbursed you. At any rate, I waited and watched as the trading price of the Baxter Marine bonds dropped and dropped until it reached a level which suggested that dealing would soon be suspended."

"You have lost me," Richard said shaking his head.

Gerry smiled at his confusion.

"Dealing suspension means something serious has occurred. In this case, bankruptcy."

"Let me get this straight. You bought Baxter Marine bonds immediately before Baxter went bust and the bonds were suspended. Why?"

"Insurance companies operate in a way that is different to other businesses. Their turnover is set by the policies they issue and has a built-in profit margin. Any claims made against policies reduces that profit margin. In the case of the Baxter Marine bond issue, the company is now defunct and the bonds represent a total loss. However, in return the insurers now have title to the properties pledged as security for the loan they had made. For the moment, that property brings in no income, but may incur running costs. It will take time to sell it and that in itself will incur substantial costs and may be difficult to achieve."

He stopped to assess whether Richard had taken all of this information in.

"The upshot is that in the circumstances that I've outlined, the company would probably be willing to discuss any reasonable offer."

"And if they aren't."

"Then eventually you would get the face value of the bonds. It's a heads-you-win, tails-you-don't-lose situation."

"So, you think we should approach them with an offer?"

"Already done. The Baxter loan has proved such a stinker, the company was anxious to expunge it as quickly as possible."

As he spoke he handed Richard the sizeable bunch of keys.

"You are now the proud owner of all the land, properties and equipment of Baxter Marine."

Richard looked at him in astonishment.

"They took your offer?"

"After a bit of horse trading. I had to add a bit more cash to what they owed you on the bonds. Overall, I would think you got the business at about thirty per cent of its underlying value."

"I see now why you called it grave-dancing."

He looked at Gerry, his head shaking in seeming disbelief.

"Thank you so much for what you have done. For years I have been thinking about the sailing boats that I would like to design. I have even made preliminary sketches, but there was always this barrier of where and how it could be done."

"No need for thanks, I've enjoyed it. My only concern was how this would square up with your plans of going back to Jersey?"

"No problems. Rob Maitland and I have always thought of working together. We can go into partnership. He will provide the practical skills and I will provide the site and initial capital. I would not need to be permanently on site. I can do all the design work from Jersey."

They were still discussing all the many factors that Gerry's investing had produced when Jenny returned from her shopping expedition.

That night, when they settled in bed, Jenny and Richard had minds occupied with very different topics. For Jenny it was wholly with the anticipation of soon claiming the keys to her Jersey property and exploring all it had to offer. Long after she had drifted off to sleep with her head filled with happy positive thoughts Richard's mind was still grappling with Gerry's latest bombshell.

Earlier their talk had been about finance and companies. Now Richard's mind turned to narrower considerations. Companies are simply names, he told himself. It is people who run them. While his initial thoughts had been about boyhood plans of how he and Rob could work together, he now began to realise that this was much too simplistic and overlooked another very important factor. Rob did not own anything. The Hamble boatyard was owned by his father.

Richard was well aware of the years of effort from Ben that had brought the yard to its present position. It was his yard in more than just the legal sense. As if that were not enough, there was also the question of personalities he reminded himself. Ben was of an older generation. He was also very much the old navy man and ran his business on the same lines. The whole subject would need careful handling. Of only one thing was he certain: the news of his ownership of the Baxter Marine assets would have to come from him. He was still thinking round all the possible scenarios when sleep finally claimed him.

The following morning, as they drove down to Hamble, he told Jenny of what was on his mind.

"It's no use looking to me for advice on any of this. I know nothing about boats or factories," she replied with a smile.

"Agreed, but you know people."

Jenny looked at him askance.

"I'm not much help there either. I didn't grow up as part of a big family. It was just Grandpa and me most of the time."

"What about Martha and Hal?"

She thought about things for a few moments before answering.

"Yes. That might help some. He could be an ornery old cuss at times. I think it was mainly a reluctance to change anything. Somehow or other she always got around him."

"How?"

"I guess it was by not pushing anything head on, but gradually getting him to see things from a different angle."

"There. That makes perfect sense. That is the approach we shall have to adopt. Thank you, my love. My mind feels easier already."

They chatted easily after that until they finally drew into the Maitland boatyard. Richard looked around as he got out of the car. It was the onset of spring and already there were spaces among the rows of parked boats where owners had already moved their craft back into the water for the start of the new boating season. It was an additional reminder to tread carefully, as this was one of Ben's busiest times. His eyes lingered for a moment on the adjacent Baxter property. Gateways and buildings had all been secured and a there was a forlorn look about the place.

As always, Lou had kept an eye on the yard from the kitchen window and was already at the doorway waiting to greet them. She flung her arms around each of them in turn.

"It is lovely to see you both. It seems such a long time since you were last here."

"There's been a lot happening," Richard said as he extricated himself from the hug.

"Well you can tell us all about it as we eat. We are having a mid-week Sunday lunch, if that is alright with you. The boys are getting cleaned up."

Richard sniffed the air.

"Roast beef!" he exclaimed. "Lead on."

"I'm really pleased to see you two back together again. You always seemed so right together."

Jenny glanced across at Richard, who nodded imperceptibly, as if sensing what she was going to say.

"We are not just back together. We have got engaged."

There was a squeal of delight from Lou, who instinctively looked at Jenny's left hand.

"We haven't got around to getting a ring yet. There's been no opportunity for that sort of shopping." Jenny explained.

Lou was already making for the hall door and calling upstairs.

"Come on down you two. There's big news."

"We are treating today as Sunday and when next Sunday comes they will treat it as a workday," Lou explained as Ben and Rob joined them.

"Before you sit down Ben, open a decent bottle of wine. We have something to celebrate. Jen and Richie have got engaged."

"There is something else to celebrate," Richard said. "I have also found my real father."

Ben found wine and filled glasses for each of them. He then raised his glass in salutation.

"Here's to Jenny and Richard. Long life and happiness and to families old and new."

After the impromptu toast, dinner was served and they struggled to tell all their news between mouthfuls of food. They nodded approvingly as they recounted Richard's arrival at the Pennsylvania farmstead and his subsequent labours storing the straw bales. In turn their response turned to howls of delight when Jenny told them of Richard's proposal on the Golden Gate Bridge. Finally, there was a more thoughtful, yet affirming, silence when Richard told them of how he had found his real father and how they had joined Richard's parents on their cruise.

It was at this point that Lou in a final twist of days and dates, served up Christmas pudding for their second course.

"I thought that you had probably missed out on this while you were in Australia."

"Too right," Richard commented in a mock Australian accent.

"Yes, it was ice cream whenever we got the chance." Jenny chipped in.

"Had you sailed before?" Rob asked.

"Rich had taken me for a short cruise along the coast in Jersey, but for Mom it was the first time on a sail boat."

Lou picked up her use of the word Mom and made a note to bring it up if she had opportunity to be alone with Jenny.

In the meantime, Ben had taken up the questioning.

"Where exactly did you go?" He asked.

"We joined Mum and Dad in Sydney and then we sailed way up to the north as far as Cairns and then spent weeks exploring the Coral Sea," Richard began to explain, before Jenny took up the story.

"At the surface the reefs look pretty enough with the sea breaking over them, but below the surface is where the real beauty is."

"Weren't you worried about sharks?" Rob asked.

"Of course, but there are areas where it is safe to snorkel."

"Eve didn't snorkel surely." Lou commented.

"No. We weren't together all of the time. There were days when we did our own thing."

"We did stay together for the boat trips in more open waters where sharks might drop by," Richard added.

"The boats were great," Jenny added. "They have glass bottoms so you can just sit and look down at everything in the water below you. The reefs themselves are beautiful and they are alive with fish of every imaginable size and colour. There were times when it simply took your breath away."

Richard nodded in agreement.

"It was unforgettable. Words don't really do it justice."

"Then, before we knew, it was time to head back to Sydney to catch our flight back to England." Jenny added sadly.

"So how long were you away? Ben asked.

"It was well over three months" Richard added airily.

"That was a hell of a long time for two rookie sailors. Didn't you have any problems?"

"Not really. We were never far from land and went ashore at every opportunity. The boat had been through a major overhaul and was in good nick. We dragged our anchor one night, but no harm done. So, on the whole I'd say things went pretty well."

"So, where did you spend Christmas?" Lou enquired

Richard exchanged a look with Jenny and shrugged

"I can't remember exactly where. We were still up in the Coral Sea area. It was mighty hot and we had fish most days and stocked up with ice cream whenever it was available."

"If there was a decent stretch of beach, we would moor the boat and go for a walk to get some exercise." Jenny added. "One day was very much like another."

"It sounds idyllic." Lou said, smiling at them both.

"Yes, it sounds like you had quite a trip." Ben added.

"And how did you all get on?" Lou asked, more concerned about the human factors than the 'why's and wherefores' of their travel. "I mean, it was a long time to be cooped up on a boat, and you scarcely knew each other."

"That's the surprising thing," Jenny said. "I think that it was because we were on a boat that, at the beginning, we made an effort to work together, and we were soon getting on fine."

"It made us into a family," Richard stated simply.

There was a pause as this last comment was made. In those few simple words Richard had effectively said all that needed to be said on that particular topic.

"That's enough about us," he continued. "What about you? How are things shaping up down here?"

"The boys are pretty busy at the moment. You know what the boating world is like at this time of year."

"Have you heard about next door?" Rob spoke for the first time. "Baxter has been arrested and his business has gone bust and been shut down."

It was the opening that Richard had patiently hoped for. Taking a deep breath, he began a short recital of what Gerry had been doing in his name in the months that he had been away. All three members of the Maitland family listened intently as he ran through all of Gerry's various dealings. When he had finished, there was a stunned silence which was eventually broken by Ben.

"Let me get this straight. You went away leaving this senior colleague to look after your affairs. Then, while you were sunning yourself abroad, he made you a pile of money by selling your shares to Brazilians who wanted to take over your old bank, which resulted in Henry Rayleton being shown the door, and then got Baxter's business at a knock-down price from the receivers?"

Richard nodded.

"Wow! Is this all legal?"

"Oh yes! I signed a legally binding power of attorney before I left."

"So, you really do own the business next door."

"I'm afraid so." Richard replied, failing to hide the smile on his face. "You will have me to worry about now."

Ben smiled back.

"Well," he said, "if we hadn't already emptied the bottle, I would raise a toast to your friend Gerry."

As the lunch party came to an end, Richard produced the bunch of keys that Gerry had given him and stated his intention to inspect his new property. Ben and Rob decided to accompany him, leaving the two females to clear the table and load the dishwasher, free to talk as they did so about more important matters.

Lou was anxious to hear more about Richard's visit to her at Hal and Martha's farm.

"Were you expecting it, or was it arranged?"

"It wasn't either really." Jenny said and then told Lou about the poems and how she had interpreted them. "Martha had collected mail from the roadside box as she and Hal had returned from town and she had just read the last of them and then suddenly there he was driving into the yard."

Lou nodded in understanding.

"It's been hard for you, but that's the way life is at times. I found it hard at times when Rob was growing up and Ben away at sea."

It was Jenny's turn to give the understanding nod of the head.

"All I can remember is this huge rush of relief when I saw him climbing out of the car."

"How long were you there afterwards?"

"Just four days."

"And that was when you did the field work?"

"That's right. I could see that Hal was itching to get back to work before his leg had properly healed, so it seemed a good way to thank him and Martha for all they had done for me."

Lou nodded approvingly.

Jenny stopped in the middle of wiping dry a large vegetable dish that had not fitted into the dishwasher.

"It was hard work. Rich had to do most of the manual

work, but he didn't complain. It's strange. It didn't feel like work. It was more like a holiday. We were so relieved and happy to be back together."

"And you are off to take over your Jersey property tomorrow. That will be exciting."

"Mm. I've only seen the driveway and the frontage of the house. Goodness knows what it will be like inside after two centuries of being leased out."

"What sort of property is it?"

"Well, it stands back from the road at the end of a curving drive. It's built of stone and has large windows either side of the front door. That's about all I saw when I cycled out to look at it with my friend Nicole. Oh, and the tenant I spoke to mentioned that there were rooms in the roof space where all the old domestic furniture has been stored."

"It sounds as if it's a big house then. It should make a good family house."

There was a smile playing around Lou's mouth as she made the last remark.

It was late afternoon when the sound of voices heralded the return of the menfolk. They seemed in good spirits as they filed in to the kitchen-diner where Lou and Jenny were sitting enjoying a cup of tea. Lou got to her feet to make more tea as they took their places around the table.

"How did you get on?" she called across from the sink, as she filled the kettle.

"The new owner muffed his lines." Rob was quick to answer. "He didn't seem to know which key was which."

"Well to be fair, there were a lot of them." His father reasoned. "Still, it was interesting. It was obviously not a planned closure."

"What makes you think that?" Jenny asked.

"Just the general mess and untidiness of the main workshop. The way tools and materials had been left lying around suggested that they had closed unexpectedly mid-shift."

"Well Baxter must have known what was coming," Lou commented, from her position at the work surface.

"Perhaps he did," Ben replied, "but he's been flying by the seat of his pants for years. He probably thought that he could wriggle out of things."

"But he's been arrested." Lou countered. "He can't wriggle out of that."

"That's a police matter. It will be months before there is any court hearing. This is purely a commercial matter, wouldn't you say Rich?"

They all looked at Richard.

"I would think so. The financial world can be very ruthless, and very quick to take action if something doesn't look right."

Lou placed a large pot of tea on the table and followed this with three clean mugs.

"This pot is all yours. Jenny and I have already had ours. While you boys have been examining your new playthings, we girls have been having a nice long chat."

Nothing more was said about the next-door property. After the latecomers had finished drinking their tea, they all moved to the more comfortable seating in the sitting room and, with much jollity, the rest of the evening passed with accounts of Jenny and Richard's travels in Australasia and the USA.

Lou had been content to bide her time and not ask any questions while they were all together. After she and Ben had closed their bedroom door and began their retirement rituals she began to probe gently for some idea of what had passed during the afternoon.

Ben waited until they were in bed together before telling her what little he knew.

"Bear in mind," he said, "Richard himself only learned about this yesterday, so he has not had much time to think about things. There was one matter on which he was quite definite. His friend Gerry had given him the option to turn down the property if he wasn't happy about the arrangement, and would refund Richard and take on the property in his own name."

"And what did Richard say to that?"

"He wasn't interested in any further changes. He told Gerry that it had all come as a surprise, but he was really pleased with the way things had turned out."

Having completed this part of his report he rolled over on to his shoulder to face her.

"He has made me a solemn promise that he will never willingly sell the old Baxter properties and there will be no more interference from that quarter."

"Has Richard said anything about what he is planning to do with it?"

"That's where things get interesting. He is anxious not to upset anything here. It's for me to decide if we simply carry on as we are or go for something different or a mixture of the two."

"What would the something different entail?"

"Designing and building our own boats. Nothing mass produced. Small scale, high quality."

"What would happen to the existing business?"

"That would remain for the time being. There would be a useful overlap with matters like boat repairs."

"And who would manage all this?"

"Until everything is well established, I would."

"And when it is well established, what would you do?"

"I shall be ready to retire by then."

"It would be good for Rob." She reflected. "I think he would like the challenge of it."

"Mm." Ben mused. "I think he would. It would allow him to use some of the things he learned at university."

Ben reached forward to give her a goodnight kiss.

"I almost forgot, there would also be a bonus for you. We would have to make use of an accountant to handle the VAT."

"If that is part of the package, then I'm all for it." Lou replied. "Lord knows if either of us will get to sleep with all of this running through our heads."

The following morning, the early stages of the drive to Portsmouth were conducted in silence. In addition to the fact that it was early morning, Jenny's mind was occupied by thoughts of taking possession of what she considered to be the family home. For Richard other matters were at the forefront of his mind. As Lou had given him her farewell hug, she had whispered her thanks and her belief that Ben was coming around to taking up the challenge of a joint operation. The implications of those few words had given him plenty of food for thought. It was only as they neared the city and the heavy morning rush that he reluctantly had to switch off this subject in order to concentrate his thoughts on his driving.

The ferry crossing was slow when compared to flying, but had other compensations. The novelty of driving into the innards of the ferry vessel and finding their way to a seat had had the effect of breaking up their earlier thoughts.

"What time do we get to St. Helier?" Jenny asked after a while.

"Around four, give or take a few minutes." Richard replied, sensing that the novelty of sea travel had begun to wear off. "Why?"

"I was just wondering if we would be in time to pick up the keys today."

"The bank closes its doors at four-thirty. If we can drive off without any hassle we might make it. If not, we can pick up the keys first thing tomorrow morning."

"Have you told Nicole when to expect us?"

"I told her the time the ferry is due to arrive."

"If I know Nicole, she will be keeping watch for our arrival."

"Mm. I'm looking forward to seeing her. It's been ages since I last spoke to her."

"You have written to her, haven't you?"

"Of course, but it's not the same," she said, noting the slightly puzzled expression on Richard's face. "It's a girl thing. You wouldn't understand."

In the event they had enjoyed a smooth crossing and the ferry docked a few minutes ahead of schedule. Disembarking was equally smooth and they made it to the bank with almost ten minutes to spare.

As they walked to the front entrance of the bank, it felt to Richard as though he had not been away. The only evidence of change was the replacement of the old brass nameplate with a new one bearing the name of the new Brazilian owners. Inside the bank the reception hall was as it had always been, with the familiar face of Tom at the reception desk giving his customary cheerful greeting.

"Hullo Mr. Rayleton. It's good to see you back."

"Hi Tom. We're here on private business. Miss Pearson is here to pick up the keys to her property."

Tom shook his head.

"I don't know anything about that, I'll have a word with Charlotte."

A few minutes later Charlotte appeared with a broad smile on her face, bearing the property keys and a form for Jenny to sign. When the transaction had been completed she accompanied them to the outer door.

"It's lovely to see you both. Is everything sorted?"

"We shall know the answer to that tomorrow when I finally get a look at the inside of the house." Jenny replied. "Heaven knows when it will be ready to move in."

"You're coming back to live in Jersey?"

"Just as soon as we are able." Richard added. "I don't know whether you had heard. I don't work for the bank any longer."

"I'd heard that things had been happening in London. Then the South Americans took over. Rachel has gone. They want staff to be bi-lingual."

"You're still here."

Not for much longer. I shall leave at the end of next week."

"That's tough." Jenny commiserated.

"I'm OK with it." Charlotte smiled. "I'm getting married at the end of August. I would love you both to come. I'll send you an invite if you give me your address."

"Oh congratulations! We'd love to." Jenny exclaimed.

"We are staying temporarily with Nicole and David Lansbury. Send it care of them." Richard suggested.

With that Charlotte left them to hurry back to her desk.

"What a lovely girl." Jenny said as they began their walk back to their car. "It will be so nice to see my first European wedding."

There was no response and Jenny sensed that Richard's thoughts were elsewhere.

"Is everything all right. Don't you want to go to the wedding?"

"Charlotte was a cracking good secretary and friend. I shall be as pleased as anyone to see her happily settled."

"So, what's on your mind?"

"It's something else. Wait till we are back in the car."

Jenny shrugged and did as she had been asked. Once they were settled in the car she turned to him with an enquiring look.

"Well?"

"It was back there. Something that was said."

"I thought Charlotte was perfectly natural."

"I didn't mean Charlotte."

"Well there was only Tom at the desk. All he said was 'Hello Mr. Rayleton. It's good to see you back.' Apart from his not being aware that you no longer worked for the bank, I can't see anything to take exception to."

"He used the name 'Rayleton'."

"I don't get it. Rayleton is your name."

"Technically yes, but I no longer feel that I am a Rayleton. In a sense, once I'd passed out of boyhood, I don't think I ever felt that I was."

"Do you want to change your name?"

"I think it is something we should talk about. Neither of us carries the name of our real forebears."

"So, what are you suggesting, that I should be called Weybourne and you should be called Keogh?"

"Yes. Why not?"

"And after we are married?"

They looked at each other and simultaneously a broad smile spread across each of their faces as they spoke it in unison.

"Weybourne-Keogh."

"It has a ring to it. I like it." Jenny declared.

"It does what a name should do. It says who we are," Richard added. "And isn't that what we have been trying to sort out for the past year?"

"I guess it is," Jenny agreed. "I'll think about it. Now we need to get on our way. Nicole will be wondering where we are."

Richard started the engine and, after negotiating a couple of central streets, turned on to the Esplanade and headed out of town.

"Ah! The beach where we used to walk." Jenny exclaimed

as they began to run alongside the seemingly endless strip of sandy beach that stretched westward. Her happy reminiscences changed to puzzlement and her head turned to look back over her right shoulder.

"Shouldn't we have turned off back there?"

"Mmm."

A smile played around Richard's mouth as he spoke.

"We have time to make a short detour. I thought it would remind you of that first bike ride you made with Nicole."

She looked across at him accusingly.

"No. You can't fool me. You're taking me to see the house."

The accusation was further confirmed when they took the turn-off road that would take them directly to St. Brelade's. Jenny watched carefully as they proceeded, looking for the screen of trees that she remembered so well.

"Here, on the left," she cautioned.

Richard braked gently and made the turn into the curving driveway. He stopped the car directly facing the front door. Since they had turned into the driveway, Jenny had been busy scanning every aspect of the property.

"The grass will soon need cutting and there are outbuildings lying back on the left side of the house that I didn't notice when I was here before," she remarked. "Otherwise, the only thing that is different is that the company nameplates here and at the gateway have gone."

"We shan't have time to go in." Richard said. "I just thought that it was important for you to see it today."

"Thank you, darling. You're right. It has been a long road, but I think this marks the end."

Richard slipped an arm across her shoulder.

"Yes. When you unlock that door tomorrow morning, it will mark the end of the whole sorry saga spread across the past two centuries. From that moment, perhaps, we shall be free to face together whatever the future has to offer."

Ingram Content Group UK Ltd.
Milton Keynes UK
UKHW020746100723
424852UK00015B/618